From the Chicken House

What a job. Tasting for poison isn't exactly a lifelong career! And what if you also live in a topsy-turvy world of swords, feuds, disguises and madcap violence – and don't know who you are? Oh, and there's a girl you are supposed to save, and you find yourself hunted by absolutely everyone for reasons that are totally unclear. Welcome to the brilliant and exciting world of Dalton Fly. You'll love it. Just don't drink the wine.

Fletcher Moss is the 2012 winner of The Times/Chicken House Children's Fiction Competition. You can see why.

Barry Cunningham
Publisher

CROIT

THE POISON BOY

FLETCHER MOSS

Chicken
House

2 Palmer Street, Frome, Somerset BA11 1DS

Text © Fletcher Moss 2013
First published in Great Britain in 2013
The Chicken House
2 Palmer Street
Frome, Somerset BA11 1DS
United Kingdom
www.doublecluck.com

Cover design and interior design by Steve Wells
Cover illustration by Chris Stocker
Map of Highlions by Joanne Phillips 2012
Typeset by Dorchester Typesetting Group Ltd
Printed and bound in Great Britain by CPI Group (UK) Ltd, Croydon, CR0 4YY
The paper used in this Chicken House book is made from wood grown in
sustainable forests.

3 5 7 9 10 8 6 4 2

British Library Cataloguing in Publication data available.

ISBN 978-1-908435-44-6

For Jo and *Agatha*; for the real Griffin brothers;
and for Mum and Dad.

ONE

When the door crashed open, Dalton Fly was holding his breath in the shadows, his back pressed against the cool marble of a thick pillar and his eyes pleading with a playing card. That lucky Jack, spattered in Bennie's blood, had somehow saved his life. He couldn't leave it. From where he was hiding, Dalton could see the Jack's face staring at him, smudged in red. It was lying face up at the edge of the rug near the fireplace, perhaps a dozen strides away, Dalton thought. He blinked and his vision smudged and blurred again; everything was a wash of swimming shapes for a moment. He rubbed his eyes. There was blood on his hands and under his fingernails.

Dalton was sure of one thing: two men had come into the room and they had pistols; he heard the click of a cap drawn back to shoot.

'Kite almighty!' one of them said as he saw Bennie Jinks, ghosted.

Bennie was face down, a bag of bones in a bloody lake. He had coughed himself inside out. He was still leaking in great scarlet pools. He was only twelve. Whatever he'd been eating had pulled his guts to pieces.

There was a long pause. Dalton's sight sharpened, his heart hammered and his poisoned belly stung. He dropped slowly to a crawl, careful not to slip in all the wet. There was a lot of blood for such a tiny, curled-up boy and Dalton was soaked in it. It was in his face and nose, on his teeth and under his tongue. It was bitter and it was dark; his hair was thick and black with it. He felt sick again.

He heard the creak of the men's leather boots as they stepped forward slowly with pistols aloft. One of them crouched by Bennie, his knees popping, and touched the little boy's shoulder.

'He's still warm.'

Dalton peered at the contents of the tasting table, now flung across the thick rug. There were scattered bowls and plates. Two gold-trimmed cushions had been spun away; a chair lay on its back. The smoky flame of a candle shuddered, making thick shadows wobble in the grey archways. Perhaps Bennie had thrashed around, screaming and gurgling as he choked. The crash and clatter of the devastation must have echoed through the halls and galleries.

'Dreck!' one of them swore, kicking something aside. 'What a mess. The marcher needs to see this.'

There was further movement. Dalton wondered whether their pistols would be down yet. His hands shook madly. Bennie's blood was cooling on his clothes and skin, his spit and guts were getting sticky. There was a chance now, Dalton thought. If the men were moving beyond the bulk of the table, searching the space near the windows at the far end of the room, he could stay in a low crawl and make it to his lucky Jack with a scramble and a stretch.

He began to move forward, struggling to focus again. There was a silver jug on its side, rolled in deep red with a blur of bloody fingerprints. From somewhere outside came the endless low tolling of bells. Church bells clanging over and over.

The Jack was still winking impassively at him. Dalton moved slowly, hand over hand, trying not to breathe. He needed that card.

'What was it? The wine?' one man asked the other.

Dalton heard him lift a stopper from a bottle. He began to inch forward into their line of sight and glanced upwards. They were only a few strides beyond the table of food; two hazy silhouettes in the shadows. All they had to do was turn round, he thought, prickling with fear, and he was stagged.

'Kite knows. The wine, the fruit, the olives . . .'

There was a pause again. One man was examining the table closely now, his wide back hunched. Dalton tried to remember what it was he and Bennie had last tasted; what it was that had killed Bennie; where the poison had been hidden. He moved forward again, crawling slowly.

'Something's killed him . . .' the voice said. 'The kid's coughed his whole belly on to the floor.'

'Ah, dreck,' said the second. 'My boots are covered in it.'

Around Bennie, food was scattered. Dates, olives, fruit, two pale cheeses half wrapped, and wine. Dalton knew he'd been drinking wine; he could taste it through the blood on the back of his teeth. He didn't usually try the wine. He wasn't old enough and neither was Bennie Jinks. Oscar shouldn't have sent them.

He moved forward again, lifting each hand carefully. His palms were sticking to the rug. Little square jellies, dusted with sugar, were cast across the table cloth. Bennie still held a twisted end of it in his little red fist. The lucky Jack seemed to grin. He was nearly there. Dalton reached forward, dripping and shaking. He was very close. His muscles burnt.

'Kite!' one said suddenly, through gritted teeth. 'Where's the other boy, the older one?'

Dalton's heart dropped. His belly hollowed itself in fear. He heard one of them take a step but didn't dare look.

'What's happened to him?'

Dalton touched the edge of the Jack with the tips of his

fingers. His stomach tightened. If they turned, he was as good as dead.

'He's not here.' This voice came from close by. A curtain was swept open and allowed to fall again. They were searching the room.

Dalton eased the playing card towards him, drawing it in slowly. There were more bootsteps. He swallowed hard. He had it. He tried to crawl backwards, to find the safety of the shadows again but his legs wouldn't behave the way he wanted them to.

'Who is the missing one?' said the voice from further away — beyond the table near the windows, Dalton guessed.

There was another pause and a shuffle of papers as one of them checked the tasting arrangements.

'It's a kid called Dalton Fly. Just another one of Oscar's boys.'

The men had come together again and were both huddled over the papers. This, Dalton knew, was the best chance he'd have to get back into cover. He willed himself to move and began a trembling retreat towards the pillar. On the floor where he'd crawled he'd left a great red smear. He pocketed the Jack, trying not to weep with fear and relief. He was hidden again, hugging the shadows of the huge trunk of marble that rose to the painted and patterned ceiling.

As he made it to his feet, he caught a sudden blurred sight of a mad demon, wild-eyed and foul, sneering directly at him. He caught his breath and raised his bloody hands instinctively. Then he saw it was himself, in a gold mirror, one side of his face darkened crimson-black and shining, as if dipped in tar. His hair stood on end. His teeth were red. He looked as if he'd been cut into ribbons. But he was still alive.

'We could have an impostor here,' one of the men said. 'The mistress could be in danger.'

'Possible.' There was an uncomfortable silence. One of them spat.

Dalton edged around the pillar and saw the door to the room was open just a crack. If he was quick, he thought wildly, and was able to run without slipping or being sick, there was a chance he could escape while they were thinking.

'The boy could know nothing,' one said. Dalton heard him leafing through the papers again. 'He's only fourteen. They're just children.' There was a pause. 'Hang on . . .' he added, his voice hardening. They'd seen something: the red trail on the floor, leading straight to the pillar. There was the click of another pistol cap being drawn back; both were ready to fire.

Dalton swallowed but the hot lump in his throat wouldn't move. His feet were cramping. There was movement in the room. They were approaching. He looked again at the door that might deliver some sort of escape, shaking his head to clear his sight. There was a sharp burn in his stomach that wouldn't shift. The door was only a dash away, he figured; he could be there as they raised their pistols, and through before they blew his back into bits.

He patted his lucky card, safe now in his coat pocket, and sent up a pointless prayer for Bennie Jinks. Then he made a run for it.

Two guns exploded with sharp cracks and the door frame at his shoulder shattered into knotty fragments. A rush of panic consumed him and he cried out in fear – then he was running, wild and gasping.

The corridor was long, high-ceilinged and very dark. There was shouting. He crashed through a heavy door into the room beyond. A square of pale moon lit the floor near a grand fireplace. Beyond a long dining table was a second door, and he made for it. Behind him there were more shouts. Dalton knew it took some time to reload the pistols; Oscar had shown him once.

He crossed the room, pushed open the door and sprinted down a long gallery, wide windows with heavy curtains giving snatched glimpses of the city below. He could get his bearings now. Down below he thought he could make out Greengoose and the Sixteen Fountains; the opera house; the city dropping down and away towards the plains, the lazy river widening. Above, half a white-faced moon.

He reached an open hall with a marble floor full of stuffed birds on pedestals, peering at him like nightmare creatures. A curved stairway with a blue carpet led upwards. Suddenly, from his left, a door burst open and a second group of men ran towards him. A broad black figure in silhouette was leading them, a wing of dark riding cape rolling around his shoulders. Someone was bawling a battle cry. Fear propelled Dalton Fly up the stairs, three at a time. At his back was the clap of a pistol shot and a shouted curse.

He rounded the stairs to a landing and ran headlong, mouth gaping, arms pumping. There was another pistol shot, and with it, the acrid stink of burnt shotpowder and smashed plaster. He thrust open a door, stumbled across a fireside rug, vaulted a bed, crashed through a bathroom sending glass vials of sweet-smelling preparations spinning and then somehow, somewhere in the half dark, Dalton came to a panting stop in a dressing room with a city view.

Madness drove him. He was sobbing, partly for Bennie Jinks, ghosted in some foreign Upper-Circle mansion, partly for fear of being blasted open with lead shot.

'Dreck!' he swore, tugging at his pocket, looking for the lucky Jack. He scanned the room as his fingers worked. He was squinting and blinking, trying to get his eyes to focus. Then, with the card held tightly in his trembling hands, he begged it for help. Blackjack Gannet, mighty King of the Poison Boys, could always be counted on in desperate times.

'Where next, Gannet?' he asked the card, his voice a scratchy growl, his throat burning. The Jack stared at him with its one eye, mute. 'Don't let me down, Gannet. Where next?'

Outside, a warm wind rattled the window in its frame and Dalton heard the bells again. There were hundreds of them clanging out across the city, their dull roll deep and slow. Dalton wiped the sweat from his eyes. What was going on out there? He drew his face close to the window, careful not to smear the glass. It was a clear night with stars. He could see a good portion of city roofs below him; domes and galleries, walkways and squares stitched and jumbled together. It seemed as if every church bell in the city had joined in the mournful choir of endless, echoing tolling. He'd never heard anything like it; as if the whole of Highlions had been plunged into mourning.

Dalton blinked, thinking.

Oscar had warned him and Sleepwell about this. Everything was about to change. 'When the old man finally dies,' Oscar'd told them, 'the city will fall to fighting itself.' War would break out. Many would die. 'Good times,' Oscar had said, with a wink, 'for poison boys.' Perhaps this was it, Dalton thought, listening to the bells. The Duke was dead.

A light wind rattled the sash again. Dalton peered at the Jack, his vision still a glassy blur, then put the card away. He had the fierce fear of the hunted in him.

'Right then,' he croaked.

Blackjack Gannet had spoken. Dalton wiped his hands as clean as he could get them, yanked open the sash window, his breath ragged and wheezing, and climbed out into nothingness.

TWO

His fingers slipped on the window stones and he skinned his knees as he hauled himself out into the warm night. Dalton could hear the whisper of tree tops, even over the monotony of those rolling bells, and knew he was high up. The trees smelt like pines. He pulled the window closed. When he dropped his flailing legs they found a foothold in something tangled and rustling – ivy, old and thick.

'Vivas Gannet!' he breathed in thanks. He let the branches take his weight and lowered himself, knuckles like iron, face pushed against the stones of the windowsill. If he fell from here, he guessed, he'd hit some grand gravelled driveway and splash into bloody gobbets like a dropped dish of tomato soup.

A light popped into life somewhere close. Dalton could hear voices at the window just above him – shouted instructions and banging doors. Another window was hauled open somewhere near and a new wave of terror washed down his back. Sweat broke out on his forehead.

'He's not here,' a man's voice said, its owner drawing back.

Dalton buried his legs as best he could in the ivy, arms shaking with the effort of holding himself. He shifted his weight and turned his face away from the light.

'Find him. The boy's not invisible, is he?' This voice was a woman's. There was the sweep of a dress.

Someone cleared their throat to speak. 'No, madam.'

'The bedrooms are clear!' said another voice, more distant.

'Is he outside? He may have left the house by a window.'

Despite his clamouring heart, Dalton found himself counting up footsteps and voices, trying to make sense of where he might be and how many people were in the rooms above. It was hard to think over the bells.

'I've checked. It's too far down. The fall would have killed him.' This voice had spoken already. That meant there were four of them, Dalton guessed.

The woman's voice came again, cold and clear. 'Check outside. Take two men, and arm yourselves. I needn't remind you, of course –' here, her voice lowered to a hissed whisper, clearly through closed teeth – 'about the danger this boy could pose to the mistress. Post a man on each stairway.'

'Yes, madam.'

A door opened.

'Could he be upstairs?'

'No, madam.'

Dalton heard again the rustle of a dress as the woman drew back from the window. He thought for a moment he caught the scent of her perfume on the night air. A lantern somewhere nearby was snuffed out and the window drawn shut.

He grinned with relief and shifted his grip to steady himself. His right foot seemed to be resting on something solid. He reached out an arm slowly, his palm inching its way across the face of the brickwork. It was a trunk. The central branches of the great plant were thick and strong – gnarled stems hidden beneath the mass of green – and they took his weight well.

Dalton thanked his lucky Jack and hauled himself across, the ivy clattering and leaves spiralling downwards. But his elation was short lived. There was the crunch of movement on the gravel below: men in the grounds; men with loaded pistols, ready to blow a boy's brains to pulp. They'd pick him off the wall of the house as easily as plucking a plum. If the poison didn't get him, these guards would.

'Dreck!' he cursed quietly, scrambling upwards. He made slow progress, each dry branch buried as it was beneath a tangle of growth. Leaves stuck to the gluey blood on his clothes. Little clouds of nightflies burst from the stones beneath the ivy leaves. They bit like mosquitoes. Sweat stung Dalton's eyes and his belly broiled. The branches weakened as he approached the overhang of the roof. It was at a dizzying height. His slippery palms were losing their grip. The only answer was a wide, top-floor balcony to the left, if he could reach it – but that meant going back into the house.

Somewhere below hushed voices were in conversation. More men had been summoned and they were preparing to fan out and search the gardens. Dalton descended an uncertain step and reached for the balcony rail. It was too far away. He stretched and flapped at it in vain. He'd have to jump.

Above, thin clouds obscured the moon. Below, torches bobbed in the blackness as men searched the foliage. He could hear someone beating the undergrowth, expecting to flush out a frightened boy for the pistol-bearers. Above all else, the moaning of the bells continued. It was as if he'd woken into some wild nightmare version of the city he knew; a bad dream in which every steeple was mournfully calling for help.

Dalton touched his lucky Jack again, held his breath – and made the leap. There was a dull crash as he hit the balcony rail but the men below weren't looking. He pedalled his legs madly and found his footing, heaved himself over the rail and straightened up.

Ahead were doors and the pale light of a room beyond.

He blinked and moved forward. There were curtains of white silk and through them, like distant lights, a pair of candles, one on each side of what looked like a bed. There was incense in the air, and incense meant people. He leant against the outer wall of the house. The stones still held some of the day's oppressive heat. He found himself wondering if he could stay hidden outside until daybreak – it was another hot night, after all – then find some escape across the roof. Dalton watched the guards working the undergrowth in pairs below. There were too many of them. He'd be spotted if he stayed still. No, the only way was into the house again.

He crept forward, cursing. He opened the door outward, leaving a swollen red smudge on the fine brass handle. There was the sound of water, and then something far worse – a girl's voice. Someone was in the room.

'Edward?' it said. There was fear in that voice, Dalton thought. For a stupid moment, he wished he was Edward, whoever that was. This was going to require some explaining. He placed an open palm across the lucky Jack in his pocket, as if waiting for guidance.

'Edward?' the voice said again. 'What's happening?'

Dalton brushed a bloody hand through his fringe, drew the curtain aside and stepped forward into the room. He froze, and for a moment his breath deserted him.

A young woman was sitting in a copper bath, the steam rising about her. She was pointing a pistol at his face.

'Kite!' she whispered. The pistol wavered in her hand at the sight of him. The fear in her voice was alive in her eyes and tight in her throat as she swallowed. There was a pause. Her composure seemed to return. 'I will shoot you if you move,' she said more firmly.

Her eyes were dark and her hair in black ringlets, wet and sticking to her shoulders. Her skin was gleaming in the steam and candlelight. Dalton felt his heart squeezed by some great invisible fist as he looked at her. She drew an arm across herself and the water swished. She kept the pistol steady.

Dalton averted his gaze, feeling the heat rise in his face. He'd never seen a girl undressed. He glanced about the room, raising his hands slowly. There was a table next to the bath with a robe and glass flicker of wine on it. Splendid items glistened in the half-light: a silver hairbrush, an elegant mask for a costume ball, a cane, a fan and, on the dresser, an oil lantern and a letter-opener resting on some scribbled papers. He looked at his boots and realised with a sinking heart that he was leaving a trail of blood and ivy on her marble floor. Still. He needed to say something.

'Can you help me?' he said. He was aiming for calm reassurance, but it was the first time he had spoken above a whisper since he woke and his voice sounded like a cracked rasp. He tried to smile but the young woman's eyes blinked in revulsion at his lopsided flash of red teeth.

'Who are you?' she said, eyeing him with horror. She moved in the water, sat more upright, reached for the robe at her side, royal blue with golden stitched edging, and pulled it up to her. Beads of moisture clung to her pale arms. The steam moved like a ghost. 'Who are you?' she repeated, slowly, as if to an idiot.

'Not Edward,' he croaked, trying his battered smile again. He cleared his throat but blood came up and he had to swallow it back, grimacing. 'Dalton Fly,' he said. 'One of Oscar's boys. You don't know me.'

Her dark eyes narrowed. She didn't believe him. 'Look away,' she said.

Dalton turned. He heard her rise and the water tumble and splash from her, then her feet on the marble floor of the room. The girl crossed quickly to the window, dripping in her robe, holding the pistol aloft. Dalton watched her, his hands in the air, arms aching. The gun was old, he noted, flogged with use but still dangerous. There was a silver seal inlaid on the ivory handle butt: a silver crescent moon. She pulled the curtain aside and watched the lanterns bobbing in the darkness below, listened to the wailing of the churches.

She had small silver rings in her ears. She was, he guessed, sixteen or so, tall, brave and fine looking. He could see her pulse push at the skin of her wrist. It was galloping. 'This is all a mistake,' said Dalton. 'I'm just a poison boy. One of Oscar's — you can ask anyone.'

'What have you done?' she said, indicating his gruesome outfit. 'Who have you killed?'

He wiped a wet sleeve across his brow. 'I don't know. I'm poisoned. So's Bennie Jinks. But he's already ghosted. It wasn't me. I swear.'

In the distance, a shot was fired – perhaps at an imagined shadow or silhouette in the oleander bushes. There was a tumble of upraised voices. She took a step towards him and brought the tired old pistol to her shoulder to rest it there, pointing it upwards. She was still steaming from the bath and a pool of water swam at her bare feet.

'It wasn't me, I swear,' he said again, watching the pistol, watching her. He tried to clear his throat, but it became a hacking cough. The horror in her expression hardened and she turned from him to check the window one last time. The bells continued their mournful song.

'She's got them all searching the gardens,' she said to herself as she watched. Her posture loosened a little. 'She must really want you.'

This was his chance. Her fear had slackened. She wasn't going to shoot him. He began to back away towards the bedroom door. She lowered the pistol, watching him retreat. A ringlet of black hair had fallen across her left cheek.

'What is it you've done?' she whispered and indicated the curtain. She meant the men in groups down there in the sticky night, hunting him.

Dalton took another uncertain step backwards. He wanted to say something brave that she would remember forever and always take courage from. But he couldn't think.

'I don't know,' he rasped. 'I'm just a poison boy.' Dalton thought of Sal for the first time that night, and added as brightly as he could, 'There's more of us. We can help you if you're ever in trouble.' It sounded hollow and stupid even as he said it.

'Well, thanks,' she said, mocking him now. 'But if there's someone in trouble here, it's probably you.' She waved the pistol at the second door. 'Go that way. Follow the steps all the way down.'

'What's your name?' Dalton said.

She pushed her hair back from her face. 'Follow the steps,' she said. 'Go.'

After a moment's hesitation, Dalton crossed the room and opened the door. A servant's stairwell fell away beyond it, secret and empty. He turned and grinned with relief, flashing blood-blackened teeth. Then he was away, his heart whirling and his pulse rushing as he clattered downwards, following the circular stairwell away from the room with the marble floor and the finery, away from the girl with the long black hair and the wet skin – down, floor by floor, landing by landing, to the shadow of the cellars.

THREE

'We can't do this without waking Oscar,' whispered Sal Sleepwell. Waking Oscar would be a mistake and both boys knew it. 'Does it help if you hold your breath?'

Dalton, having eventually made it home, was huddled below the first floor window of Oscar's place in a pale pool of moon. He shot his friend a look. 'It helps, dreck-wit, if I know what the poison is.' He managed a smile, though his teeth ground together fiercely. 'We need to go upstairs.'

'Right. Right. I know that,' Sal said and crammed his spectacles into his huge thatch of wild hair, his eyes still wet with tears for Bennie Jinks and his voice an uncertain tremor. 'But he's asleep up there and it's Kite knows what time of night. We can't get the stuff without waking him.'

'Come on, Sleepwell,' Dalton said, louder than he should. The other boy's eyes widened and he held his shaking hands aloft in warning. 'You're better than all of us at this,' Dalton continued in a whisper.

Sal wiped his nose and peered out into the empty street. The bells were still going; a ceaseless tolling that echoed out across the city's districts – out across Angels and Geswick and Yelder – over the split roof tiles of the cramped houses of the Lower Circle.

'Kite!' he said, looking up at the ceiling. 'How can the old man sleep through this noise?'

'Fever-tea, dreckwit. Can we speed this up? I'm getting gutted here.'

Something shuffled in the shadows below – a rat, picking its way through the dust. It hadn't rained for weeks. A single shutter banged aimlessly in the warm wind. Under them was the ever-present creak of the swinging iron sign that declared, 'Oscar's Honest Dozen. Anti-venom and food tasting for the people of Highlions.' But there had never really been a dozen, Sal knew. There'd only ever been three, and now Bennie was ghosted.

Oscar sometimes spoke of his 'Honest Dozen' with a blind, half-dreaming look in his eyes. Names that the boys didn't know were incanted like an old spell: Starmint, Rakes, Moorepeach, May, Swales. Dead boys or grown-ups far away now from the baking back-alleys of the Lower

Circle. Above them, the old man would be sleeping, his huge old body rolled over, his sheets thrown back, deep in a fever-tea dream, sweating. Sal turned from the window.

'All right. We'll go up.'

'Thanks.' Dalton wiped his hot face with a heavy sleeve, his guts knotted and shuddering.

'So Bennie was sick?' Sal said, crouching beside him to begin his diagnosis.

Dalton nodded, his fingers tracing the outline of his lucky Jack tucked in his inside pocket.

'How much? All at once? Was it like river-sickness?'

'I don't remember,' whispered Dalton, his eyes tight shut. 'I woke up like this,' he indicated his jacket, creased and filthy.

'Have you coughed blood yourself? Or is this all Bennie?'

Sal kept probing, tugging at the yellow straggles of his fringe and closing his eyes from time to time, trying to remember all he had learnt from his limited time at the books. The important elements needed to be determined: time of sickness, type of sickness, heat, reaction to close candlelight . . . 'Shivers?' he asked in a dry whisper. 'Tremors in the arms and legs?' With each response he would move closer. 'What kind of headache? At the top of the neck, here?' The bells continued their ponderous clang. 'What about your eyes? Show me your eyes.' He peered in close. 'Dreck!' he swore, his voice a pitch higher.

'What? What's wrong?'

'Can you still see with these?'

'Not well. It's better now. What do you mean *these?*'

'Your eyes are flogged,' Sal said and gave a low whistle, looking as if into two pools of ink. 'All the white's gone black.'

Dalton held the other's gaze. Only one poison did that, and they both knew it.

'Have you a burning throat?' Sal asked.

Dalton nodded, grimacing.

'And you can't remember what happened.'

'No,' Dalton said. 'I just woke up and Bennie was ghosted. I didn't know where I was. It took me hours to find my way back here.' He folded his arms across his belly and closed his eyes.

Sal studied his friend – a pale-skinned poison boy, feverish and fading. 'Blurred vision,' Sal said, raising a thin finger, his face a picture of concentration. 'Flogged memory.' A second finger went up.

'And Sleepwell,' said Dalton, forcing a smile, 'can you feel this?' He placed his friend's palm across his chest. Sal felt the mad stutter and gallop of the other boy's heart. 'It keeps doing it, then slowing down again. I can't make it stop.'

Sal rose to his feet, wiping his red palm clean. 'We need Calabar beans,' he said firmly. 'And we need to get the right number or . . .' He faltered. Dalton grunted, trying to stand. Sal held his hand out.

'So – it's belladonna poisoning,' Dalton said.

Sal nodded, sad and frightened, hauling his friend to his feet. He wiped his eyes again for a moment or two and sniffed loudly, then perched his glasses back on his freckled nose.

It was dark and the stairs creaked. At the top, Oscar's door was ajar. Sal pushed it gently open but it struck an object behind it with a thud and the two boys winced. If Oscar had been drinking fever-tea heavily, he often carried on seeing things for hours. He could mistake a frightened boy for a bandit or burglar – and gut them while they tried to shake him awake. It had happened to Rakes. Everyone knew – Oscar had cut the kid's belly open in a panic when the boy, a new one who'd only arrived a matter of days before, tried to wake him up in the night.

Sal swallowed hard and shouldered the door further, widening the gap. Both boys slipped through. The room was lighter than usual. A blanket, normally hung over the window to block the moon, had been cast aside. An oil lamp guttered low, nearly dead. The place smelt of sweat and fever-tea. As their eyes adjusted, the boys saw him, a great dark shape under the sheets; and over on the desk where the shrine was, the heavy stoppered bottle with its glaze of green liquid, the silver slotted spoons, the sugar, the candle and the swirling glass flicker: all Oscar's fever-tea equipment.

'He's drunk a lot tonight,' Sal whispered, indicating the bottle. 'He might sleep through this.'

The boys gazed at the chaos of the room; Sal alert, Dalton hunched and clumsy. Sometimes, late at night, Oscar seemed to fight himself, stumbling and raging above the bedroom the posionboys shared. It looked as if he'd been angry at something. Above the desk, where his hospital was usually kept in neat and polished order, the bottles were disarrayed like crooked teeth, some spun around lidless, some on their sides. Sal began a quick search, replacing stoppers and caps as he went, checking labels and sniffing at the powders, roots and berries.

'Here,' he whispered suddenly, raising a jar with a pale smile. 'Calabar beans. Sit down.' Sal ushered Dalton to a chair near the window.

'We need to be quick,' Dalton rasped, his fists balled and his eyes tight closed. 'I'm getting gutted here.'

'Right. Hang on.' Sal held the bottle firmly in both hands and studied it as if looking for instructions. Of course, there were no instructions for the strange collection of poisons and antidotes in Oscar's hospital. No substitute, the old man would say, for time at the books. 'Belladonna and Calabar,' Sal breathed, wishing he had read more. 'The trick with Calabar,' he whispered, even though both boys knew about the trick with Calabar, 'is to get the amount right. It has a balance with belladonna.'

Dalton nodded at him, wincing. 'Three-to-one, I think.'

'Or is it three-and-a-half?'

'Yes. That.' Dalton held up a hand. 'Too much and I'm ghosted, though. Let's go for three.'

'Right. So how much belladonna have you eaten, do you think?' Sal pulled the stopper from the bottle and shook the beans: small, paired nuggets, each joined by a dry stem, like little red hearts.

Oscar twitched and smacked his lips. The boys froze. All was still again.

'Listen, lackbrain,' Dalton Fly whispered, pressing out a bloody smile. 'I don't know, do I?' He rolled himself forward into a ball and sat with his arms gripping his stomach. 'Let's try and do this quickly,' he rasped.

Sal grinned, sweating, eyes on Oscar. 'Of course, but you're going to have to guess. Enough to gut Bennie. How old was he – twelve?'

Dalton nodded.

'Eighteen belladonna berries to kill a full grown-up, perhaps five for a baby.' Sal removed his glasses and wiped his face with a sleeve. His heart thumped. 'So, Bennie gets ghosted on, say, ten. But you're older. Fatter.' Sal grinned, looking for a response, but the other boy was pale and beginning to shiver. 'And you've been tasting since you were . . .' Sal's voice drifted off as he tried to guess the level of resistance a poison boy might develop after training and working with Oscar for as long as his best friend had.

All the potions and syrups the old man made you drink . . . The grim tinctures and tonics that tasted like death; the hours awake at night plagued by delusion, fever, cramps and tremors as the body developed its defences. The agonies, the swelling, the bleeding. Some boys got stronger, others weakened. Sal knew he was one of the weak ones; he was Dalton's age – but Oscar wouldn't risk him like he did Dalton Fly.

Sal shook the jar again and the beans jumped and

clattered. Oscar didn't stir. Sal knew he didn't have much time. 'Sixteen' he whispered to himself. 'Three-to-one belladonna to Calabar. So that's five Calabar . . .' he palmed a few, and rolled them gently in his fingers. 'No – six.'

He bit a fingernail, his eyes checking the room again. They stopped at the shrine.

Oscar's shrine. A private clutter of impenetrable objects, all empowered with strange significance. You had to believe – trust and believe, as the old man was fond of telling them. The shrine had given Oscar many wonders and signs, so the boys were told, and these messages would often come dressed in unexpected ways: mysterious, disguised, obscure – but there, nevertheless. Sal suspected it had less to do with the mad scatterings across this makeshift tabletop, and more to do with drunkenness and fever-tea.

Still, it was worth a try.

Sal thought for a moment, his hand on his sick friend's feverish forehead. He cleared his throat. 'Fly,' he said. 'I've got an idea. Where's your lucky Jack?'

FOUR

No one was allowed too close to the shrine. Sal approached, clutching Dalton's playing card, with heart racing. At the centre of the gathered oddities was the pen-and-ink picture of Blackjack Gannet, King of the Poison Boys. It was the famous picture, the one everyone knew, where Gannet, dark-skinned, his hair escaping from beneath the brim of a ridiculous hat, was raising an eyebrow and flashing a bold grin – a face often imitated by the boys.

Gathered around this centrepiece were a range of strange curios: seeds in dusty glass dishes, two small ivory figurines, a crowd of stoppered bottles with nameless unguents in them, a locket, a seabird's wing-tip feathers, a monocle, two iron dice and a heap of coins, and two pages torn from a book with a scrawled list of names on them – Sal drew closer – names like Starmint, Rakes, Spooner, Fox. Poison boy names.

'Sleepwell,' hissed Dalton. 'Give me the Calabar, will you?'

'Hold on,' Sal said, his voice tight. *Trust and believe*, he heard Oscar say, his voice a wet slur. Sal shook his head clear. 'Ah, flog it,' he whispered, fixed Gannet's gaze and cleared his throat. He held up Dalton's card between thumb and forefinger and pointed it at Gannet. 'Where next?' he said to the picture in a low voice, casting an embarrassed glance over his shoulder. He'd seen Oscar do this – swaying slightly, his back to the door, washed in moonlight. 'Where next?' he'd say, always the spluttered, tired voice he had late in the night, waiting for his sign, his guidance.

'I don't know,' whispered Dalton. 'How about I eat Calabar, and don't die?'

Sal held a hand up. He rolled his eyes and tried again. 'Where next, Gannet?' he said, more urgently. Nothing except that shutter banging out in the street again, the perpetual rolling of distant bells, then Dalton, twisting his legs together and cursing quietly. Sal looked at the playing card in his hand and shook his head at his own stupidity. *Wonders and signs indeed.* 'Come on, Gannet. Don't leave us now,' he said through gritted teeth.

'Give me my card back,' Dalton hissed, his breathing

unsteady. 'That card only works for me. Get your own lucky card.'

Sal looked at the jar of Calabar and bit his fingernail. 'Right,' he whispered. 'I'll borrow Oscar's. It'll work with Oscar's.' He reached carefully across the bottles and jars and picked up the deck of cards there. The bottom card slipped from his grip and remained on the table, face up. It took a moment for Sal to see it.

Five of hearts.

Sal stared for a moment; looked again at Gannet's picture, framed by its family of random objects. The flat smile remained, impassive and empty. Five of hearts; five little paired beans, joined by a stem. He shook his head in disbelief. *Wonders and signs.* A small smile grew as he palmed out Calabar.

'Vivas Gannet,' he whispered, making a silly self-conscious bow to the King of the Poison Boys. Then, turning to Dalton Fly, he held out his palm. 'Eat these.'

They were on the roof, backs to the chimney, watching the sun creep above the wall of the Middle Circle; washed and famished, heady with relief. Fat wedges of shadow retreated as morning came. The bells had stopped and an empty dawn silence had replaced them. The city would soon be stirring.

'What about that cat?' Sal said, pointing.

Dalton squinted. 'No.' He was eating an apple.

Sal studied the Lower Circle streets again, mazy knots of dusty cobbles. 'Count the windows in that house there.

Just the top floor.'

Dalton peered, pulling a face. 'Seven?'

'No, five. Your lucky number.' Sal laughed. 'See that elephant down there?'

'Wet yourself.'

'Seriously. Just there.'

Dalton laughed. 'They're improving, anyway. What do they look like?' He offered his eyes up for inspection.

Sal leant over. 'Better. Your pupils are shrinking. The light should be less painful by now too.' Sal turned, his attention caught by the appearance of a group of figures: a huddled gang marching purposefully from the market squares near the main gate. They were making swift progress, picking a route through the alleyways beyond the church. 'Right,' he said, pointing. 'Your last test. How many Streetwatch are there in that patrol?'

Dalton followed the outstretched arm, frowning. 'Four? Plus dogs.'

'Right!' Sal slapped him on the back. 'You're getting there. They'll soon be back to normal. Of course, if it hadn't been for the quality of my calculations . . .' Sal smoothed the front of his shirt and pulled the Gannet grin. The boys laughed. 'Give me a bite of that, will you?'

'Trap it, Sleepwell.' Dalton smiled, tossing the apple core from the roof. He was watching the distant patrol.

'It's quiet now the bells have stopped,' Sal observed, following his friend's gaze. 'You think it means the Duke's finally gone?'

Dalton nodded. 'There'll be a big funeral.'

'Then what?'

'Then, trouble,' Dalton said, remembering Oscar's words, 'and good times for poison boys.'

The dogs were audible now; two broad-backed hunting hounds that pulled their handlers hard forward. 'There's six, actually,' Dalton said, pointing them out. 'Look. Two have moved across to that street over there. Down by the bear pits, see? The other four are coming in this direction.'

'Holy Kite,' whistled Sal, wiping his glasses. 'Your eyes really are improving. What are they up to?'

'I've seen them do this before. Someone's going to get their door kicked in.'

'How do you know?'

'Well, these two,' Dalton indicated the breakaway pair who had come back into view, past the fountain, 'will take the alleyways at the back in case the murderer jumps out of the window. Whereas these four −' the other group were closer now, the dogs lively and muscular, tugging at their ropes − 'will thump his door in and drag him from his bed. Should be a good one to watch!'

Both boys rose to standing, holding the chimney pots for balance. A moment or two passed as they studied the patrols. Dalton seemed to be right; the two groups were converging, perhaps on some nearby point, in a pincer movement.

Two streets away now.

'Must be somewhere round here,' Sal said quietly. He cast Dalton a quick glance. The two looked briefly at each other. The patrol approached the end of their street.

'Yeah,' Dalton said, his voice faltering a little. 'Luckily for us, we haven't done anything wrong.' There was a silent moment of watching.

Sal ran his hand through his hair. 'Good times for poison boys . . .' he said in a half-whisper. In the streets below, the patrols continued their progress. They were close enough now for the boys to hear the low snarls of the dogs, the boots of the Streetwatch on the cobbles.

'Piss,' said Sal Sleepwell, his face blanching.

'We need to go in,' Dalton said. 'Quick.'

In the kitchen, all was still. No one had washed up. The previous night's food caked cheap tin plates and blackened pots. The long table where the boys ate was empty. Both looked at the large, high-backed empty chair at the head. But Oscar wouldn't be up for hours.

'Sleepwell, we need a plan.' Dalton was checking the windows, rubbing a hand across panes so grimy that spotting an approaching threat was difficult. Cobwebs choked the view. 'We're going to get stagged here.' Dalton paced, the card held tightly between finger and thumb. 'Look, we've not got much time. We'll have to—'

A volley of thuds broke suddenly from the direction of the hallway. The front door groaned in response. Sal leapt like a spooked child and Dalton dropped his card.

'Dalton Fly!' a voice bellowed from the street. 'Streetwatch. Open the door immediately!'

There was a short pause. The dogs were growling sloppily, their claws skittering and scratching as they reared to paw the door. Dalton and Sal gawped wide-mouthed at each other, pulses charging.

'Dreck!' Sal cursed hotly. 'What do we do?'

Again, the voice from the street. 'Dalton Fly!' Hardened fists battered the door once more. The dogs yelped and spat, fighting against their ropes.

In a haze of fear, Dalton bent to pick up the lucky Jack. Then something caught his eye. 'Sleepwell,' he said, looking up. 'What about the kiteholes?'

Sal grinned with relief. 'Good idea,' he breathed.

'Let's go under,' Dalton said, a mad fire in his eyes. 'Sleepwell. Say you know a route. Tell me you know a route.'

The old trapdoor to the kiteholes, long forgotten, was a heavy slab of damp wood beneath the dining table. The floor about them was dusty and cold as they clawed at its edges with trembling hands. They worked quickly and quietly save for whispered curses as they broke their nails and bruised their fingertips. Sal eased his fingers beneath a corner, and Dalton prised open the gap, holding his breath against the gasp of sour air.

As they struggled, it happened: a single blast from a pistol, followed by a crash of ripped hinges as the front door folded inwards. Beyond the kitchen, they could hear the choked growling of dogs fighting for position in the tight corridor.

'Dalton Fly!' an indistinct silhouette bellowed from the hallway, the shadow of a pistol raised in anticipation of a mighty scramble. 'Surrender yourself! No one is to leave this building!' The heavy shapes of a barrel-chested crew of Streetwatch shouldered their way into Oscar's hall, their thick legs visible from beneath the table where the boys worked frantically.

Dalton had the door raised now, straining to lever it upwards and hold it long enough for Sal to slip through. In the hall, the men advanced, pistols aloft, and there was the crash of a door being shouldered in.

Sal was through now, and down into the darkness below. Dalton dropped his legs through the mouth of the kitehole, held his breath, rolled on to his belly and lowered himself. His last sight was that of a tangled gang of boots moving in wide strides into the kitchen. He lowered the door as gently as he could, arms burning, and found himself in tar-black darkness.

There was a moment of horrible silence. Then, the scrape and shuffle of heavy feet on the stone floor above them and the growling of dogs. The voices were clear and distinct.

'There's kiteholes in here,' someone said. 'Bring the dogs through. Get ready to rip this room apart. And watch for the boy. He's dangerous.'

FIVE

They were in a dank stone cell.

Foaming with fear, Sal spoke at a whisper. 'Fly.' He drew breath through gritted teeth. 'We have to find the right tunnels.'

Above, the boys heard the sound of wood being drawn across stone. There was a roll of thumps from the kitchen as something tumbled on to the floor. Sal peered frantically into the blackness beyond them. The whole of the Lower Circle was a web of passageways. Smuggler's towns were built like that. The trick was to be able to navigate them, to head for the river, master your fear and pilot your way through the ink. A crash of tin pots overhead made them jump. Something else came down on to the kitchen floor.

'They're pulling the flogging room apart!' Dalton hissed, squinting into the dark around him. 'Come on, Sleepwell! You're the Mapmaker's youngest. Where do we go?' He peered into the shadows, breathing hard. 'We need to trick the dogs.' He pulled his jacket off and tore at the shirt beneath, balling it up.

Sal began shuffling forward, arms ahead of him. 'This way,' he said.

'Wait.' Dalton Fly had moved forward in another direction, feeling his way around the outer wall of the room.

'Fly!' Sal whispered fiercely. 'Not that way – we need to make for the river!' But the poison boy had gone, pushing his way through a gap in the broken wall into a chamber beyond.

Sal stared agog, heart hammering. Then, a spear of light widened suddenly across the brickwork behind him. For a moment, he continued to stand, stunned, watching it thicken as the trapdoor was raised. From the kitchen above them came the jumps and scratches of angry dogs and a voice shouting, 'Over here!'

Then, in the half-light, Dalton emerged from the next chamber, tugging his jacket over his under shirt, his face a white blur and his eyes illuminated like a cat's. He was holding the lucky Jack between his teeth.

'Follow me!' Sal gasped, a rush of relief warming him into action as the rising trapdoor dropped pale light into the hidden chamber, illuminating the mouth of a passage-way. 'It's this way!'

Dalton followed. Ahead, Sal moved quick and low, passing from cellar to cellar through the collapsed brickwork passages of the sub-street trading routes. Sal knew these passages. The Mapmaker's youngest, he was often called, the boy who learnt everything at the knee of his father, a master of the art. The blackness about them was broken occasionally by a brave stripe of light offering a temporary signpost, thrown through a floorboard crack or storm-drain grill.

Behind them both, echoing in the tangle of inter-locking rooms, Dalton could hear the dogs mauling his shirt, slobbering and fighting their way through that tight hole in the broken wall, following the wrong scent. Soon the growing distance between them dulled all sound, and the claps of kicked stones, the harsh barks of straining dogs or the fizz of boots slipping in gravel somewhere in the cellars behind them faded altogether. The two boys stayed low, pushing forwards, legs aching, fighting exhaustion and keeping a steadily swift pace. In time, the ground beneath their feet changed, and the boys stopped, panting for breath.

'Thank Kite,' Sal said wearily. 'These are the pipes. We're nearly at the river.'

'That,' said Dalton Fly, sitting at the mouth of the storm pipes and dangling his legs over the edge, 'was close.' They were bathed in sunshine, side by side above the river that cut its deep slice through the city, tossing sticks from the pipe-mouth down into the water below. The day was heating up and the sun stood high in the white-blue sky. Above and around them, Highlions rumbled and shouted; ostlers and hawkers, smugglers and bandits, street gangs and beggars all joining the ceaseless song of trade.

'The Streetwatch won't give up that easily,' Sal noted, picking through the debris that had gathered at the edge, collecting chinkers. Upper Circle socialites threw away small coins − chinkers or bone − Sal had discovered. A poison boy could live for a day on finds, scattered in gutters or washed by rain into the pipes. 'They'll have Oscar's guarded now, waiting for us to go back.' He paused, looked at his friend. 'What is it you've done?'

'Sleepwell,' said Dalton, turning his palms upward in a shrug, 'I told you everything. I don't know. I woke up − Jinks was there on the rug, rolled in a ball. My eyes were mad. I was poisoned. My head was empty. I ran.'

'But you might have done something − and forgotten.'

Dalton kicked his legs in frustration and threw a handful of sticks, watching them spiral down to the rolling water. 'When I try to remember, nothing comes back,' he said. 'I must have gone there last night. Oscar must've sent me and Bennie. We were tasting. But I can't remember anything else.' He bit his lip. 'And what did that Streetwatch guard shout? "The boy's dangerous." Where's that from? Someone's given them a reason to get me.'

Sal cleaned his glasses on his filthy shirt. His skin was

dark with dust, his hair an ill-tamed fuzz. He propped them on the tip of his nose. 'You've been in trouble before,' he began, remembering a thousand wild misdemeanours all undertaken in the spirit of Blackjack Gannet: a jumbled sequence of Fly-born scrapes and injustices, fights and misunderstandings – most of which Dalton had long since forgotten. Sometimes, being someone else's memory was a tough job. 'Who's doing this to you?' he asked. There may have been a whole host of scrambles in the past, but never anything as bad as this.

Dalton fell silent for a moment. 'The people in that house last night . . .' He shook his head, frustrated. 'I don't know,' he said eventually. 'I escaped. If they wanted me back quickly, they might have called the Streetwatch in to help.'

Sal cleared his throat. 'What about the undertaker?'

'Wet yourself!' Dalton gave an empty laugh. 'Just some stranger in a black coat who thinks he knows me. I've only ever seen him once!'

'Three times in a week, you said.'

'Once – three times . . .' Dalton began, his voice fading. He remembered the undertaker, even if he'd forgotten everything else. Belladonna was like that. 'It's nothing.'

'What about that stuff he said to you, then?' Sal persisted.

The other boy fell silent. The first time he'd seen the undertaker, as they called him now, had been a few days ago. Dalton had been on the Laceway down in Yelder, buying spices for Oscar's collection; clinging to the palmful of dirty chinkers the old man had given him and hoping he'd got the right type of incense; staying clever among the spice traders and pollen smugglers; watching his pockets for dippers; swimming the thick crowds; breathing the heavy, ripe smells of saffron and cardamom.

Then, a hand on his shoulder. Dalton had turned, one arm raised defensively, jumpy, expecting a scramble.

Above him loomed a tall, sharp-featured old man who quickly withdrew his hand. His eyes had widened and he'd brought his other hand up to his chin, as if in an instinctive, shocked movement, and then seemed to recover his senses. He said something at a whisper as if gripped by amazement – a single, odd word which Dalton hadn't heard before and couldn't now remember. Then he reached a hand into the deep pocket of the black greatcoat he wore – an unusual garment on such a hot day among the spices and pollens.

Something had made Dalton bolt as he did this; duck low into the legs of the crowd and scramble for safety beneath a trader's wagon then out into an alleyway beyond.

'Just an old market dipper,' said Dalton.

Sal shook his head. 'If you say so. But three times? You must have something he really wants to steal!' Sal tried to laugh as he spoke, but it came out mirthless.

'That second time was strange,' Dalton conceded.

It had been past midnight; he was making for home, weary after a tasting in Greengoose, steering his way back to the shop, down the hill through Geswick, the river slopping and gurgling to itself some streets off to his right, clouds of mosquitoes drifting. The coat caught his eye first – the dark undertaker's coat billowing behind the man as he rounded the corner in the shadow of the bear-market buildings. There was a moment's silence; a flash of recognition. Then, for the second time, the word, shouted, barked almost, as if it were an order. What was that word? The figure had raised his arm in a wave or a command, and begun to run towards him, taking long, agile strides across the moonlit cobbles. Dalton had turned on his heels and fled; a side alley, a flight of slippery steps and a charge across an empty square to the safety of Yelder's streets.

'How did he know I'd be there?' Dalton said, recalling the event. 'I suppose it's possible he was following me . . .'

Sal nodded. 'So it could be him, then. Raising the Streetwatch to get you.'

'It could,' Dalton conceded. 'But what for? I've never seen him before in my life.' He scowled. Bennie Jinks ghosted, the undertaker – it was as if his old, familiar life was unravelling around him and he didn't know why.

'So what's next?'

Dalton fixed his gaze on the storm pipes across the river, thinking. 'We can't go home,' he said. 'Well, I can't.' He rubbed his eyes, shook his head clear and stood up, ducking slightly beneath the curved roof of the pipe.

'Where will you go?' Sal asked.

Dalton put his head in his hands and stared at the water. He found himself, inexplicably, thinking of Rakes.

How old had the boy been when Oscar had carved him open? Seven or eight? The rain had lashed down the night they dug a hole for him, its walls a sheer slick of greasy clay. And Rakes, floating in the bottom of it, his skin going black. The kid wouldn't sink, just kept bobbing back up in the muddy water.

Dalton blinked the memory clear. At the moment, Bennie Jinks was rolled up in a bloody rug in the house of a stranger.

'To start with, I'm going to get Bennie back,' Dalton said. 'We're going to have to dig a hole for him.'

Sal fingered the coins in his palm. After a moment, he looked up at his friend. 'So, let me see if I've got this right,' he said levelly. 'Bennie's ghosted. The Streetwatch want your arse for an ornament. We're homeless. The undertaker's out there somewhere, looking for you. And you want to go back to a mansion full of pistol-waving bandits.'

Dalton considered his position for a moment, one hand across the Jack in his pocket. Then he nodded. 'That's right,' he said. 'Are you coming?'

Sal looked at his hands. 'Dreck,' he sighed, flexing his fingers. Being around Dalton Fly could be exhausting. There was always something: some lunatic plan; some stand-off with local street boys; some hastily assembled solution, forged in the fire of a moment. His friend certainly had a talent for making things dangerous.

'Sleepwell,' Dalton said, and gave him a nudge and a Blackjack Gannet grin.

Sal held up his hoard; a pocketful of grubby silver chinkers, gleaned from the pipe debris. 'You're going to need me,' he said. 'I'm in.'

SIX

Out in Geswick, the streets were busy.

'Where do we start?' asked Sleepwell, one hand across his eyes, shielding them from the late morning sun. 'If it's mansions with gardens we're after,' he said, squinting into the distance, 'then we're going to need to be checking places like Ivyhill or Purslane.'

Dalton pulled Sal clear from the bustle of the street into the shade of the buildings that hugged the carriageway. 'Careful, Sleepwell,' he said. 'We don't want those Streetwatch guards recognising us again.' He ground his teeth, scanning the crowds. 'Anyway,' he added, 'I remember seeing the opera house from the windows of the hallway.

The flags above the cathedral were low. I could hear the bells. So, Mapmaker's youngest, where was I?'

Sal adjusted his spectacles and ran a hand through his stiffening, mud-caked hair. His eyes went loose and dark as he thought, imagining the city's packed districts stitched together like a patchwork quilt. 'If you could see the cathedral,' he said, 'you were north of Sixteen Fountains, probably west of the river; Skillet or Ivyhill, I'd guess.'

'That's a mighty mess of streets to search,' said Dalton.

Sal nodded. 'We need help. Someone who can tell us where to start.'

Dalton laughed. 'Wet yourself! Who'd help us?' He shot his friend a black look.

Sal wiped his glasses on the torn corner of his shirt and replaced them, meeting Dalton's gaze evenly.

'No,' Dalton said, realising what Sal was thinking. 'No. We're not seeing Eyesdown.'

Sal shrugged. 'Big city,' he said, 'little Flyboy.'

'No, Sleepwell. Not Eyesdown. He'll have my plums for a lucky charm. He hates me.'

Sal frowned. 'That was a long time ago now. His hair will have grown back. He doesn't have the nightmares anymore. It's forgotten.'

Dalton kicked his heels. 'He said he'd never forgive me.'

'He's over it, Fly. I swear. It wasn't your fault he had an allergy, was it? Besides, the boy knows everything. He'll have heard something from someone – he'll know where Bennie is.'

Dalton checked the bobbing heads of the crowd around him. It would be a long and fruitless search without some help. And Eyesdown was the boy who knew everybody's business – the perfect place to start. There was just the small matter of the disagreement to contend with. Dalton thrust his hands into his pockets, his mind made up. 'Right then,' he said. 'Eyesdown it is.'

Down by the Laceway, the broadest bridge in Highlions, the air was heavy with flies and the sour smell of fishmongers trading in the sun. Two Streetwatch guards were moving through the crowds at the markets, a dog on a leash between them. The boys kept their heads down and stayed shoulder-to-shoulder through the ruck. Spice merchants shouted over the crowds in heavily-accented voices. Oil traders unloaded carts of lamp resin and hawkers selling the *Advisor* and the *Circle* held up copies of their papers and called out headlines. 'Tributes pour in for Highlions Duke!' one shouted. 'Duke dies childless!' chimed in a second. 'Accession already debated!' another declared, waving the paper above his head. 'The senate calls for any potential heirs to make themselves known!' They were doing a roaring trade; a ruck of city folk were forming disorderly lines, blocking the street as they queued for news.

'Down here,' Sal said, steering his friend away from them, and indicating a coil of slippery steps that dropped into the shadow of the bridge arches near the river's edge. Dalton followed, holding his breath. Beneath the bridge in the damp darkness was a muddy ledge. Halfway along it was an open door and, within, a pair of oil lamps illuminating a short passageway. Only one was working; the other spluttered and smoked in the fetid air.

Dalton peered into the recess. 'You really reckon he's forgiven me?'

'Absolutely,' said Sal. He slapped his friend across the shoulder. 'I bet he'll be pleased to see you.' Sal cleared his throat and spat. 'Nice place he's got here.'

Dalton dried his palms on his undershirt and tapped his lucky Jack. 'After you,' he said. Sal pulled a face and ducked through the doorway.

Inside, Francis Eyesdown was standing, feet apart, in a cramped, windowless room amongst a huge pile of letters. He was holding a silver letter opener like a weapon. He was a broad-shouldered boy of fifteen with strong arms. His knuckles were white, his fist closed tightly around the blade. He was completely bald, his small head a shiny dome. Beads of sweat prickled his smooth scalp.

'Dalton Fly,' he said, breathing slowly. 'I thought I heard your voice. Come any closer, dreck-for-brains, and I'll cut your fingers off and feed them to you one by one.'

There was a moment of clammy silence. Dalton shot Sal a glance and tried to make a smile arrive. 'Eyesdown,' he said. 'You look well.'

'Get flogged,' Eyesdown said bluntly, and wiped his forehead with the back of his spare hand. 'Do you know what I'm still suffering 'cause of you? I get these shivers all the time. I can't sleep. I'm up all night in this Kite-forsaken little hole. You said the hair would grow back. It hasn't, in case you hadn't noticed.' Eyesdown paused for emphasis, adjusted his grip on the letter opener. 'It hasn't grown back anywhere.'

Sal took an uncertain step forward and held a pacifying hand aloft. 'Listen, Eyesdown. Sometimes oleander honey is like that. I swear we didn't know it was so strong when we tried it out.'

'Yeah, thanks, antidote-boy. Last time I take your advice. And it's not done Kite's arse here any harm, has it?' Eyesdown indicated Dalton with the sharp tip of the blade.

Dalton bit his lip. It had, actually. But he'd been working on building a resistance to it, taking just small amounts each evening, following Oscar's instructions. The pain had been acute to begin with, but he was getting stronger. Honey made from oleander pollen could deck a man in a large enough dose. This variety clearly hadn't agreed with Eyesdown. Then again, Eyesdown shouldn't have asked to try it. He'd been bothering them for weeks about it. Good oleander honey helped you sleep. And if there was one thing Eyesdown had trouble with, it was sleep. It never visited him. Often he spent the whole night trying to hunt it down.

'It'll take time,' Sal persisted, 'but you'll be all right. The hair thing – it's not permanent. Honest.'

Eyesdown sneered at Sal, but lowered the weapon a little.

Dalton sensed his chance and took it. 'We need your help, Eyesdown. We're trying to find someone. You remember little Bennie, don't you?'

'Word is he's ghosted,' Eyesdown said. He certainly had a remarkable talent for staying abreast of the news. 'Something else to do with the boy calamity, I'd guess. Feed him bad honey as well did you, Fly?'

Dalton clenched his fists at his sides and swallowed hard. 'Leave it, Francis,' he said, keeping his voice level. 'We just need to find Bennie again. I'm sorry for what happened. But you've got to help us. What do you know?'

'Nothing I'd want to share. You trail a big black cloud of trouble over your heads wherever you go, you two. I don't want it pissing on me.'

Sal fished in his pockets and pulled out the palmful of chinkers he'd rescued from the storm pipe. 'Listen, Eyesdown,' he said. 'You could take a couple of these coins.'

Eyesdown weakened. He was imagining bread and cheese, Dalton thought. A cup of beer, perhaps, or a sleeping draught.

'You could get yourself a nice hat,' Dalton suggested evenly.

Eyesdown didn't smile. But he lowered his arm and transferred his attentions to the letters around his feet — great piles of them. He stole a lot of letters, mostly from bins. Eyesdown was always saying how amazing it was what people threw away. Their whole life stories, sometimes. Stories, he had discovered, could be valuable; once he'd been paid fifteen guineas for a single letter. Dalton remembered it fondly; Eyesdown had been a generous friend. He'd lived on pies and wine for weeks and took to smoking a pipe. Then, inevitably, he went through a bad spell, things went quiet and his sources dried up.

Dalton peered into the shadowy recesses of Eyedown's room: a bed with a driftwood frame and straw mattress, a flogged shoulder bag and riding coat over the back of a tired chair, rolls of pamphlets and handbills, wanted posters stripped from the walls in districts like Down-holland or the Dips. And of course, letters and notes – mountains of them, some curling and yellowed, others smudged and torn, some still sealed with wax crests. This, Dalton concluded, was one of Eyesdown's bad spells.

'I've probably got something in here that can help you,' said the boy, running an open hand over his smooth head. 'But it'll cost.'

'This is all we have,' Sal said, his hand still extended. 'Come on, Francis. We need your help.'

Francis Eyesdown nodded. 'All right,' he conceded. 'But only 'cause I need the bone. Pass it over, Sleepwell.'

Sal tipped the coins into the other boy's palm and watched as he counted them greedily and thrust them into his pocket.

'Where do we look?' Dalton said, indicating the scattered masses of material heaped on the damp floor of the little cell.

'Don't touch anything, dreckwit,' Eyesdown said, raising the thin silver blade once more. 'It's all in order, this lot. Don't even move.' He began to pass between the piles, walking on the balls of his feet, hunched over and squinting, muttering to himself: a low whispered discussion with his memory, Dalton thought. He dropped to a crouch and checked the document that topped a pile, then moved on again.

'Here,' he said eventually, unrolling a crumpled note that had evidently been rescued from somewhere unsavoury. Eyesdown held it close to his face, scanning it. 'This little note here's an interesting one,' he said. 'Found it last week. It's a request from someone called Gellis for the services of Oscar's Honest Dozen. You're still with Oscar, I'm guessing?' Both poison boys nodded, expectant. 'Right,' said Eyesdown. 'Well, this asks for the services of two p-boys for a food tasting. Last night. That wouldn't be you, would it Fly?'

Dalton felt a dry lump in his throat and tried to swallow. He blinked away a sudden and vivid image of Bennie Jinks washed in a sea of spit and blood. 'That'd be me,' he said.

'Well then. This is your lucky day,' Eyesdown said. 'There's an address on it.'

SEVEN

'So' Sal said, hand against the high wall that surrounded the house. 'This is it, you think?' He checked Eyesdown's letter a third time.

Dalton looked again along the tree-lined avenue. They were in Ivyhill. The streets were clean; the houses had gardens lined with big, broad-leaved bushes. The view was good and the late afternoon air was clear. He nodded. 'Yes,' he said. 'This is it.'

There was something about the shape of the trees along the perimeter of the house. Flickering memories surfaced and flashed briefly: sprinting low across a lawn with the moon at his back; trying hopelessly to climb a tree before finding a low branch near the wall; mosquitoes in the oleander; the infinite sadness of the booming bells. Bennie Jinks, a bag of bones in a bloody lake . . . This was the house all right. Dalton blinked away the visions, feeling his heart race at the memory of them.

'How do we get in?' Sal asked, squinting along the street. Lime trees in full leaf punctuated the view, throwing grey pools of shade. The day of searching had been a hot one; now the sun was dropping a little and the shadows thickening and cooling.

'Over the wall,' Dalton said. 'Let's climb one of these trees.'

It was easy enough. The streets would stay quiet and clear for an hour or so yet, and no one spotted the boys shinning up the trunk of a street tree and edging their way out along one of its prominent lower branches. From their vantage point, the house looked different.

'You sure this is the place?' Sal said, hands white-knuckled.

Dalton checked it over again. A fine three-storey mansion in large grounds; lawns to the front and side, a pale orange gravelled drive and a large iron gate. An outhouse for the gardening staff; a set of stables beyond the main house. There didn't seem to be anyone patrolling the grounds and the windows of the house were dark. Some were shuttered.

Dalton nodded, pointing. 'When I escaped, I came out through that service entrance there. The girl's room was on the top floor, with a balcony. It's over the other side of the house. There's a view down across the city from there.'

'This is madness, Flyboy. We're both going to end up dead.'

Dalton shot his friend a look. 'Wet yourself,' he said.

'You wet yourself,' Sal sneered. He bit his lip. 'Who are we expecting to see in there?'

'Like I said,' Dalton replied, checking the house over carefully, remembering as much as he could of corridors, window views, layout, 'there were a lot of guards – not Streetwatch – private guards, with a woman in charge. She was angry at me escaping.'

'And this girl?'

Dalton licked his dry lips. In his imagination, she was stepping out of the bath, wreathed in steam. His pulse pounded at the memory of the water tumbling off her pale skin as she rose up and pulled on her robe. He couldn't find any words. 'Let's work on getting inside,' he said in a cracked voice. 'It'll be evening soon.'

The branch hung close to the wall and, with a leap and a scramble, it was possible to make the top of the wall, kick up and over, and drop into the bushes below. Both boys squatted in the shadows, safely concealed from view. It wasn't long before there was movement.

'Look!' Sal pointed through the thick foliage. The boys watched as the gates of the house swung open. A horse-drawn carriage pulled up on the hissing gravel drive. A figure emerged from the house and opened the passenger door. A woman with a sweeping gown descended. Greetings were exchanged. Laughter.

'There's another,' Dalton said as a second carriage arrived. 'We need to get moving or someone'll spot us.' The light was fading as the sun dropped closer to the city's roofs. 'Let's head for that doorway there.'

A small door that looked as if it had a set of steps ascending to it was partially hidden by a scramble of ivy. Sal nodded his agreement. When the second carriage had emptied of passengers, the boys broke out across the lawn, running low.

'Can we get through?' Sal said as they reached the house wall and pressed their backs against the warm stones. Dalton was at the door, rattling it. The wood in the frame was soft with age. This was an entrance that hadn't been used in some time. 'Come on, Flyboy!' Sal hissed, checking about him with wide and darting eyes.

For answer, Dalton pulled hard at the edges of the door. He managed to prise open a gap between the door and the frame as the soft wood yielded and, with his arms pinned against his sides, he wormed through the gap and into the darkness beyond.

Sal ducked close to the doorway, checked the lawns behind him remained empty, and followed. Soon the two of them were inspecting a cellar – a connecting series of dry and dusty rooms containing wooden racks of spider-webbed bottles, barrels, crates and dust-sheeted furniture. Near the ceiling was a small window through which the fading evening sun shone. In the third room, a short flight of steps led to a hatch in the roof, and the house beyond.

'Listen!' Dalton said suddenly, palm raised. In the

house above, fiddle music had begun. The two boys listened intently, their eyes on the ceiling, following the winding dance of violins. 'There's a band of players,' Dalton said. 'People talking. What is this? A party?'

Sal cleared his throat quietly. 'Hang on. What were you tasting last night?'

'Wine, cheeses, sweets and jellies . . .'

Sal nodded and cocked his head, listening. 'So – a celebration? A special occasion?'

They listened, faces upturned, as the noise of congregation grew – raised voices, laughter, the drum roll of feet on the floors above. The music wound its way through the chatter and buzz of the gathering. It was getting louder as more guests arrived. Corks popped. There was a flurry of polite applause.

'Dreck!' Sal cursed. 'It's busy up there.'

'We need to take a look,' said Dalton. He made his way carefully up the steps and crouched beneath the hatch in the roof, then pushed it gently open, peering through the crack. The swell of the music grew louder. 'A kitchen,' he whispered down. 'Empty. Sleepwell, let's go.'

Sal made a hopeless attempt to flatten his hair; he rubbed his forehead. 'You're mad,' he said.

The cellar hatch opened in a shadowy corner of a high-ceilinged kitchen with a heavy table running along its centre. A fire flickered in a grate beneath a huge chimney. Great haunches of glistening ham were drying on hooks. A vast tureen of soup popped and bubbled. The table was spread with a glowing banquet of fine foods: fruit, cheeses, carved meats, cooked birds. The heavy scent of the feast tugged at their stomachs and their mouths watered. They hadn't eaten all day.

'This isn't the stuff from last night,' Dalton said. 'It's different. They must have replaced it all. This stuff looks clean.' He leant over the table with bright-eyed relish.

Sal's attention was quickly elsewhere. He paced to the door, ajar on the passageway beyond. 'They'll come in here to take all this through to the house. We'll get caught, Fly. We need to stay moving; find Jinks and get out again.'

Dalton looked up briefly. 'Look at this cheese,' he breathed. 'I could eat it all to myself. Gannet, I'm starved!'

'Hey. Lackbrain. We need to move . . .'

'I'm just going to take this bread. No one'll notice. Just the bread, and something to go with it.'

'Dreckwit! Come on.' Sal checked the passageway again.

'Which cheese? This soft one, here?'

'The red one,' Sal pointed. 'No, that one. Good. Now, can we get moving?'

'Follow me,' Dalton grunted, his mouth crammed.

They shared the bread greedily as they made their way along the sparse passageway. At its end was a heavy door, half open, through which spilled warm light. The music grew louder. From the shadow of the door they could see into the corridor beyond. It was richly decorated. Dark paintings hung in gold frames; rugs ran the length of the space; candles glowed in filigree baskets. Craning their necks, the opening to a ballroom was visible. A group of figures was gathered at its doors: three women in long white robes, each holding a flicker of wine, and each with a great white pair of wings on her back.

'It's a costume ball!' Sal said, observing the angels with wide, excited eyes. 'Look at those wings!' The boys stared in wonder at the winged women, watching them bob discreetly to the rhythm of the fiddler's song.

'Careful, Sleepwell . . .' Dalton hissed, and the boys drew back as two men passed by – tall figures with decorated top hats, eye masks and gaudy jewellery. One was casually swinging a gold-tipped cane.

'What are they dressed as?' Dalton whispered, peering out into the corridor again, the men safely past them. 'Sleepwell, what are the costumes?' A pause. 'Sleepwell?' There was no reply, and Dalton turned, edgy.

The other poison boy was working through a swag of riding coats hanging from a hook behind the door, rifling pockets, absorbed in his task. Suddenly, a grin warmed his face as he pulled something from a coat pocket.

'Praise the mighty Kite!' he grinned, waving a pair of glittering eye masks. 'Someone's spare costume!'

Dalton beamed. 'What else is there? Cloaks? Hats?' The boys slipped their eye masks on and stifled their laughter. They were big, covering their eyes and cheeks but leaving their mouths exposed. 'These are good disguises,' Dalton said. 'I can hardly recognise you!'

'Yes, well . . .' Sal said, slipping his glasses into his pocket. 'I can hardly see.'

There was an elegant mirror, and Sal admired his

reflection as he swapped a hunting hat for a scarf he could wind a number of times round his neck. Dalton swung a cloak over his shoulders and joined his friend. For a fleeting moment, he saw himself as he'd been the night before: a red-skinned kid with filthy clothes and a grin like a mouthful of blood; one side of his face darkened crimson-black and shining; hair on end; looking as if he'd been cut to ribbons. He blinked the vision away, wiped his eyes and looked again. There he was, shoulder-to-shoulder with his friend: just an ordinary boy – a tall boy with sunburnt skin, a serious face and dark hair that fell into his eyes. The cloak looked comically big on his thin shoulders. His fingers, unpicking the knot at his neck, were thin and delicate. He didn't like his hands. He pushed them into the pockets of the riding cloak, flashing a grin at his friend.

'Hang on.' Dalton tugged at a folded piece of paper and pulled it out of his pocket. 'What's this?' He opened it up and raised his mask so he could look at it more closely. Sal did the same, putting his glasses back on.

'Gannet!' Dalton breathed. 'It's an invitation.' Dalton looked up at Sal, excitement dancing in his dark eyes. 'This could help answer some questions.'

Carefully, he unfolded it in his palm. The two boys read.

EIGHT

A bove the text was an embossed silver seal — the crescent moon Dalton had seen on the handle butt of the girl's pistol the night before. Below this, words followed the edge of the design in a tight circle: 'House of Dropmore: Honour and Courage.' Dalton pointed, quizzical; Sal shrugged back at him. Beneath the seal the folded card read:

Dearest Edward,
Your company is requested at a night of revels
celebrating Scarlet, the foremost daughter of this house
being fully sixteen years on this day.

Dress for the evening will homage Alstaff's Deadnettle at Dusk.

The boys looked at each other, masks raised, brows furrowed.

'What does it mean?' Sal said.

'Which bit?'

'The words.'

'I'm not sure,' said Dalton, running his fingertip along the invitation's edge. 'But I know I'm wearing this man's cloak,' he prodded the phrase Dearest Edward, 'and we should be dressed as characters from this play,' he indicated Deadnettle at Dusk, 'and that it's this girl's birthday.'

Sal peered into the corridor again, then returned his attention to the invitation. 'Any idea who she is?'

'Yes,' said Dalton, folding the paper and putting it away. 'I think I met her last night.' He felt that sudden and strange pull at his stomach, the heat below his ribs. He found himself inexplicably tapping his lucky Jack.

Sal replaced his mask and blinked at Dalton. 'Ever seen Deadnettle at Dusk?'

Dalton gave him a sideways look. 'Wet yourself.'

'Right. So. Minor problem,' Sal said, checking the corridor again, squinting through the eyes of his mask. 'How do we know if we look like characters from it, then?'

Dalton sighed. 'Well, if it's a story of two homeless starving boys who really need a bath, we're laughing,' he said. 'Come on, let's find Bennie.'

*

The trick, they had decided before emerging, was to look confident and relaxed. Dalton would have the invitation to hand, or leave it peeping from a pocket; they would keep their masks on at all times, hold a flicker of wine comfortably and sip it steadily as adults did; they would smile broadly, move slowly, talk only with each other, and be entirely inconspicuous.

In the ballroom, the music leapt and jigged. It was a grand and golden space, high and glittering, lantern-lit and blinking with a thousand candles. The wide windows were black spaces, painted by darkness as the sun dropped. The place was packed. Two doors along the far wall were flung open to the night beyond and revealed busy balconies of guests pointing out over the city. The band of players, a pair of violinists and others, had drawn a crowd of dancers to another corner of the ballroom. Near a vast fireplace, chairs had been arranged and wealthy guests in all their finery smoked cigars and drank blood-red wine. Older women wore feathered hairpieces and great sweeping dresses; men looked stiff and red-faced in formal wear; children with painted faces screamed in delight and, all about, young and old wore costumes and masks.

'Kite!' Sal said under his breath. 'Where do we start looking in all this?'

'I don't recognise this room,' Dalton breathed back. 'I was somewhere else. Where might they be keeping Bennie?'

Sal stood on tiptoes and scanned the crowd. Dalton yanked at his scarf. 'Careful. Don't look obvious.'

'Wine, sirs?' A voice at their backs startled them. A member of the house staff, maskless, was stooping towards them with a cold-eyed gaze and a tray of drinks – delicate flickers of a gluey-looking wine. Dalton forced a smile. Sal, nervous, executed a smart bow and clicked his heels. Dalton took a pair of flickers and the man withdrew.

'What was that about?' Dalton said, holding one of the flickers out for his friend.

'Sorry.'

They sipped, grimacing. 'Right,' said Dalton, wiping his lips with a sleeve. 'We need to split up. There's a room full of stuffed birds somewhere – eagles or something. I was running, the guards were chasing me. But I swear that room of birds was near where I left Bennie. Let's try and find it.'

Sal nodded agreement. 'Meet you by the clock over there,' he said, pointing, 'in an hour. Good luck.'

Sal snaked his way into the crowd of costumes, his flicker held before him inelegantly, and vanished from sight. At first, Dalton did nothing. It was a shock to be back, he found suddenly. For a strange moment, he felt the sticky blood of the dead boy still on his skin. His costume clung to him and he felt a trickle of sweat run between his shoulder blades. He wiped his forehead. A bubble of applause broke as the music stopped and an indistinct announcement was made. More corks popped. There was a flurry of laughter and the music began again; this time, a slower tune, the violins duetting.

He watched the swell of the crowd for the duration of

the tune, listening to the ebb and flow of voices. He sipped his wine, shifting from foot to foot. Then Dalton realised, all at once, what he was doing; he was looking for the girl – expecting to see her as she had appeared the night before: long blue robe, bare feet, pistol in her hand.

Ridiculous. Without knowing why, he began to make his way towards the balcony doors. There were tables on the balcony overlooking the gardens. It was another hot night. He felt a glow tug at his belly and followed it.

The small outside spaces were crowded. He turned back and dithered for a moment or two, the heat under his ribs growing. Outside once more, he leant on the iron-work and assessed the people about him. A group of men were talking in the sort of hushed tones grown-ups reserved for politics. Since the Duke's death, it was all anybody was discussing, Dalton guessed. He bowed his head and stared into the darkness of the garden below. He needed a moment to piece together a plan, but he didn't want to look conspicuous, so he swirled his wine and listened. It was hard to pick out what was said, harder still to understand the references to people, places, alliances, wars.

'Now Elber is dead, expect trouble. The two Houses will battle it out until one is defeated,' one said, exhaling smoke through his teeth and grinding a cigar into an ashtray. *Elber.* That was the Duke's family name. 'It will be worse than last time, believe me. There's more at stake now. Have you seen the papers? The senate are requesting all potential heirs to declare themselves. These are trying times.' The man's dark eyes blinked beneath a black mask. Another figure spoke urgently in a low voice, disagreeing, perhaps – it was hard to hear.

'But surely the House of De Bello has sufficient support from the senate to just arrange an heir to the Dukedom now Elber has finally slipped away,' a third offered.

The first shook his head. 'Not necessarily. Dropmore has a greater influence than you might think,' he said. The others leant in, tall hats touching as they exchanged stories.

'I'd question your faith in Dropmore to steady this particular ship,' one whispered. Names were mentioned, some tossed aside as if they didn't matter, others repeated: Dropmore; De Bello; Elber.

Dalton fished the invitation from his pocket and unfolded it. *House of Dropmore: Honour and Courage.* What was going on? He took a sip of his wine. The taste reminded him of blood. There was something big here: Houses, alliances and conflicts he'd never heard of. And presumably the girl upstairs belonged amongst it all. *These people,* Dalton thought bitterly. *None of them cared a jot for a poison boy fighting for a living in the Lower Circle.* These were the names of the high and mighty: Houses trading in power and favours. What kind of Duke, Dalton thought idly, would help a boy like him? He knew little enough of the city's senate – that he admitted to himself. But whoever was to follow old man Elber had to be different. Surely.

'Stephen De Bello will fight tooth and nail for power,' one said, as another placed a calming hand on his shoulder.

'There'll be blood on the streets tonight, you mark my words.' A moment later, drinks were offered from a silver tray and talk drifted to costumes as the men turned to face the ballroom and the band.

Dalton scanned the other guests on the balcony. There was the clatter of dice and laughter, the clink of flickers and a 'Congratulations!' for someone. All about were ornate, jewelled masks – one nearby trimmed with fur or velvet, framed by a woman's blond curls. The smell of bath oils and perfume. Again the rattle of dice. This time it caught his ear, and he moved over towards the gaming table.

He stopped suddenly.

She was there, her back to him, shaking dice in her cupped hand and laughing. They were playing sevens, he noticed. A simple old game. There were two other figures at the table – one absorbed, the other rising to go else-where, a tall flicker of sparkling wine in his hand. The girl laughed and leant forward. Dalton watched for a moment, unnerved by the strange churning of his stomach. He breathed, took a deep drink of his wine, and stepped forward, hardly knowing what he was doing or why. A seat was free.

He steered for it, wondering what on earth he was going to say. He placed a hot palm across the Jack in his pocket. *Gannet, help me now.*

The young man noticed him first – initially with a disdainful glance, Dalton noted, but then with a harder expression, one of amused shock, as the curiously dressed poison boy drew a chair up and joined them.

The girl looked up from the dice. She had a glittering sequinned mask that covered her eyes and cheeks, but Dalton saw her eyes widen through the holes of the mask.

He took a deep, shaky breath. 'Happy Birthday,' he said.

NINE

Across the table from Dalton Fly, the pale young man raised his nose and looked down it, his top lip curling. The moment of silence grew uneasy.

'Do I know you?' the girl said, but her voice gave her away; she knew exactly who he was.

Dalton smiled and raised his mask for a moment by way of answer. 'We met last night,' he said, pressing his damp palms against his costume. 'You gave me some helpful advice.'

'About?' Her curls bobbed as she spoke. Her face was impassive, her eyes empty. She was a good actor.

'The way out,' Dalton said.

'And yet you're back so soon,' said the girl. She was wearing a long white dress with lace edging. She had a silver bangle on her wrist and wore a ring with a red stone set in it. She smelt of soap.

'I'm looking for a friend,' said Dalton.

'I don't think there will be many of those,' said the pale young man, 'in this room.' He rolled the dice casually between his finger and thumb. His nails were painted black. His gaze was cold and penetrating. 'Tell me,' he continued with relish, 'do you have an invitation?'

Dalton cleared his throat and raised the invite from his pocket, enough to flash its serrated edge at the young man. He forced a steely smile.

'No – I mean an invitation of your own,' the young man said coldly. 'That's my invitation. At least – it's my riding cloak, so I presume it's my invitation in the pocket.'

The girl laughed at this: an empty laugh. Dalton felt his face heat quickly, and ground his teeth together in a vain attempt to stop it. He had chosen to sit across from *Dearest Edward*. The young man's name was on the invitation. And the name – Dalton remembered this suddenly, like a firework blooming – was the one the girl had used when she was in the bath. 'Edward?' she'd called. And, when she saw Dalton, 'Who are you?' Dalton recalled himself, battered and blood-splashed, saying, 'Not Edward.' Here they were then, both at the same table – Edward and Not Edward. Dalton squirmed silently, cursing his luck and thinking of something to say.

But the young man was bullish. He sat forward and

continued. 'I think you also need advice about costume. You see, I am dressed well.' Here he indicated his own clothing: a heavy, velvet-lined military jacket hung with chinking medals and a fob watch. 'Everyone knows who I am.' He sipped his drink. 'You, on the other hand, seem to have dressed yourself as a barrow boy.' He made a thin, malicious grin. 'Have you even seen *Deadnettle at Dusk*, barrow boy?'

The play mentioned on the invite. Dalton's heart shuddered in anger and shame. He pulled his mask back down to hide his flushed face and plucked at his clothes. 'Barrow boy?' he repeated levelly. 'I knew I should have stolen a better cloak.' He saw the girl cover her mouth with a hand. Was that a smile behind there? Her eyes flashed, but he couldn't read them. He had the advantage now, however weak, and knew he must seize it. 'As I was saying . . .' he began, turning away from Edward. Across the table, Dalton was aware of the young man rising – the clatter of the dice as he dropped them on the tabletop.

'I'm going,' he heard him say. 'Something round here really stinks. Have you washed, barrow boy?'

'I'm here to find a friend,' he said to the girl, paying no attention to the departure of Edward, swallowing a smile at his minor victory. 'Bennie Jinks,' he continued. 'A dead friend.'

She looked him up and down from his boots to his mask. 'Who are you, exactly?'

'I introduced myself last night,' Dalton said.

She shrugged, the coldness returning, and sipped her

wine, looking at him over the rim of the flicker. 'I've forgotten your name,' she said with the wave of a hand. 'A boy dipped in blood broke into my bedroom. If I'd have been calmer, perhaps I'd have asked for an autograph.'

'Dalton Fly,' he said.

She tilted her head and gave him an odd look, unreadable under the mask. 'You were tasting for me last night,' she said, putting her flicker down and sitting forward. There was, Dalton thought, a sudden frailty in her voice underneath the disdain. 'I'm afraid your friend died because someone's trying to kill me.'

She was calm on the outside, Dalton thought, with her curls and jewels and ivory-white gown and coldness. Her fingers were steady as she slowly rotated the ring with the red stone on it. She was looking at her hands as she did so.

'What have you done,' Dalton asked, his voice low, 'that someone might want to kill you?'

She looked up, suddenly sad in her glittering silver mask. 'It's not what I've done,' she said. 'It's who I am.' Then her lips thinned and she was in control again. She gazed again at her hands. 'What a dull evening,' she said, collecting the dice in one hand and shaking them. 'All these tiresome people.'

Dalton had no idea what he could say. He tried a smile but it wouldn't come out. She tossed the dice in a clatter across the tabletop. They fell at five: a three and a two. *Like the Calabar*, Dalton thought briefly. There was a thrill in the air, like a plucked string shaking, and a frozen moment of silence. The music seemed to stop. He tried to catch her eye, but she was staring at the dice.

Then – the explosion.

A bellowing roar picked them up and threw them into the ballroom – a hard fist of heat and noise that tore the balcony into bits and turned each window into a sharp white shower of heated glass. Everything spun outwards from the roaring centre; the floor bucked and rippled, walls shifted, furniture pitched; a grand chandelier held its baubles momentarily like glass stars, then flung them. Torn curtains flapped like flags, then balled and drifted into the garden. Everywhere, dust and smoke, the hoarse, empty shouts of the disorientated, the wordless screams of the injured.

The room was an inky crimson, choked in smoke and fire-flooded. Dalton heard nothing but a high, sharp scream in his ears, saw nothing but great pillows of purple smoke ripple across the shattered ceiling, making for the wide black eyes of the empty windows. He was coated in something: a thick dust. His mouth was full of it; he spluttered and retched and struggled for breath, found his feet and made it upright. He was, he realised, at the far end of the ballroom, among the crushed instruments of the band. Gouts of smoke pulsed outwards as if the whole room were breathing. *Gannet*, he thought. *What about Sal? Where is Sal?*

All around him, indistinct grey figures stirred and struggled, some standing – coughing and vomiting. Others were motionless and broken like dropped dolls. A paper mask spun and drifted on the haze of heat. Part of the far wall had gone, and a great ragged hole opened on to the night air and the garden below, its edges burning. Dalton felt his face and head for holes or blood, checked he had his arms and hands, unsteadily counted his bloody fingers. At his shoulder, he saw wild white eyes in a face of soot; a partygoer with wine on his breath and cracked teeth trying to speak through split lips.

Dalton stepped forward carefully, fearing the floor would collapse. A central section of it had slumped downwards, so the whole room seemed to tip into a hot orange plug of flame. He slipped, made it to his feet again.

By the time he'd edged around the wall of the room, past the fallen chandelier, which had ditched like a great silver ball gown, the air was clearing. People were on their feet; crowds were clotting about doors and windows as the survivors spilled out into the safety of the garden. Along the room's edges, figures were gathering, pointing, shouting, guiding the frail or blinded. Even through the wobbling haze of heat, Dalton recognised the guards from last night, working quickly to re-establish control.

He knew her dress before they did. It was still white, despite the filth and grime of the smoke. Her mask, like his, had gone.

He knelt and pulled her upwards, looping his arms beneath hers. She still smelt of soap. Soap and mint. He felt her fingers curl behind his neck, and knew she was alive. Her legs worked. She sagged weakly for a moment, then she was up, pushing him away, rising to standing, flattening her hair back, checking her head and neck, uncurling her shaking fingers. She turned to face the room, leaning against him as her balance wavered. He placed an open palm between her shoulder blades. Her skin was hot. He thought she might have said something, but he couldn't hear. She wiped her face with the back of one hand.

Across the room, the guards had seen her. One of them was waving, eyes bright with relief. Another had raised a pistol and was approaching carefully, checking his footing and signalling the advance of his comrades. The men closed about them swiftly, their attention devoted entirely to the girl and to the poison boy at her side.

She leant into his shoulder and put her mouth to his ear. 'Someone's trying to kill me. I need your help.' Dalton stared at her, wild and ragged in the heat haze. It was like a dream. The men circled them, pistols aloft. Repeaters, Dalton noticed – two shots before reloading, rather than one. The girl stepped forwards then, accepting the arm of one of her rescuers, and was led away, her head dipped as she listened to their urgent instructions. Three guards remained, hard-faced and armed.

'Dalton Fly,' said one, his voice familiar above the roar of the fire and the cries of the suffering. The man opened the cap on his pistol and aimed it, calm and steady. Dalton found himself tapping his lucky Jack, checking its presence in his top pocket as he raised his palms in surrender.

'That's me,' he said, distracted. Beyond them, he could still make out the bobbing retreat of the girl in her white birthday dress, and his belly burned.

TEN

D alton leant forwards and spun his lucky Jack on the table before him. The room was cool and small, one of the cellar-stores, smelling of firewood and leaf mould. Judging from the flickering light that washed the wall beneath the high window, the fires were not yet out, though the shouts of the injured and the barked instructions of the rescue parties had long since faded. A squat candle burnt on the table before him. It had been hours. He guessed there were a lot of people that needed talking to. He thought about Sal, calculated hopelessly where he might have been when the explosion happened. He thought of the girl in the dress, heard her voice whisper urgently in his ear.

Sometime later, pale moonlight at the window, the door was opened and his interrogators entered. He straightened in his chair, and placed the Jack in his top pocket. Two men in formal wear, faces darkened with grime and streaked in sweat, waited by the door. A woman stepped forward. She was tall, ice-faced with a steel glare. She tucked her short grey hair behind her ears, opened the buttons of her coat and sat. She smiled at him, her eyes creasing, then took a repeater pistol from her inside pocket and placed it carefully on the table. She looked tired in the candlelight. Her hands were dark with soot, and the shoulders of her coat, dusted with ash. She nodded to the man by the door, who produced a notebook with a weary look.

'Dalton Fly,' she said. He recognised her voice. In a moment, he had placed it; she had been at the window the previous night. He had clung, trembling, to the ivy below the sill as she had spoken to her guards – 'The boy's not invisible, is he?' – and sent them outside to search the gardens. She smelt the same as she had then: a rich and exotic perfume.

'That would be me,' he said tiredly.

She spoke slowly and clearly. Dalton got the impression she was repeating a patient speech she had made endlessly since the explosion. 'A case of shotpowder was ignited below the ballroom earlier this evening,' she said. 'Many innocent guests have been hurt or killed. I am Marcher Gellis and it is my job to talk to those I see as important in the matter, and to determine the perpetrator of the attack. You are one of the people who interests me – you and your friend, Mr Sleepwell, who, you will be glad to hear, is safe and well and sends you his best.'

Dalton smiled, a warm bubble of relief rising in his chest.

'I would ask for your co-operation in answering any questions,' she said. 'Mr Sleepwell has certainly been of much assistance.'

Dalton nodded.

'You found a way in tonight,' she began. 'Tell me about it.'

Marcher Gellis was determined and tireless. Questions came quickly in a clipped, precise tone. The small service door they'd squeezed through, the disguises, the places and positions in the ballroom, the sights and sounds, the quality of the air, the temperature, the masks and costumes on the balcony, the chatter, the dice-games, the young man called Edward – all were sifted and turned, examined and probed. The candle guttered; another was brought. The room grew cold; bread was ordered, and a blanket for the poison boy.

The questions continued in a stream for over an hour. At this point, the marcher's manner suddenly changed. Her eyes glistened and she sat back, one boot against the table leg. Then, very deliberately, she leant forwards, peering at him closely. Her face warmed in the orange glow of the candle, and her features seemed to soften, though she still frightened him. She held his gaze for a moment, lips tight together, thinking.

'Where were you born?' she said.

Dalton, exhausted, was taken aback by the question. He found himself laughing.

'What?' he said through a fading grin.

'Where were you born?' she said again, expressionless. She was studying him with an intensity he had not felt before.

His jaw tightened. He coughed. 'Yelder,' he lied. 'In the Lower Circle. It's poor – there's not much to it, really . . .'

'And you're quite sure of that story, Mr Fly?' said the marcher, leaning back a little. There was a pause. 'Because I have reason to suspect otherwise.'

'What's this got to do with tonight?' Dalton tried. Gellis seemed excited and he neither understood nor liked it. Confusion upon confusion – he was exhausted by it all. 'I wasn't the one playing with shotpowder.'

'No,' she said. 'I believe you weren't. But I'm trying to untangle a knot. And you're part of the knot. If I'm to help you – and believe me, Dalton Fly, you really need my help . . .' She stabbed the table with her finger in emphasis. When no response came, she took a patient breath. 'I sent the Streetwatch to get you after you escaped last night. They have . . .' she paused, looking for the right word, '. . . occupied your employer's house to ambush you on your return. My fault. I needed to speak to you. So, you have nowhere to go. You're going to have to be honest with me if you want me to call them off.'

Dalton looked at her. Her tone – urgent, cold –

reminded him of the girl's words, *If there's someone in trouble here, it's probably you*, and the marcher's pale grey eyes glowed like pearls. He felt the creep of fear at his neck, the fear of uncertainty. What was all this about?

'I don't know where I was born,' he admitted.

'That's better,' said Gellis. She turned, shot a glance at the man at the door to check he was writing. He was scribbling hard, Dalton noticed. 'Now. Tell me the whole truth. And bear in mind I ask because I already know it, and I want to hear it from you. Not because I'm seeking information.'

Dalton felt the sweat prickle at his scalp, and rubbed his eyes. He was hungry. 'Will you help me, if I tell you?'

She shrugged. 'If I can, then yes. But there are others I am charged with protecting first.'

'The girl,' Dalton said. 'Are you her mother? She mentioned her mother.'

'No, I'm her marcher.'

Dalton looked blankly at her.

'Like a guard. She is my responsibility while she is a sentaway. Now, let's begin. Tell me the barrel story.'

Dalton's heart hammered suddenly, and he flushed. She knew the barrel story? His mind raced. Even Sleepwell didn't know the barrel story. No one knew it. Apart from Oscar. Oscar was in it. How did Marcher Gellis know it? Who had told her?

'Oscar Wright found me in a cellar,' he said.

'Go on.'

'Oscar is my employer. He—'

'Yes, yes, I know of the Honest Dozen,' she said, waving away the detail. 'Kite knows we spent long enough checking we were using a reputable company for such an important client. We met last week, Mr Fly, before the party.' She cocked her head. 'To discuss the tasting. Do you not remember?'

Dalton stared at her. He'd never seen her before. At least, that's what he thought. But the belladonna had done for him badly. He'd nearly died. His memory was flogged – he couldn't trust it any more. 'The poison,' he said, tapping his temple. 'My memory isn't good. Sleepwell remembers things for me.'

Marcher Gellis stared at him. She seemed fascinated – it was an uncomfortable feeling. 'Continue,' was all she said with a wave of a hand.

Dalton sighed. 'Oscar found me in a cellar. I don't know when, exactly. I was a baby – I can't remember it. It was one of the smugglers' cellars in the Lower Circle, Oscar says. He can't remember which one. Those Lower Circle tunnels are like a huge underground maze where smugglers sell their contraband out of the passageways and storm drains under Geswick – Sal knows them really well.'

'Go on.'

Dalton felt as if his muscles were iron. He tried to relax. He had never told the barrel story before, though he had heard it; it felt strange in his mouth, as if it wasn't really his.

'I was in a barrel,' he said. 'It was a cask, for wine. It had been passed around between pirates and smugglers. I was in it. No one seems to know why.' He took a deep breath. 'Oscar kept me as a poison boy. He used to say that, if I had survived in a barrel, I must be strong. He said Blackjack Gannet had sent me as a lucky charm. But that meant I had to take more poisons, to build up resistance. I was his lucky charm, he used to say.'

'What else do you remember?'

'About the barrel story?' Dalton said. 'Nothing.'

'Early memories?' she probed.

'There's nothing else,' Dalton said, trying not to think about the undertaker. Why he had crept back into his thoughts, he didn't know. 'My first memories are of Oscar telling me the barrel story. It's like it happened to another person, not me.'

Marcher Gellis bit her lip and looked at her hands. She clenched them closed then opened them, clenched them then opened them. She was disappointed, Dalton could tell.

'What did you want me to say?' he said.

She stared at the window for a moment. 'Never mind. I thought you might remember more.' She breathed out slowly, through her nose, then made a decision and nodded over at her assistant, who snapped his notebook shut. 'I need you to come with me.' She rose from her chair, checked the cap and catch of the pistol, and placed it in her pocket. 'You and Mr Sleepwell can still be of great help to me tonight.'

Dalton struggled to his feet. The two men fell into line behind him as they made their way into the corridor and up a flight of stairs.

'I want to show you something,' said Gellis over her shoulder as she walked, 'though I'm afraid it will bring back some unpleasant memories.'

Dalton followed, fear clammy at the small of his back like a fever. It was going to be a long night.

ELEVEN

He recognised the door by the shattered wood-work. He had been there a matter of hours ago. The guns had punched an angry hole above shoulder height at the moment Dalton had ducked to run from the room. He suddenly thought how close he had come to dying.

'Is Bennie still in there?' he said, his mouth dry.

The marcher smiled sadly. 'No. He's at rest now. You can see him later. But for now, we have all the food and drink from last night. We need your help tasting it.'

The first thing he saw as he entered was the marble pillar, his hiding place. A sudden rush of dizzy heat overwhelmed him. The tasting table had been straightened over the rug and surrounded by chairs. The table was spread, the resin lanterns low, the heavy curtains drawn. The silver jug was rolled red with bloody fingerprints. Dalton moved to the table uncertainly, the marcher close by.

'I know this will be difficult for you,' she said. 'But the stronger your memories, the more accurate you can be. I need you to tell me which item is poisoned. Then it's my job to try and locate the poisoner.'

Dalton drew the chair back and sat, looking over the food before him – the dates and olives, cheeses in wax paper, bowls of citrus fruit, cold meats, sweets and jellies, wine . . . Bennie lying on his face in a spreading red pool.

He swallowed hard. 'Marcher,' he said, trying to keep his voice even and his fear marshalled. 'Sleepwell could help me here. We can get this done quickly together.'

She seemed briefly to consult her men with a glance – then she nodded to one, and he left, drawing a gun from his jacket as he did so.

A moment later, Sal was with him, looking exhausted, his face blurred in ash, his glasses thick with grime and his hair wild. He still wore his party scarf, and his mask was pushed up over his tired eyes.

'Flyboy!' he said with a grin. 'You're alive!'

They worked quickly, one from each end of the table. The marcher stood over them, her hands in her coat pockets, her pistol glinting at her hip. Next to her, an assistant with a notebook and pencil scribbled. Gellis tugged at her grey hair habitually and hooked it behind her ears, her face wrinkled in concentration as she observed the poison boys proceed.

'Talk as you work, gentlemen,' she said. 'I need access to your thoughts.'

The boys looked at each other. Sal spoke: 'Belladonna is the poison,' he said, pushing his glasses up his nose. 'The roots are the most poisonous, but more difficult to disguise. In food, it's usually the juice of the berry.'

'Or a leaf tincture,' Dalton put in.

'But mostly berries. Oscar used to call belladonna "black cherry" because of the juice.'

'It's quite sweet,' Dalton added, 'so the victim doesn't taste it clearly. So it's better than castor or wake-robin, which have a stronger flavour.'

'Tell me more,' the marcher instructed, bending closer. 'How do you know what's poisoned?'

Dalton stopped his work, carefully counting off a number of items as he did so. 'Fruit's easy,' he said.

Sal nodded his agreement.

'Poisons are usually pushed through the skin with needles. But the breaks in the skin cause bruising. So, to check this, say,' Dalton rolled an apple between his palms, 'we can look at the points around the stem and base where the entry wound will be less visible.' He peered at it. 'This one's safe,' he said with a quick smile. He offered it to the marcher, who halted him with a raised hand.

'Go on,' she said. 'What about other foods?'

Sal indicated a jar of preserved lemons, bobbing in

pale-green oil. 'The juice of belladonna is purple,' he explained. 'So we look for pockets of colour. A shutter won't go for this jar, I don't think—'

'Shutter?' Gellis cut in, frowning.

'Shutter,' Dalton repeated. 'A poisoner.' He shrugged. 'It's Oscar's word.'

Sal continued. 'A shutter wouldn't go for these cheeses either, because the colour will be too difficult to disguise.'

'Clever boys,' Gellis said. 'So what about the wine here?' She nodded towards the stoppered bottle at the table's centre.

'It's possible,' Dalton said, eyeing the cork. He could taste it through the blood on the back of his teeth.

'We'll save it till last,' Sal said. 'Dangerous stuff goes last.'

'Why?'

Sal smiled. 'So we can eliminate the clean stuff first! That's why we haven't tasted the olives here. They look . . . difficult.'

'Kite!' said Gellis softly, leaning over the shoulder of her note-taker. 'This is tricky work.'

'It's even harder first time through,' Dalton said. 'Last night, I didn't know I was looking for belladonna.'

Sal replaced a plate carefully. 'These figs look clear,' he said, examining the cut fruit on the blade of a knife and grinding seeds between finger and thumb. He brought his tongue carefully to the point of his finger and tasted, his eyes distant in concentration.

They worked their way through the cheeses and

finished the fruit. Dalton began studying a bowl of glistening olives, smelling the oil around them, stirring them and looking for changes in colour.

'These are clear,' he said, chewing one confidently.

Sal, finishing the sweets, wiped his knife. 'Fly – it's time to check the wine.'

Dalton leant over and raised the bottle by its neck.

Marcher Gellis crouched beside him. 'The seal is broken. Was that you, last night?'

'It's possible. I don't know,' Dalton said. He tapped his temple once more. 'No memory.'

Sal passed him a flicker and cleared his throat. 'A wax seal doesn't tell you anything, anyway,' he said. 'A decent shutter can needle poison through the seal and cork, then melt it shut. A seal doesn't mean it's clear.'

The marcher gave a low whistle. 'Well, well . . . Our enemies are clever,' she said, pulled a chair from beneath the low table, and sat. 'What happens if the wine is bad? Will you need help?'

Dalton poured a small measure of wine and swirled it, then placed the flicker on the table. 'Not this time. To kill Jinks, there must have been – what, sixteen berries?' He looked at Sal, who nodded. 'So it's strong. I'll only take a little.'

He took a deep breath, clearing his senses, then picked up the flicker. He dipped his nose quickly. The scent was deep and leathery. There was an acrid tang, like woodsmoke; no lingering sweetness. He sipped.

Dalton spluttered suddenly, retched and kicked. The

flicker was on the floor, the wine spilled. Sal held his shoulders and shook him gently. Dalton coughed, his chest heaving. 'I'm all right. I'm all right,' he said. He could feel his skin prickle and rash, raised blotches on his cheeks and neck. But he'd sipped only a little, he knew. Not like last time.

'I'll get water,' Gellis said, rising from her chair and barking a swift order. Her note-taker scribbled at her shoulder. 'It's the wine,' she said to him, peeling the label off and handing it over carefully. 'Check the inventory,' she said, stabbing her finger at him. 'I want to know who gifted this bottle, when it arrived, how it was delivered. We need to speak to every belladonna trader in the city.' She paced eagerly. 'And get this boy some water!'

Sleepwell and Fly slept for an hour or so, head to toe in a bed with an old feather mattress, locked in a room with the curtains drawn. Famished and exhausted, they had been allowed to say a farewell to Bennie Jinks after the tasting. A Middle Circle undertaker's assistant had dressed and cleaned him. His face was white and cold, his clothes untangled and neatened, his hands by his side, fingernails washed and pared. He looked like a reclining marble statue: unreal.

Dalton woke, feeling Sal kick and twist and hearing him mutter wordlessly in his dream. The room was dark slate-grey, with a thin vein of fading light glowing at the gap between the curtains. There was something wrong. Dalton could feel it – a warmth in the air, a movement. He raised his head from the pillow, breathed in silently. His eyes adjusted. He placed the scent.

'I know you're here,' he said at a whisper, feeling foolish.

There was no response. Dalton moved again, thinking he'd perhaps mistaken her presence – dreamed it. Then, a faint footfall. His heart galloped. Sal stirred, turned in his sleep, and Dalton worked his way free, rising from the bed. A moment later, he saw her break the strip of night sky between the curtains.

'I want your help,' she whispered.

Dalton moved towards her, eyes growing accustomed to the dark, trying to guess the time. An hour before midnight, perhaps? 'Get us out of here first,' he said. 'Gellis wants us locked up.'

He heard her laugh gently. 'My marcher is very keen on my safety. It gets frustrating.' She paused. 'Looks as if she likes you two, as well.'

Dalton thought of the interview in the cellars, the barrel story. 'She knows a lot about me,' he said. 'Why?'

He made out a shrug in the half-light by the window. She'd tied her hair up, wrapped it under a headscarf. 'Look,' she said. 'Wake up your friend. We don't have a lot of time.'

'The shotpowder bomb?'

'Yes. Someone's trying to kill me. I'm a danger to this house –' she opened her palms with an exasperated gesture – 'and to all the people here. If my Marcher had her way, we'd move on, try another district, keep ourselves hidden. But it'll just keep happening. They'll find me eventually. That's why I need to leave. The longer I stay, the more people suffer. I'm harder to find with less of all this around me.' She waved a dismissive hand at the room; the walls that confined her. Then she reached into her pockets - Dalton could pick out her clothes now: a long riding coat, rolled-up trousers, heavy boots – and produced a pair of silver-butt pistols. 'Here,' she said, holding one out, handle first. 'I need you and your friend with me. You're both . . .' She studied him a moment, looking for the right word. She gave up, wrinkled her nose, plucked the curtain's edge and checked the street below. 'Anyway.'

'What's the plan?' Dalton said, pulling his boots on.

'Aha!' she whispered, brightening. 'That's the good bit. We escape. We leave Gellis and all the others behind. We find the shotpowder gang –' she spun her pistol – 'and we get 'em.'

Dalton watched her. 'Right,' he said slowly. 'Any more details?'

'Working on it,' she said. 'You and your friend would be a big help. Come along. What do you say?'

Dalton placed his fingertips across his jacket pocket, feeling the stiffness of the lucky Jack there. He thought a moment. 'Fine,' he said. 'But why not leave this to your marcher and her armed guards?'

'I can't. I need to move. Everyone is safe once I'm gone.' She paused a moment, listening, then continued. 'How many people have died tonight because of me? It has to stop. Help me.'

Dalton had to smile at her there in the half dark. 'Sleepwell!' he said, turning. 'Wake up!'

TWELVE

She flashed the keys at them, hurrying them along as they dressed. 'I have to give these back, you know,' she said. 'Someone might miss them.' One grated in the lock as she turned it, flinching. The door opened silently. 'The advantage of being trapped here for nearly a year,' she whispered, 'is that I know this house backwards.'

Sal checked the corridor, nervous. 'Where are we going?' he said.

'The gardener's gate. Keep quiet and don't flog things up.'

She was nimble, walking delicately on the balls of her feet, and they passed swiftly along the landing above the stairs. She paused, raising her head slightly at a noise in the rooms below them, then turned into a gallery that ran along the side of the house facing the gardens. The poison boys followed a few paces behind her, jogging lightly across the sprung floors. Sal gazed about him, catching tantalising glimpses of huge oil paintings, hanging tapestries and stately furniture splashed in the glow of street lamps.

They skirted the shattered ballroom from above, following a wide walkway that ran its length. Below them, the space was broken and blackened, a dark well at its centre where the floor had been blasted upwards. The far wall of the house was open to the night like a ragged mouth. The wind stirred dust and glass.

'Kite!' breathed Sal as they hurried on. 'What a mess.'

'Look,' said Dalton. Through the smashed hole of the house wall they could see the city below them. There were fires in the streets, two drifting palls of smoke coming from somewhere under the Middle Circle, the sound of distant pistols and the roar of a crowd. 'What's happening?'

The girl shook her head. 'It's started,' she said. 'I'm surprised the truce lasted as long as it did.'

'Truce?' said Sal.

The girl regarded them both for a moment and rolled her eyes. 'You don't know?' She shook her head. 'Follow me.' They descended a set of back stairs, slowing as they did so. Dalton recognised them: the servants' stairway she had pointed him towards on the night they first met.

Soon they were out into the gardens. The girl held a hand up in warning, watching the guards swap positions at the front of the house, then she was off, low and graceful, skirting the edge of the lawns. The poison boys followed, fear and exhaustion dogging their steps. Through the gate and on to the streets of Highlions they ran alongside each other, directionless to begin with – driven by fear. As they dropped away from the Upper Circle, their pace slowed. The air drifted with the fine sharp fog of shotpowder. It was surely midnight but there were men on the streets, armed and running. Somewhere, a fight had broken out. Pistols cracked and shouts and calls echoed. There was a thrill in the air, a tight tension, as if something somewhere was on the edge of snapping. It was just like Oscar had said, Dalton thought as they ran: *When the old man finally dies, the city will fall to fighting itself.* Somewhere below them in the Lower Circle streets, there were pistol shots, calls and clamour. It seemed suddenly as if, all his life, Duke Elber had been holding a pack of baying hounds apart. And now he was gone, they were free to savage each other.

'What in Kite's name is happening?' Sal said. 'Why all the fighting?' Sal's gaze met Dalton's. 'Will it be safe to go home?' he said hopelessly. Dalton didn't answer.

'If you two don't know why there's violence on the streets tonight then someone needs to give you a serious history lesson,' said the girl. 'Where've you been for the past ten years?'

'Sleepwell,' Dalton said, 'find somewhere we can sit and talk.'

Sal mopped his brow and put his glasses back on. The Mapmaker's youngest could always be counted on at times like this. 'Follow me,' he said.

They wove through a maze of Greengoose backstreets, with the quick, slim figure of Sal in the lead, until they reached a public bar, its bright windows throwing squares of light out into the alley. 'Oscar's brought me here a few times,' he explained as they approached. 'It's open all night. The Harriet Air.'

'Will they let us in?' the girl asked.

Sal nodded. 'I think so. Chimney boys drink here. And most of them are younger than us.'

They moved through the bar, a hot and noisy place even at such a late hour, towards a table at the back. The owner glanced up as they entered, blinking tiredly before returning to wiping flickers. A group of sweeps' boys were eating in a corner, their masters swapping stories and smoking. Gangs of traders huddled in corners. Hard-faced women dealt cards at the bar. The rattle of dice games echoed – traders playing sevens or blackball. Towards the back, fever-tea drinkers sat hunched over their spoons and fans, sharing sugar and getting ruined.

They chose a table away from the adults and stretched their legs out. Sal paid for bread and milk with the last of the coins he'd found in the storm pipes. A friendly woman with fat hands dropped an oil lamp on the table and brought them cups. For a while they were quiet as they ate and drank, listening to the rumble of activity about them, watching a ginger cat circle their table.

Then Sal said suddenly, eyes wide, as if he'd surprised himself with his question, 'What's your name?'

She looked blankly at him. 'Dropmore,' she said. 'Scarlet Dropmore.'

Dalton sat forward. *House of Dropmore: Honour and Courage*, the party invitation had said.

'Sal Sleepwell. This is Dalton Fly,' he heard Sal say.

She looked carefully at them both. 'Thanks for the milk.'

Dalton forced a smile. 'Scarlet. You've got to tell us what's happening. Everyone understands but me and Sleepwell.'

She placed her hands on the table, one over the other. 'What do you want to know?' she said. The cat squeezed between their legs, purring.

'Right.' Dalton held up a fist and raised his fingers upwards as he spoke. 'Who's trying to poison you? Why? What happened with the shotpowder bomb?' He paused, three fingers raised. 'And all the other stuff,' he said, uncurling a fourth.

Sal cleared his throat. 'There's more,' he said. 'The Streetwatch are trying to arrest us. They've occupied our home and we can't go back. And there's a man in a black coat following us.'

'Yes. What he said,' said Dalton, pointing at Sal. 'You've got to tell us.'

Scarlet looked beyond them, across the room, checking how close other drinkers were. She twisted her fingers together, her knuckles whitening, deciding something.

After a moment, she looked up.

'Right,' she said, resting her head on her palm. 'This is everything.'

The friends leant forward.

'It's about the Houses,' she began.

The boys looked at each other. Sal raised a shoulder and turned his palms out. 'Sorry,' he said. 'Houses?'

'Kite! Poison boys really are backwards, aren't they? The Houses of Highlions,' she said, exasperated. 'The House of De Bello? Dropmore? Bad blood and civil unrest? Duke Elber's death? Any of this sounding familiar?'

Dalton cleared his throat, drank some milk. He knew the last bit. 'Look,' he said. 'We're just poison boys. We don't know what's happening in Geswick or Angels most of the time, let alone the rest of the city. Duke Elber's dead – we've figured that much. But anything else . . .' His voice trailed off. He felt small and stupid. Oscar's kitchens, his borrowed bedroom shared with Sal, the cramped alleys of his grubby district, the street dreck and smugglers – this was the futile reach of his world. He was an orphan nobody, born in a barrel. 'Everything important that has ever happened to us,' he said, surprising himself with his own sudden sadness, 'has happened in the last two days.'

Sal nodded. 'Imagine we know flog all,' he said, 'and you won't go far wrong.'

Scarlet shook her head in disbelief. 'You two really know nothing . . .' she said to herself, leaning to stroke the cat absently. 'The thing you need to remember about Elber,' she went on, 'is that he died childless. So no one knows who's going to take over. The senate are arguing about it. My mother is Loyola Dropmore. Senator Dropmore?' The boys looked at each other and shook their heads. Scarlet issued a frustrated sigh. 'Never mind. My mother is head of the House of Dropmore. We're a wealthy family. Also on the senate is Senator De Bello. You'll know him, surely? The man in charge of the Streetwatch. The guy with the beard. He's in the papers.'

This was more familiar territory, Dalton realised. He'd heard the name, and he'd read about Senator Stephen De Bello, someone who made regular proclamations in city newspapers like the *Advisor* and the *Circle* about additional Streetwatch patrols, crackdowns on the trading of unlawfuls, curfews or bans, arrests, that sort of thing. An arrogant and violent man, Dalton thought. He looked at Scarlet, nodding his understanding.

Scarlet seemed relieved to have found a little common ground at last. 'Now the Duke is dead,' she said, 'chaos will break loose. Senator De Bello will want his son to take charge of the city. He'll be desperate for it. Mother won't let him: she can't stand him. The Houses of Dropmore and De Bello –' she clenched her fists and brought the two of them together, knuckles touching – 'they're enemies. Bitter enemies. Mother won't speak about it.' Scarlet picked up her milk, the mug held tight in both hands, and swirled it.

'How did it start?' Dalton said.

'What, the De Bello thing?' Scarlet made a bitter smile. 'Long time ago,' she said. 'I was only a baby, but Mother mentioned it once. Duke Elber was taken ill. He had a stroke and nearly died. There was this big scramble for power – arguments about who would take his place. He had no children, so various names were put forward. The senate argued over who should succeed. Senator De Bello supported one candidate – Mother and others disagreed. Another name was proposed; I don't know who.' Here she paused, pressing the tip of a finger against the table-top. 'I'm not sure of the details, but something terrible happened. People died and the rumour was the House of De Bello were behind it. And then Elber recovered and it was all for nothing.' She shrugged. 'That's when we started the whole thing with sentaways.'

Dalton recognised the word. Marcher Gellis had used it. 'What's a sentaway?' he said.

Scarlet sighed. 'An important child, kept hidden' she said. 'Kept safe, away from its parents somewhere. Especially in difficult times – like these.' Scarlet looked across at the windows of the Harriet Air, out into the streets beyond. 'They're fighting down there tonight because some districts are loyal to De Bello, and some to Dropmore. Greengoose always support De Bello, the fools. And, as for the Upper Circle – well . . .' Scarlet studied the table before her and swirled the milk in her cup again. 'But others are loyal to Mother. So the streets will go mad in the next few days. These fights we've seen – they're just the beginning. Until this mess is sorted out, there will be terrible bloodshed. And the senate won't have a leader. They'll argue amongst themselves endlessly.'

Dalton wiped his eyes. This was all new to him. He'd never before had any time for the politics of Highlions. And no inclination, either, to listen to empty promises or tedious proclamations. It had never been his concern. Now, he realised, it was.

'And the poison? The shotpowder bomb?'

Scarlet looked dreamily into her cup and shrugged. 'My mother says it's a betrayal: a breaking of trust. They don't usually go for sentaways like me.'

'Who don't?' Dalton asked. 'The other Houses? The De Bello family?'

Scarlet opened her mouth to answer, but suddenly stiffened, sitting back in her chair as someone approached. A second jug of milk was deposited on the table's edge, and more bread.

Dalton ripped off a hunk and chewed thoughtfully. There were so many questions. 'What's a sentaway?' he said.

Scarlet looked distracted and tired. 'A hidden child,' she sighed. 'The son or daughter of someone important. I'm stuck in that Upper Circle mansion because I'm a sent-away. I'm not allowed out for my own safety. But they've found me. I should never have talked my marcher into letting me have the party . . .'

'Someone's been watching the house?' Dalton said, forehead furrowed. 'Waiting for a sign that you might be there?'

'Right,' Sal finished. 'So the poisoned wine was meant for you. And the shotpowder bomb, too.'

She nodded. Dalton stared at her. He saw her again suddenly in her bedroom the previous night, trembling but brave as she held the pistol up, watching as a boy dipped in blood broke into her room. His heart charged. She must have thought she was about to die. And yet – so calm and clever.

'You let me go,' he said, his throat tight.

'You didn't look like an assassin,' she said. 'You looked like a disaster. I knew it wasn't you.'

'Thanks.'

She poured some milk on to her plate, then lowered it carefully on to the floor beside her. 'This cat won't leave us alone.'

Dalton watched her, poured himself another cup of milk. He brought the cup to his lips, took a mouthful. The milk was warm, nutty, with a sharpness at the back of it.

It tasted wrong.

He spat it back, scowling. 'Gannet!' he coughed. 'That's not good milk.'

He looked up suddenly.

'Scarlet, don't touch the milk!' He lurched to his feet, the chair spinning from under him. 'Some shutter's been at the milk. It's flogged.'

Scarlet's eyes widened. 'Dreck!' she said. The three of them stared at the jug. Then Scarlet brought her legs up with a jerk, wrapping her arms around them. 'The cat!' she hissed, peering beneath the table. Sal jerked himself from his chair, his face white, and followed her gaze.

Something was still writhing under there in the shadow, gagging and spitting.

'It's dead,' Dalton said quickly. 'Leave it, Scarlet. Someone's followed us from the house. Come on.'

The clatter of their sudden movement had attracted attention. Sleepy drinkers looked up, sensing trouble. The talk at the bar died; inquisitive eyes peered. Dalton's attention was turned to the door. It was still swinging in its frame, having been barged open.

Someone had just left.

THIRTEEN

D alton broke into a run, making directly for the way out. Sal looked about him for a second, dazed by the thud of his heart, then followed. Scarlet gave chase, and the three of them crashed from the Harriet Air and into the lamplit streets of Greengoose.

Off to their left, a man was following the edge of the street under the eaves of the houses. He was running low and fast.

Sal arrived at Dalton's shoulder. 'Let's go!'

The boys sprinted across the street in pursuit, Scarlet at their heels, their focus on the figure ahead. Here was a clue, Dalton knew. They had to follow. The street lamps were dimmer in the early hours – their skirts of yellow light smaller. The man ducked and wove, quick and agile. They were heading downhill, the river on their right; down through the streets of Jacksonbridge and out into the Lower Circle. Somewhere nearby, Dalton realised as he ran, a fight had broken out. Another one, just like Scarlet had said. There was a volley of pistol fire, and it was surely only a few streets away.

Soon they were passing down through the edges of Geswick, the river drawing closer. Dalton's legs were burning with fatigue, his lungs raw and empty. Still the figure ran ahead of them, gaining ground. Dalton pushed himself on, pumping his arms hard, but as the moments passed, he gave in to the growing feeling that he wasn't going to catch him. This was a darker district, a maze of meaner streets. Even Sal looked lost. Scarlet was behind them now. They couldn't afford to leave her. Dalton slackened his pace, hope fading.

Then they were out on the river's edge and he realised where they were. They'd reached the Lower Circle now. Midwater West rose out of the river to his right, and the bridge to it, pooled in lamplight. Dalton came to a stop and bent over for a moment, hands on knees. He breathed hard. The figure was crossing Midwater Bridge to the island, and the river below shone like a mirror in the warm moonlight. That's where he was going.

'Kite!' Sal gasped as he pulled up. 'He's gone over there?'

Dalton nodded, his breathing evening out. Soon, Scarlet was with them, her face glowing red with exertion. The three of them stood together, leaning against the wall that marked the river's edge, panting hard and looking out at the island fortress.

Midwater West. Dalton knew something of the place, but only what Oscar had told him: a walled island accessible by a single bridge on its east side that ended in a pair of regularly patrolled heavy gates. Beyond those walls was the Skeltonyards, Highlions' prison, and the Palace of Justice, its court of law. Only three types of people visited Midwater, Oscar used to say: lawyers, Streetwatch and criminals. When Oscar told his night stories, he often gave the impression of having a number of acquaintances who had ended their days on the wrong side of Midwater's walls. There wasn't much to be seen from where the three stood now. The walls were high. The towers of the Palace rose above it, outlined against the stars of the night sky.

'De Bello runs Midwater,' Scarlet said. 'This makes perfect sense.'

Dalton watched her tuck her hair back under her headscarf. 'Are you sure?' he asked.

She sighed. 'Stephen De Bello virtually lives out on Midwater. The House of De Bello is behind this, I swear.'

Sal replaced his glasses, his crazed mop of hair tangling in his eyes as he wiped the sweat from his brow. 'There's no way we can follow him in there,' he said.

Dalton stared at the river, wide, deep and slow, and at

the steep-sided island at its centre. He tapped his lucky Jack. 'There might be a way,' he heard himself say. He hardly knew what he was doing.

On the bridge, they paused. Dalton's gaze followed the cliff down to the water below. 'Look. There's two just on the cliff face here,' he said, pointing out the black mouths of the storm drains. 'They'll lead us inside.'

Sal gave a hollow laugh. 'Don't be a lackbrain!' he scoffed. 'Look at the drop!'

Dalton studied the rocks around the bridge's edge. The fall to the water was indeed dizzying, but the cliff face wasn't quite sheer; a handhold here, an outcrop there, a scruffy scab of grass clinging to the stone, a thin perch stained in bird dreck. Then the storm drain itself, big enough to climb inside, a passageway into the rock of the cliff. There'd surely be access somewhere in there.

'It's quiet,' Scarlet said encouragingly, looking at the gates. They weren't guarded at this hour of the night. 'No Streetwatch to bother us.'

'Kite!' Sal said, shaking his head. 'You're insane. How are we going to get down there?'

Dalton looked up and away, studying the Lower Circle streets. Somewhere beyond the houses that faced the river, a fire was burning and an eddy of smoke was coiling upwards into the darkness. There was a stuttered exchange of pistol fire. On one of the streets, a chain of paper lanterns bobbed on a rope strung between the dark faces of the houses, the remnants of some party or celebration. 'I've got an idea,' he said.

Dalton lashed their climbing rope tight to one of the columns of the bridge's parapet. Below them, its far end was jumping on some current of air above the emptiness.

'Right,' he said, a quiver of tight fear in his voice. 'As long as we hold on hard, we'll be fine.' He was facing Scarlet and Sal, having backed himself carefully over the bridge's edge. He wrapped the rope around his wrist a number of times and swallowed hard, his mouth dry.

'Just watch the pipe,' Sal said. 'Don't look down.'

Dalton nodded, and began to lower himself, arm over arm, legs pedalling in the huge gap beneath him. Under the bridge, in the shadows, the stones were damp and green. The river was deep and wide and black like ink. Above, Sal was calling something but he couldn't make it out. The pipe was a dark blue yawn just below him, its edge a tangle of weeds and flotsam. He couldn't quite reach the pipe edge, but the action of reaching for it sent him spinning and swaying: back to the cliff face now, arcing out away from his goal and over the gulf. He heard the creak and shudder of the rope as it swung, and a plucked noise like the string of a musical instrument. Then he was turning again, and the pipe was looming, and his outstretched arm felt the cool of its clay rim. His fist gripped, his feet clattered the rock face, the rope groaned again, and he was in, folded over on his belly, legs pumping as if at a sprint, face in the storm dreck, safe.

He found his feet uneasily and, too scared to stand fully upright at the edge of the precipice, crouched near the mouth of the pipe and waved up at Scarlet. She came next, and the dizzying descent was repeated. She was brave and silent, spinning calmly on the end of the rope and swinging over to catch the lip of the pipe. Dalton pulled her in and, for a moment, she was in his arms again like she had been as he'd lifted her after the shot-powder blast. Her skin was warm, her heart hammering with fear. She pushed him away gently.

The two of them watched as Sleepwell turned his back, swung a leg over the parapet, secured the rope in both hands, and began his descent; all too quickly, Dalton thought, his palms prickling with fear, as if his friend were needlessly rushing. The rope was juddering as Sal moved awkwardly down it. Dalton shuffled forward to shout encouragement, but his eye was caught.

A figure had moved into view above them – a figure making its way along the bridge.

Sal, bobbing on the rope's end, looked to his friend for encouragement, and saw his attention was elsewhere. He craned his neck upwards, then looked back at Dalton.

'What is it?' he shouted above the rush of the river.

On the bridge, a tall dark outline had detached its hat, and was peering downward, trying to make out the figure squirming on the end of the rope. Dalton felt his stomach tighten. *The undertaker.*

'It's him, isn't it?' Sal shouted, sharp fear in his voice.

Dalton beckoned him wildly. 'Come on!' he yelled.

'Who's that?' Scarlet was saying. But Dalton's attention was on his friend.

Sal flapped and paddled, doing what he could to bring himself closer. Dalton looked up again. The undertaker was leaning over the parapet, a silhouette too distant to read or understand. Was he shouting? Had he something in his hand?

'Come on, Sleepwell!' Dalton bellowed. For a moment, he looked down, and his belly lurched at the sight of the river and its drift of spray far below them. His knees weakened, but he held an arm out as far as he dared.

Sal was trying to create enough swing to reach the grasp of his friend. Suddenly he slipped, one arm outstretched, and his face became a white shout of terror as he began his fall – but somehow he held on, wriggling like a hooked worm, and clattered into the cliff wall just below the pipe.

Dalton dropped to his knees and grabbed Sal's shoulders, heaving him upwards as Sal shouted wild and wordless curses and scrabbled at the pipe's rim. With a pull that emptied him of strength, Dalton yanked Sal clumsily in, and the two of them pushed themselves away from the edge and lay for a moment, exhausted, on their backs.

Through half-closed eyes, Dalton saw the dark figure on the bridge above them withdraw. He swore he heard again the bark of his voice – a shout, blurred and ragged; a word he couldn't understand. It came again, and then again, and each time Dalton listened harder, trying to calm the thumping of his blood in his ears. The distant voice was dying, the words too indistinct. A moment or two passed and Dalton's breathing slowed, his head beginning to clear.

The three of them got to their feet. There was a long silence – just the dry rhythm of tired breathing and the roll of the river.

'Who was that?' Scarlet said eventually.

Dalton looked at his hands, rope-burnt and trembling. 'That was the undertaker,' he said.

FOURTEEN

The storm drain cover shifted. Dalton put his shoulder to it and lifted, then pushed it aside. He heaved himself up and out, keeping low. They were inside the walls, in an enclosed square. Moonlight illuminated the face of a tall building with high arched windows. Inside, lamps flickered through the glass. Behind them, Dalton noticed, was the high wall which he saw every day from the Lower Circle, soaring up to the walkway that crested it. There was no one around. Judging by the face and position of the moon and the relative coolness of the air, he guessed it was after midnight now. Little bats swooped in circles, hunting insects.

He waved the others up and crossed quietly to the wall of the building, pressing his back against it and tucking himself in next to a delivery of stacked barrels. He ran a hand along the rough wood. They were still warm from the day's sun. Each barrel was neatly branded: Griffin Brothers, Wine Merchants, Ivyhill. An Upper Circle district; this was fine wine indeed. Perhaps they were used to such luxury on Midwater West, Dalton thought, looking up at the vast frontage of the high-windowed hall.

Scarlet pulled herself out of the drain and scampered across to him. She adopted his position and sat, breathing hard. 'You smell nice,' she said, wrinkling her nose. Her face was a smudge of sewer dreck, her coat scuffed and dirty. Shuffling through the storm pipe in the blackness hadn't been a pleasant experience.

Dalton watched as Sal pushed the drain cover back into position and came to join them. He cleaned his glasses hopelessly on his filthy shirt. When he propped them on his nose again, the lenses were two wet smears of grot. He looked over them at his companions, brushing dreck from his tangled hair. 'Midwater!' he whispered excitedly. 'Over there will be the Palace of Justice, beyond these buildings here. Beyond that will be the Skeltonyards, I should think.' Sal furrowed his brow and squinted, calling to mind the little ink images of the island he had stared at as a child while his father worked. The Skeltonyards – the city's famous prison – was double-walled and sealed with a heavy iron portcullis. Next to them, the Palace of Justice with its towers and halls, its galleries, staterooms and, if

rumour was to be believed, its secret chambers for tortur-
ing spies and gutting renegades. 'Yes,' he confirmed as the
shape and arrangement of the island clarified in his head.
'So this —' he patted the wall behind them — 'is the Senate
Hall.'

Even as he said the words, the light from its windows
dimmed suddenly, then swelled again. The unmistakable
shape of a figure was passing in front of a candle or lamp
inside. They could hear muffled voices.

Dalton pulled himself up to his feet and the others
followed suit. Together, they picked their way wordlessly
along the length of the hall, staying beneath the windows,
until they reached a door with a rusted iron handle: a
servants' entrance or service point.

Dalton tried it. The door opened into blackness with an
ominous creak. He turned to face his friends. Scarlet
nodded. Sal shrugged. Inside, it took a few moments for
their eyes to adjust. Sal gave up cleaning and pushed his
glasses up, burying them in a thatch of wild fringe.

Dalton tapped his lucky Jack. 'Which way, Gannet?' he
whispered to it.

Scarlet groaned. 'Forget the flogging card,' she
whispered. 'You've been fired on, poisoned and blown up
with shotpowder. Aren't you getting the message yet?
Ditch it!'

Dalton forced a patient smile. 'You wouldn't understand,' he said. 'Step out of the light. I can't see.'

Scarlet pressed her back to the door. Inky blackness
became slate grey. Spiral stone stairs, church-like, led up.

'See?' Dalton said. 'Follow me.'

'Does he always make choices this way?' Scarlet said over her shoulder as she followed him quietly upwards.

Sal thought about the five of hearts and the Calabar beans, and said nothing.

At the top was another door. Dalton held his breath and pressed his ear to it. Voices bubbled low beyond it, like secret water. How close they were, he couldn't tell. He wiped the sweat from his hands on his trousers. Thanks to their grime-encrusted bodies, the air in the passageway stank of storm dreck. He tried the handle. The door opened a crack and a thin blade of orange light dropped into the darkness of the passage. The voices grew louder – three of them, by the sounds of it. Dalton pressed an eye to the gap.

They were at the back of a meeting hall, under an over-hanging gallery. There was a long central table, partially obscured from view, and, fanning out around it, a series of chairs. Two oil lanterns suspended from the ceiling above dropped choppy, bright circles of light around them. This was the Senate Hall, just as Sal had said.

Dalton couldn't see the owners of the voices yet. Conscious that a sudden movement might alert them, he inched his way into the room and dropped to his knees behind rows of chairs. Soon, his friends were beside him. They edged forward until the speakers were in sight. They were close – so close Dalton felt the sudden fear of discovery catch in his throat.

There were two men leaning over a document spread

out on the large meeting table, their backs to the intruders. One was tall and apparently youthful, with short, cropped dark hair in spikes. Next to him was a broad-backed, heavy-set man.

A third figure was leaving the room, walking towards the huge doors that marked the state entrance to the hall. It was the man they had followed from the Harriet Air. He slipped out into the night. The larger man watched him go, then reached for a metal pitcher, poured a flicker of thick liquid, swirled it with slow pleasure and drank. After a moment's pause, he smacked his lips and sighed. The two resumed their conference, their voices guarded but clear.

'So we're back where we started with Scarlet Drop-more,' said the younger man, touching a section of the document. He seemed to be indicating something impor-tant. Dalton risked a stretch upwards, but couldn't make it out. He felt Scarlet tense beside him, and saw her steady herself with a hand on the floor. 'Your man really should have done better. See that we don't use him again.'

The second man spoke then. His voice was mauled and strange; it seemed to come from somewhere broken inside him. 'Of course,' he said. 'There are others we can be working on.'

His intakes of breath seemed to rattle; it was a discon-certing sound, sticky and ugly. He took another draft of the thick liquid. It was fever-tea; Dalton could smell it. Somewhere on the table would be the sugar and spoons. The big man looked as if he enjoyed a drink. Dalton fixed his eyes on the table and watched the two of them place their fingers on the paper as they spoke.

'These, you mean,' the younger man said, touching three or four points. Dalton squinted. *Some kind of diagram with people's names on it?*

The second man nodded confirmation. 'Here,' he pointed. 'Dropmore first. This young man next. Then Eppington, Eden and Honeycut.'

'Let's move on to Knox,' said the younger man. 'We need to do him quickly.'

'Speed is of the essence, that's true. But three days is sufficient to deal with them all.' Again, the ragged intake of breath; again a mouthful of the liquid. He poured another flicker.

Sal touched Dalton's shoulder lightly. Dalton turned and Sal leant forward. He mouthed slowly and carefully, 'I think it's a map.' If ever anyone could spot a map, it was Sal Sleepwell, the Mapmaker's youngest.

'Why am I on it?' Scarlet whispered. Her face was drawn. She seemed fixed by some horrible realisation.

Dalton turned to face his friends. 'We need to see it,' he mouthed as firmly as he could. Whatever was going on, the answer was on that paper, he was sure. He glanced around him, taking in the features of the Senate Hall. The gallery looked too high to allow them to study the document from a safe distance. The light was too low anyway. They needed to be up close. Dalton realised the two men were speaking again, their voices a low murmur.

'Thank you, Tench. So we have a direction: Dropmore,

Knox, Eppington, Eden, Honeycut,' the younger man said, placing a hand on the back of the larger figure.

'And, of course, our friend Holt,' the larger man replied.

Low laughter. 'Right,' said the younger man. 'Dropmore, Knox, Eppington, Eden, Honeycut and our friend Holt.'

The broad-backed older man nodded in agreement, threw back the fever-tea in one deep gulp and moved away from the table towards the doors. Dalton felt his muscles relax slightly and his courage strengthen. This was better. With just one of them, they had a chance. He felt the pistol Scarlet had given him pressing against his thigh. He'd only held a gun before – never fired one. The thought of it made his throat dry up. He turned his attention to the figure at the table, assessing a possible approach.

But then the big man glanced back, just once, and Dalton saw his face.

It was a sight he wouldn't soon forget. One ear was only half there, the lobe gone, as if ripped off; and a ragged white-edged scar crawled across the cheek, rendering that side of the man's face utterly broken. There was something wrong with his throat and neck, and his lips seemed somehow torn. Dalton placed a hand across his mouth involuntarily.

'I'll return presently,' said the man with the shattered face. Then he was gone.

Dalton drew breath and turned to Scarlet. She had her pistol in her hand and was weighing it, swallowing nervously, her face pale. She wanted that map, it was clear. Dalton gave her a reassuring nod, hoping to calm her. They were ready. They had pistols. They had a way out.

Dalton rubbed his eyes. He could hardly believe what they were about to do; but then so much had changed since the night before. His life seemed to be rolling and spinning like a leaf in a storm, hopelessly beyond his control. His face must have said as much – Sal and Scarlet were staring back at him with expressions which registered fear, disbelief and determination in equal parts. They seemed to be looking to him for guidance. But then, he was the boy with the lucky Jack, after all. He pressed a palm against the jacket pocket where the playing card was stowed, gave them a wink and brought a hand upwards, three fingers raised. His companions nodded their understanding. He made a clumsy countdown, steeling himself, until his hand was a clenched fist.

Then he rose to standing, and cleared his throat.

FIFTEEN

The young man spun round at the sound. He was older than Dalton – older even than Scarlet – eighteen, perhaps, with elegant features and finely made clothes.

'Who are you? What is this?' he said. He was calm, Dalton thought – straight backed and courageous, appraising his options with an intelligent gaze that leapt quickly around the hall as he watched the remaining intruders emerge from their hiding places. Scarlet held the pistol steady, levelled at his chest.

He was armed, Dalton noticed: a neat little silver-butt pistol, like the one Scarlet had given him, tucked into a hip-holster. He was going to be quick and slippery. 'Raise your hands,' Dalton said as confidently as he could. He wished his voice was deeper and stronger.

To his surprise, the young man did as he asked. 'This is going to be the biggest mistake you ever make,' he said. 'And, I suspect, one of the last.'

'Save your breath, De Bello,' said Scarlet.

Dalton made the connection suddenly, and cursed himself for missing it. Standing before them with his hands aloft was Stephen De Bello's son – the handsome young man being groomed for a position on the senate: Doone De Bello. The calm confidence, the fine suit of clothes and the gold bangles and rings – they all made sudden and horrible sense. Dalton felt his stomach tighten with fear. They were robbing Doone De Bello, at pistol-point, on Midwater West, in the middle of the night. It was utter madness. *The biggest mistake he'd ever make* began to sound pretty close to the mark. He tried to swallow but his mouth had furred up.

'Come on,' Doone De Bello said. 'The quicker we get this over with, the quicker I can get Tench to track you down. And kill you.'

His self belief was disorientating. Dalton took a step forward, swallowing back his fear. 'We want the map,' he said.

'Thought you might,' said De Bello, but he didn't move. Such was his poise and certainty, Dalton wondered if there was some sort of trick lying in wait for him. He paused. 'What?' De Bello said with a sneer. 'Are you waiting for my permission? Take it.'

Dalton crossed hurriedly to the table and rolled up the document, checking it as he did so. Sal had been right – a map of the city, an old one, inked in with lots of writing. He moved clear of De Bello and passed it to his friend who unrolled it and examined it eagerly. 'Thanks,' he said. This time his voice was firm, matching the calm of the De Bello boy. 'It's time we were leaving.'

Sal looked up from his assessment and nodded, folding the map and jamming it into his jacket pocket. Dalton dropped back as slowly as he dared, step by step, to join them.

Doone De Bello was brushing down his jacket now, not even concerned enough to keep his hands up. Whatever advantage they'd had at the opening of this encounter was slipping away.

Dalton checked his exit route one more time. Scarlet and Sal were ready. He gave them a nod. Then the three of them turned and broke into a run.

Doone De Bello issued a murderous cry: 'Tench! Tench!' he bellowed, as they hammered down the stairs and out through the door into the moonlit square.

They'd have to make this a swift and intelligent tactical retreat, Dalton thought as he ran. Back through the storm drain and along the pipes that—

Guards. Four of them, crossing quickly from the far corner of the square to the grand doors of the Senate Hall, their boots clattering and their coats billowing behind them. The one in the lead was pulling a pistol from his belt. Their eyes were on the doors of the hall as they followed the sound of De Bello's furious call, but, when they drew nearer, one spotted the three youngsters spilling out of the side door. He called out. The others pulled up, assessed the distance between them and their new target, and changed direction.

Dalton heard Sal swear violently. They wouldn't reach the storm drain now; they'd be stagged as they tried to lift the cover clear.

But Sal could get them out of this. 'New plan, Sleep-well!' Dalton said, skidding to a stop. 'We need a new plan!'

Sal seemed stunned, feverishly trying to recall the shapes and sizes of the squares and alleyways of Midwater West. There was no time. Pistols were upraised as the guards ran towards them. Tench surely couldn't be far behind. The thought of suffering the anger of that man made Dalton's blood turn to ice. A shot was fired, the bullet skidding off the stones near their feet.

'Scut and feathers!' swore Scarlet Dropmore, and then the three of them were running again, directionless, propelled by the pursuers at their backs.

Another shot. Dalton ducked as he ran, tried to weave to avoid a bullet in the backside. Sal was leading the sprint – arms pumping, wild hair streaming. He was babbling incoherently. Dalton had a vague impression of a high stone wall massing to his right – the Skeltonyards, perhaps: the prison Sal had mentioned – of the alleyways dropping now via a series of shallow steps, of oil-lamp light dimming and darkness descending. Still the guards followed.

There seemed to be a greater clamour of bootsteps; more of them had joined the chase. Even as he ran, Dalton found himself placing a hand across his lucky Jack and hoping his fear alone would be sufficient to summon Gannet's protective power. Or at least plant an idea in Sleepwell's bobbing and empty head.

Then things got suddenly and immeasurably worse.

Dalton's heart skidded and his belly flipped. The moon had dropped a skein of pale light across the street ahead of them and a section of shadow had uncoupled itself from the black walls of the buildings and made itself human. A tall, thin shape, swathed in an inky cloak, legs apart, head raised, was waiting for them.

For a mad moment it didn't make any sense. But it was the undertaker. Sal actually screamed – a high, hoarse shout of terror.

They darted left into a shabby passageway, reached a sprint again, slowed, crashed through a gate into a tiny yard and skittered down a set of stairs into pitch darkness. Sal was tugging at a bolt, scratching at a doorway and shouldering something open. Then they were through and inside a building – into old and damp air, into sightless blackness.

Scarlet sobbed and sniffed, gasping for breath. Sal retched. Dalton's blood thumped in his ears. For a while, only the slow calming of their breathing could be heard.

A little time passed.

'It seems quiet,' said Scarlet at length. 'We've lost them.'

Dalton could feel her shoulder against his. The hot smell of her breath. Her skin. Mint and soap.

Sal was moving about nearby. 'A candle!' he whispered. 'Are we safe to light it?'

There was a pause. Scarlet tapped Dalton on the shoulder. There it was again — that tendency for everyone to turn to him, as if he knew anything more than anyone else. He ran a hand over his sightless eyes, trying to clear his head. Perhaps this was his contribution, he thought. They needed someone strong enough to make some choices and take the blame? He could do that. The three of them couldn't crouch in the dark for the rest of the night. Escape was necessary, and for that, they needed light. And if it all went wrong?

He tapped his inside pocket. Gannet would see them through. 'Go on,' he said.

The low glow illuminated Sal's glasses and washed his face golden yellow. 'Fly. That was the undertaker,' he said, his hands trembling.

Dalton grimaced. 'I know,' he said. 'Where are we?'

They were huddled at the doorway of a vaulted cellar with a huge, high roof and, as they rose to standing, their steps scattered little echoes. The walls were patterned by strange grey-black blooms of mould and moss. Stagnant water pooled in the worn centre of the stones that made up the floor, little bits of broken candlelight dancing in them. They must be close to the edge of the island, near the river, Dalton thought. He could feel the rattle of its sour breath. Sal cupped his hand and attempted to conjure a stronger flame. Against the wall near the doors were three boats, old skiffs propped upright with their hulls outwards, rusted metal spines running their length. A stand of oars leant against the wall nearby, fogged in spider-webbing.

Dalton moved tentatively forward, and his footsteps pattered out a coded echo. 'Some sort of underground store,' he whispered. His voice danced and jumped in the chamber. 'What are the boats doing here? Something to do with the old wars?'

'Perhaps. We could always check the map,' Scarlet said, eyeing Sal. Her name was on that document. She needed to know why.

Sal nodded, drawing it out and unfolding it. 'Well – it's Highlions,' Sal said, leaning over it, his voice soft with wonder. 'But I don't know this version.' Sal knew all maps of the city, right from the earliest folios – those that were pictures more than maps – his father's favourites. He'd studied them all: ones that stopped at Geswick, ones that only mapped respectable streets, maps by district, political maps, maps that showed mermaids singing in the river. Sal's father had owned every version and edition there was.

'Sleepwell,' Dalton said, breaking his reverie. 'It's incredible. Who made it?'

Sal wiped his eyes. The artwork was unfamiliar, the faded pen-lines more graceful than any others he'd seen. He shrugged. 'Nothing like the Chisnall's folios,' he said. 'And better than Stretton's fourth and fifth editions.' He leant closer. 'Look at the detail!' he said. 'Every fountain, every well . . .' He gave a short laugh of admiration as he studied the knotted walkways and alleys.

'Fine,' interrupted Scarlet. 'But what's the writing?' There was a lot of it – cramped and spidery, some red, some black. There were names: whole lists of names, with numbers and symbols alongside them.

'Look,' said Sal. Scarlet and Dalton followed his finger, and he held it steady, eyes bright behind his glasses. 'Here's Scarlet's house. There's "Dropmore".'

'What's this?' Dalton said, pointing at a symbol perched above Scarlet's house. 'A crescent moon. What does it mean?' He stared. *A crescent moon* . . . He looked again at Scarlet, his heart leaping as he made the connection. The mark on the pistol the night he first saw her. 'A silver crescent moon . . .' he said. 'That's you.'

Scarlet nodded. 'A coat of arms for the sentaway,' she said. 'We all have them.'

'All have them?' Dalton said. 'How many of you are there?'

'Here's another crescent!' Sal stabbed the map with a finger. 'This one's Eppington. Another one next to it: Eden. And here's Knox. They've all got crescent moons.'

Dalton stared. 'The city's full of these sentaways!' What had Scarlet described them as? Hidden children? Dalton tried to marshal his thoughts, to make sense of what he was learning.

'And these are the names De Bello was reading out,' Sal said. 'Aren't they?'

Dalton nodded. 'There was Scarlet, and then – what was it? Knox?'

'Dropmore, Knox, Eppington, Eden, Honeycut, Holt,' Scarlet repeated tiredly. 'It seems there's something about sentaways that De Bello doesn't like . . .'

Dalton ran a hand across his face. The undertaker wouldn't leave his mind. And Tench with the smashed face. What was going on? 'We need to move' he said. 'Let's look for a way out. I can hear the river.'

He padded further into the gloom of the cellar and the others followed. It was colder here and the low roll of the river was louder. He saw something swim up from the gloom. There were steps, falling away in a deep downward tunnel, and a rusted metal trackway running down the centre of them that looked as if it were designed to hold something straight and true as it descended.

Then, above the river noise, another sound. They all heard it. Sal blew out the candle and thick darkness swallowed them whole.

Dalton heard Scarlet's breath catch in her throat. There they were again – footsteps somewhere close by – out in the yard, back near the door. There was another sound now, the sound of two men whispering in low voices. And there was the unmistakable click of a pistol catch being drawn back.

They needed to hide. 'The boats,' Dalton said hoarsely.

SIXTEEN

I t was a struggle to make it in time, moving as swiftly and quietly as they dared in the pitch black, running their hands along the cellar walls as they progressed. Then they struck the hull of the skiff, upstanding against the stone, lifted it clear and slipped behind it. There was just room enough for the three of them. Despite its size, it was frail and easy to move – the wood spongy and rotted, the boat held together by its flaking iron backbone. They let it lean again, its prow balancing against the wall above their heads as they cowered, crouching. It smelt of river mud and dead fish. And fear – the sharp tang of fear in the black air.

Then the cellar door swung open and an echoing tattoo of bootsteps accompanied a group into the chamber. They spread out quickly then paused. The intruders had lamps – light leaked through the gaps at his feet, Dalton noticed, and next to him, Scarlet's profile emerged from the blackness. Outside, the men were checking the shadows, thinking through the possibilities. Someone was breathing heavily. Pistols were drawn.

'More lamps!' barked a mangled voice. It was Tench – the man with half a face.

Dalton shifted his position silently, feeling Scarlet press against him in the dark. The light from the lanterns patterned the floor in stripes as the shadows of men passed before them. He counted: three, four, five of them, perhaps, though they were passing back and forth like shades, pacing the room. This was a foolish place to hide, Dalton thought, searching for ideas.

Then, his mind made a sudden connection. The metal spine running down the centre of the skiff and the rusted channel dropping down the steps out there in the darkness. It was an ancient launch chute for emergency boats. He knew then that the iron backbone of the skiff would fit the trackway and that, if he could get there in time with the boat and not get ghosted, they could perhaps ride the chute downwards and out into the river. His fingers flexed with the pins and needles of terror and hope. It was a plan. A lunatic plan, that much was certain – but options were limited and his friends were relying on him. He felt a curious surge of pride for it, reckless and idiotic as it was.

Dalton craned his neck and found that he could observe some of the movement outside through the gap between the boat and the wall. De Bello's guards were fanning out across the room, their footfalls nothing more than whispers now. Sal twitched at the click of a pistol nearby. Someone was very close. Then the skiff next to them was being lifted back from the wall. Someone was checking behind the boats. Dalton could almost feel the breath of the searcher at their necks. He listened, panic flurrying in his throat, as the adjacent boat was lowered again. He pressed an open palm across his Jack. They were next. There would be no escape. They were doomed to die.

A voice came through the darkness, and it saved them.

'Don't move, Pallis Tench,' it said. It came from the door out to the yard.

Tench came into Dalton's line of vision as he stepped forward towards the voice. His face, already split by the jumbled weave of scars, was thunderous. He held his pistol high in the air.

Dalton could hardly believe what he was seeing. From the doorway, a repeater pistol emerged, followed by the hand that held it. A strong, old hand with a grip like iron. Then an arm, the sleeve of a black coat.

It was the undertaker.

Dalton stared, lips parted in amazement.

'Call your men off, Tench, or I'll blow your brains out,' the undertaker said. He never looked towards the boats. But somehow, Dalton realised, he knew that's where they were hiding.

Pallis Tench didn't move. His blasted face darkened. 'Applefell,' he said in a flat voice, but his eyes betrayed surprise. 'I was hoping you were dead.'

The undertaker – Applefell, Tench had called him – took a step forward and the cellar fell silent but for the distant and rolling roar of the river. 'Well, Tench,' he said, 'I thought the dogs had got you. But here we both are – still alive. Call your men off their search or I'll put a hole in your forehead.'

Tench made one of his twisted smiles; the kind that split his face. *Dogs*, thought Dalton. He didn't dare imagine what horror Tench might have suffered. The big man lowered his arm.

'Ah, ah!' the undertaker said, his voice bright. 'Keep the pistol up!'

Tench raised the arm again, suppressing a scowl. There was a moment's unbroken silence.

'I'm here for the boy who calls himself Dalton Fly,' said the undertaker.

Tench grinned. 'I think you'll find that particular problem falls under De Bello jurisdiction now.'

Dalton blinked in the darkness, mind racing. *The boy who calls himself Dalton Fly?* What did the old man mean by that?

'He belongs to me,' the undertaker said, his voice steely. Dalton watched the stand-off from his painful crouch, helpless. It made no sense: he belonged to Oscar. Or to no one. 'Come out, boy!' the undertaker called, his gaze never leaving Tench's upheld pistol. 'Bring your friend. Come slowly.'

Scarlet gripped his arm tightly. Dalton had no idea what her fingers, hard above his elbow, signified. Was she holding him back? Urging him into action? Dalton squinted at Sal. The poison boy's face was a dark mask in the shadow behind the boat: unreadable. This was a decision he would have to make without them. What made him stand up, he couldn't tell, except there was, somewhere in him, a sudden and unexpected connection with the man trying to save him. The undertaker had said 'friend'. But he surely knew there were three of them. Which meant this stranger was helping to keep one of them concealed – giving them a chance. Dalton pushed the boat away from the wall and squeezed out into full view.

There were five of them: Pallis Tench in the centre of the cellar facing the undertaker, four of his men circling him from a distance, each with a lantern and a pistol, each making their own slow search of the chamber.

The undertaker seemed suddenly transfixed by his emergence, gazing at him with an uncomfortable intensity. The old man's cheeks were sallow and unshaven, his hair thinning, shoulder-length and grey. His eyes were deep set and his jaw clenched hard. He looked like someone who knew he was facing his final moments. And his gaze was like that of a bird of prey: a hunter, fierce and dark. Full of sadness and anger, Dalton thought. Behind him, he heard Sal emerge too, and watched as the guards adjusted their positions and pistol grips to cover them.

'Master De Bello needs his map back,' Tench said,

watching Dalton with his one good eye. 'Hand it over.'

Dalton found he was mute, his tongue dried to the roof of his mouth. He swallowed hard. Sal took a step forward. Scarlet had been clever. She'd kept herself concealed. Dalton looked at the undertaker. The old man knew she was still hiding – he could tell. Had Tench noticed, though? Had his men mentioned there were three of them?

'Pass me the map. Now.' Tench raised a crooked finger, the pistol in his other hand trained on Applefell. One of his men began to move in, tightening the circle. Another took a step forward.

Dalton looked at Sal. His friend's face was a pale disc in the lantern light. It took Sal two attempts to draw the document from his jacket pocket, such was the tremble of his hands. He held it up. Dalton could tell he was trying not to cry.

'Don't,' Applefell said.

'The map,' Tench repeated, louder.

Sal winced and took a step forward.

'No!' This time, Applefell yelled.

Sal fumbled, terrified, and dropped the map. Dalton's gaze was drawn to it as it spun. One of the guards lunged for it. Applefell shifted his footing—

The crack of a pistol came from somewhere off to the left. A crunch of bone – the gurgle of blood-filled breath. Dalton watched in frozen horror. The undertaker was down on one knee. His pistol hit the ground. He must have looked away from Tench for just a moment as the map fell. And that moment had killed him – Tench had lowered his arm and fired.

The undertaker was choking and his neck and chest were black with gluey blood. It looked as if the bullet had passed through his throat. Still kneeling, he cupped his hands under his chin but couldn't stop the flow.

When he spoke, he looked at Dalton, and his voice came through bubbles of blood. 'I told them you were dead,' he said. His eyes were glassy and fierce. Dalton watched him, rigid with shock. 'I told them you were dead,' he said, again, this time fading.

Then he crashed forwards on to the cellar floor, his jaw striking the stones hard and his eyes rolling upwards and closed. The undertaker – Applefell – was ghosted. Dalton felt his eyes sting and realised tears were streaming down his cheeks.

'Well, that's torn it, boy,' Pallis Tench said calmly. 'I've just killed your marcher.'

SEVENTEEN

D alton hated the slowness of his thinking. Trying to work out what had just happened was like wading slowly forward, waist deep in mud. The undertaker – the man who had stalked him from street to street, passing from lantern to lantern through the dimly lit Lower Circle – was his marcher? His protector? Not his enemy.

In an elongated moment, he remembered the first time the old man had seen him that night near the bearmarket, the way his wrinkled eyes had widened instinctively – shock, was it? – and the word he'd said in a dry voice. Had it been a name? He'd reached for something in the pocket of his jacket. Not a pistol, Dalton now realised. Had he been about to show him something? But Dalton had run away. And Applefell had been patiently tracking him ever since. Dalton felt the axis of his world tip. He had a marcher. Then that made him—

A high scream shattered the still silence of the moment. Dalton spun round, senses alive again, seeking its source. One of the boats seemed to be moving on its own, floating towards them. Then he realised what was happening – quicker even than Tench and his men. Scarlet was making a charge, holding it before her like a huge shield. She couldn't see where she was going. She was running blind, holding the boat at its edges with a white knuckled grip.

Sal Sleepwell, on fire with a kind of deranged terror, issued a coarse bellow, dipped quickly to scoop up the map and began to run with her. He was alongside her as the pistols began to crack. Voices clamoured and clashed, and Dalton rode a fierce burst of energy and ran towards the boat, which bobbed like a huge upright insect in the direction of the steps and the launch chute.

Tench roared. A pistol clapped and a bullet punctured a tattered hole in the boat over Scarlet's head. They ran forwards into the darkness of the cellar, the three of them as one now, all howling and horror-stricken. Scarlet's grip was slipping, and the boat dropping from vertical like a spear dipped by a warrior before a charge into battle. It thumped their shins as they went. Sal grabbed its edges and it squirmed from his hands, smashing to the floor and skidding along its iron spine.

Another pistol shot was followed by the drum of pursuit and high shouts of rage. Sal ran on, low, pushing the boat from behind. Dalton did the same. The skiff's base sparked and screeched across the stone, as if they were launching a mighty sledge at a hill of ice. Scarlet screamed and, with a dive, was in the belly of the battered boat, her pistol clattering down somewhere behind her. A bullet fizzed off the stones at their feet.

With a great, rending screech, the boat's iron spine found the trackway at the top of the steps and it straightened suddenly, then tipped at the lip of the drop. Sal hurled himself in. Dalton lost his footing and fell backwards into the boat on top of his friends.

With a volley of sparks and a howl of rusted metal, the boat began to fall. At the top of the chute, the men appeared. Dalton scrabbled for Scarlet's pistol, his nails breaking, and found it. He made it to his knees, balanced himself, and managed to fire it upwards at the figures there, pounding the trigger with hot, bleeding fingers. The silver-butt reeled from his grip, jumping like a fish.

Somewhere above, a figure dropped to his knees with a shout. The last thing Dalton saw, looking upward as the boat sped down into the dark, was the silhouetted figure of Pallis Tench holding a pistol high and firing wildly at them.

Then they were plummeting downwards, the stone walls of the stairwell flashing past on either side. Sal's long shout became a victorious scream. Dalton was aware of his friend somewhere at the front of the skiff, hanging onto the prow and howling like a blind pilot.

The craft's weakness was evident as it hurtled down its launch track. Its edges were shattering and flaking against the stone walls, the wooden slats cracking. Scarlet was screaming as the belly of the boat beneath her began to disintegrate, torn away in splinters. There was light ahead. They gathered speed. The three of them clung madly to each other as the sides of the boat broke away in spinning shards. The launch ended ahead. The river was a low roar. The skiff barrelled out of its tunnel like a bullet and, for a moment, seemed to hang in the spray above the river and fly. Then it ditched, nose first, and broke into pieces as it hit the water, sending its passengers into the air.

Dalton hit the water backwards and the cold knocked the breath from him. He whirled, submerged in a sea of bubbles and mud, and was sucked forward with the force of the current. Someone's boot caught him in the face. He kicked his way upwards and broke the surface, gasping. The sharp night air filled his senses and he pulled in a deep breath. His lips were bleeding

His friends. He blinked the water out of his eyes and flapped his arms, supporting himself above the surface of the river. It looked low and glassy from the city's bridges, but down here at its heart it was a fast-flowing beast, rocking and spinning and kneading. His clothes stuck to him uncomfortably; his boots were lead weights as he kicked his legs.

There was Sleepwell, one hand raised above his head, the map flapping like a victory flag as he paddled for control with his spare arm, his hair flattened across his cheeks. He was blowing hard, spitting water, coughing and beating the surface, trying to keep his beloved map dry. He whooped at the sight of his friend. 'I've got the flogging map!' he called with a stupefied look. 'Are you all right?'

It was a strange conversation, conducted as the companions were swept downriver, the city dropping closer to them on either bank as they moved further into the Lower Circle and the houses and lights came into view. Scarlet was calling to them and chopping at the surface of the river as she made her way towards them, her coat billowing up around her in the water, a grin of triumph on her face.

'Can you swim well?' Dalton called.

Scarlet spat a jet of water in his direction. 'Well enough, poison boy,' she said with a lopsided smile. 'Though not usually in my clothes.' She twisted her way towards Sal. 'Where are we?' she called.

Sal was watching the buildings slip by on the west bank, one arm trembling with the effort of keeping the map raised, a grimace of pain plastered across his face. 'Over there's the church in Angels,' he said, flinching as the water caught the edges of the map. His eyes narrowed and his smile faded. 'Kite!' he said. 'Look at that.'

Dalton and Scarlet watched a procession of Streetwatch gathering at the corner of a square, oil lanterns raised and dogs on leads. One of them, the leader by the look of his uniform and stature, was dispatching a gang in each direction. They had pistols – the repeaters that Lower Circle

Streetwatch were apt to carry.

'Is that for us?' Scarlet said. The boys swam closer to her until they were drifting together as a group, arms linked, watching the guards making their preparations. Scarlet took a turn with the map.

Sal brought an upraised finger to his lips. 'Looks like De Bello's been quick off the mark,' he said, his face close to the water and his voice low.

'He must really want this back,' Dalton said. 'Let's make for the other bank.'

They emerged, spitting and coughing downriver by a broad cobbled area of upturned boats in Snortehill, and crawled from the muddy edges of the river, gasping. The milky light of the moon picked out the shapes of fishing gear: eel traps, nets for trout and coiled chains, thick with rust. Behind them, the river guttered and chattered. Nightflies dozed in clouds over their heads as they dragged themselves clear and lay panting on their backs.

Dalton rose to his feet, and leant for a moment on his bruised knees, water pooling in the mud beneath him. 'We need to move,' he said. 'They'll be looking for us soon.'

'Have you still got that silver-butt?' Scarlet asked.

Dalton felt his pockets for the heavy curl of the pistol handle. 'Yes,' he said. 'But I fired it. And we've no shot-powder. Come on, let's keep moving.'

They struggled up from the river's edge, exhausted, to the empty streets of Snortehill, a place that, by day, at least, meant rats, dippers, brawlers and trouble-rousers.

The dark houses were low and mean. Walls were daubed with slogans; shutters were missing or broken. Somewhere, a stray dog sent a volley of barks into the night. At least the street fighting seemed to have stopped.

'You boys bring me to the nicest places,' said Scarlet, looking around her. Her clothes, slaked in dreck, clung to her and water dripped from them round her feet.

The three of them kept moving, trying to stay warm, sticking to the shadows under the eaves, heading anywhere away from trouble. But trouble was hard to avoid, they soon found. Despite the early hour and the silence of the empty streets, Streetwatch patrols were numerous. Twice, the friends had to cower, shivering in an abandoned alleyway while guards patrolling in pairs passed within a few strides of them. Eventually, Sal led them to a stables near the city gates and they crouched in the straw where the horses whinnied and stamped, unpeeled the damp map from itself and lay it out to dry, hung up their dripping coats, kicked off their boots and curled up in the straw, hollowed out with fatigue.

Dalton couldn't sleep, though. It was partly the pain from his bruised and bloodied hands, aching joints, split lip; partly the stink and discomfort of slowly drying river mud under his arms and between his legs; and partly the close buzz of gnats and horseflies. But mostly it was the undertaker, Applefell, haunting the edges of his thinking to start with, and then striding unbidden into the centre of his mind. Dalton saw again the buckling knees as he was hit; the bib of black and gluey blood draining from the old man's throat across his chest; and he heard the meaty thud of his face against the stones as he plunged forward, ghosted. The old man's voice echoed too: 'The boy who calls himself Dalton Fly,' he'd said. 'I told them you were dead.' The memory of Pallis Tench drifted up out of the darkness like a black ghost wearing a mauled grin. 'That's torn it. I've just killed your marcher.' Dalton found himself turning it over and over, shifting in the crackling straw and listening to his companions' breathing.

He slept fitfully at last. And by morning, he knew what he had to do. There was only one person who could tell him more about 'the boy who calls himself Dalton Fly', he figured, and that was Oscar. He hadn't seen his master since the night of Bennie's death, and the numbers of Streetwatch would be a problem, but the risk was worth it. He needed to know what was going on.

EIGHTEEN

Sal was hunched over the map, brushing caked mud from the torn knees of his trousers. His eyes were bright with excitement. Scarlet sat herself next to him, swatting hopelessly at gnats.

'Fly,' said Sal, beckoning, 'it's as clever as I remember. Pen and ink, like Stretton's best. But much more detailed. The scale is incredible.'

His eyes had glazed a little, Dalton could see. This was Sleepwell in a mapmaker's world of folios and editions, a little boy with round glasses gawping by his father's side again.

Dalton rubbed his eyes, groaned and pushed himself

up on to his elbows. Everything ached. He brushed off some straw and propped his head on his scabbed hands.

'The list of names,' he reminded Sal and Scarlet, indicating them. 'Remember what De Bello and Tench were discussing?'

Scarlet nodded. 'Knox, Eppington, Eden, Honeycut, Holt,' she said, omitting her own name. 'Sentaways. De Bello's targeting sentaways.'

'So it was definitely him who poisoned the food at your party?' Sal said.

Scarlet nodded. 'And when that didn't work . . .'

'. . . the shotpowder bomb,' Dalton said. He found himself grinding his teeth as he made connections, saw some strange and dark purpose opening itself up before him. 'So he's tried to kill you twice. And he's after the others too.'

'Three days,' Sal said suddenly. The others looked at him. 'Didn't he say three days would be enough?'

'He did,' Dalton confirmed. 'He's looking to get to the sentaways on this list as quickly as he can. To poison them. Or, if that doesn't work, to blow them into bits.'

'But why?' Scarlet said, exasperated. 'What have I done? I've never even met him.'

Sal bit his thumb, thinking. 'Has your family wronged him in some way? Your mother?'

'Not that I know of. My mother doesn't share senate business with me, though. Marcher Gellis keeps me away from all that.'

Dalton found himself thinking of marchers all of a

sudden, imaginings crowding his head again. Marcher Applefell: guardian to the boy who calls himself Dalton Fly. 'We have to get to the others on the list,' Dalton said. If he was going to bring anything to this endeavour, he figured, it could be a bit of direction. Gannet knew, it needed it.

To his surprise, the others nodded. 'Agreed,' said Scarlet.

'There's something else before we start,' Sal said, hesitation in his voice. Dalton nodded at him to go on. Sal scratched his head, unsure of what to say. 'If you've got a marcher, Flyboy, doesn't that make you a sentaway?' he managed, giving voice to Dalton's own thoughts. 'Could you be on this list too? But in a different name?'

Dalton closed his eyes for a moment, trying to get control of his pulse and slow his breathing. He was Dalton Fly. Just one of Oscar's boys. Sal gazed at him, unblinking. Scarlet was looking at her fingernails.

'We'll get to the names on the list,' Dalton said. He swallowed, trying to moisten his dry mouth. 'But I have to see Oscar first.'

Sal nodded his understanding. 'I'll track down the first name. It's Knox, isn't it? Leave me with the map. You go.'

Dalton smiled his thanks. He needed to resolve this.

'I'll come,' said Scarlet. Dalton's surprise must have been painted across his face. Scarlet placed a hand on Dalton's shoulder. 'I'm a sentaway. If you are too, I'll know the signs.'

'Signs?' Dalton said.

Scarlet brushed her hair back under her headscarf. 'It's more than just silver crescents, poison boy. There's stuff. Sentaway stuff. Your man Oscar might have it.'

Dalton felt his heart sink. The old man would probably be drunk. There were a million ways this could go badly.

He sighed. 'Let's go, then,' he said.

'This is it?' The alleyway was cluttered and dusty. The houses either side were covered in a rough plaster which was crumbling in cracked sections. Much of the street was in shade despite the climbing morning sun, and flies buzzed incessantly. The sign creaked above them.

Dalton wiped the sweat from his forehead. 'This is it,' he said. Scarlet wrinkled her nose.

Dalton pushed open the door and followed the steps down into the cool of the kitchen. He felt a wriggling knot of discomfort in his stomach and it took a moment to identify its source. Then he placed it – shame. Shame for the broken little house where he shared a room; shame for the rats in the alleyway, the creaking sign with its silly lie – *Oscar's Honest Dozen* – embarrassment at the smell of the kitchen, the low ceiling, the fat man snoring in his chair, his head on the table, balding scalp exposed.

Scarlet followed him down. Dalton heard her hold her breath. Trapped flies spun in aimless circles in the half dark of the room. There was a stale loaf of bread on the table, and a wedge of hardening cheese. And, of course, Oscar's spoons and flickers scattered about an empty bottle. The old man was half drunk, as usual. Pots and pans, black with grime, huddled in the low sink. Oscar raised his head at the sound of Dalton's steps, blinked and rubbed his eyes – ground at them with the heels of his hands – and licked his cracked lips.

'Kite, boy,' he managed. 'Where've you been?' He wiped his face with a greasy palm. 'There's been Streetwatch everywhere since you left – all demanding to see you. None of them looking happy, either.'

Dalton looked at his hands, struggling to find his voice. He didn't know what to say.

'I'm Scarlet,' Scarlet said, raising a hand in expectation of a greeting.

Oscar gave Dalton a sneer. 'What's the missy doing here?' he said.

Dalton felt his face warm with embarrassment and swallowed back his anger. 'There's something I need to ask you,' he said. The words came quicker now. 'When you first found me – did I have anything with me? Any identification?'

Dalton noted the change in Oscar's expression, the eyebrows hiking at the unexpected question.

The old man puffed out his cheeks. He was still orientating himself; coming round from the fever-tea. 'I don't know what you mean,' he said.

Dalton was expecting this. He'd never known honesty from the man; his existence was a drugged haze of half-truths and borrowed memories. 'Yes, you do,' he said.

'Who've you been talking to?' Oscar said. He was shifting in his chair.

'Never mind,' said Dalton. He was feeling stronger now. 'Just tell me, sir. Just tell me.'

Oscar's face softened and fell a bit. He looked at the floor. 'How old are you now?' he said. 'Still fourteen?'

'Yes, sir. Still fourteen.' In truth, Dalton didn't know how old he was. Fourteen was the answer he always gave. He'd been giving it for close to two years now. When he was a little boy, he remembered, he'd decided to be one year older than Sal, partly so he could win arguments and boss his friend around. If that were true, it would make him at least fifteen now. But at some forgotten point in the past, the two friends had fallen into the habit of claiming to be the same age. At least Sal knew when his birthday was – it meant Dalton could borrow the same birthday and make a meagre celebration of reaching the same point.

Oscar examined his fingernails for a moment. His tongue ran along the underside of his yellow teeth. Then he swallowed and placed both hands carefully on the table. His mind seemed suddenly made up. 'I've something to show you,' he said. 'Follow me.'

NINETEEN

The big man tramped upstairs, Dalton and Scarlet following. The wood creaked ominously as they made their way up to Oscar's room. Dalton hoped fervently it was going to be tidy and decent for Scarlet.

The old man pushed the door open. 'Come in,' he said. They entered. The curtains were drawn; even the morning sun couldn't penetrate the gloom.

Scarlet issued a little gasp. Dalton knew she'd be scanning the shelves, taking in the array of bottles that made up Oscar's hospital – the oils and unguents, seeds and leaves, crushed fruits, powders, dusts and ointments. Snakeroot, hemlock, mandragora, Calabar, of course, oleander, poppy seed and wormwood – all labelled and sequenced, dated, weighed and measured.

'The tools of our curious trade,' Oscar said to her, noting her wide-eyed interest. 'Don't touch a thing, missy. Only my poison boys get to taste these.'

Scarlet looked at Dalton. 'You eat this stuff?'

Oscar laughed. 'To strengthen the body against poison, you need to accustom yourself slowly – build up your resistance. Fly's a strong young lad. He's doing well. Sleep-well, too. But Jinks . . .' Oscar paused and ground his teeth together. 'Not so well.'

A bag of bones in a bloody lake. Dalton ran a hand across his face, trying to shake off the memory of the boy with his belly inside out. He could still taste blood at the back of his throat. 'You've something to show me,' he reminded Oscar.

Oscar stepped across to his shrine – the tangled collection of trinkets, keepsakes and charms he amassed to ward off ill luck. He selected a key from a hook and opened the drawer beneath the desk. Dalton hadn't been in Oscar's room very often – most times he'd been there because he'd over-tasted and needed a tonic or antidote – but he'd never even noticed the locked drawer before. Oscar withdrew a package wrapped in a grubby-looking cloth.

He turned towards the boy.

'I haven't been entirely honest with you, Fly,' he said. 'Sit down.'

Dalton felt his legs weaken. He sat next to Scarlet on

the bed. She put a hand on his arm. The sheets were filthy. He wished he could open a window, clear the air. He felt sick. Oscar pulled up a chair and began carefully unwrapping the package, his fat fingers moving gracelessly.

It was a silver box the size of a small pistol case. It sat neatly in the palm of Oscar's hand, light and durable. Dalton felt Scarlet's grip tighten, as if she'd seen one like it before. His heart raced, though with what, he couldn't tell. He wondered for a moment if he was scared or excited or still feeling belladonna hammering through his veins.

'What's this?' he managed.

'Now there's a question,' Oscar said. His fingers paused. 'Let me tell you the barrel story.'

'You've told me the barrel story.'

'No, I haven't. Not all of it. Let me tell you the whole barrel story.'

'What's the barrel story?' Scarlet said, her fingers still tight around Dalton's arm.

'You don't mind the missy listening?' Oscar said.

'Tell it,' said Dalton. He hated Oscar calling Scarlet 'missy'. He hated the blank-faced rows of bottles in Oscar's room. And, more than anything, he hated the barrel story. This, he swore, would be the last time he was ever going to listen to it.

'Once, I found a little boy in a barrel,' said Oscar, and his voice assumed its slurred and sleepy story-telling quality, like it did when he was getting drunk. Dalton made fists with his hands.

'I was trading spice and pollen in the cellars under Downholland,' Oscar continued. 'It was late in the year. The days were short and cold. It was a frosty night and I was in need of a drink. Some trader called Loades – a bandit and a no-good brawler, if there ever was one – had a quantity of fortified wine he wanted rid of. I was his man.' Oscar laughed wheezily and rubbed his hands together. 'It came in these barrels, little wooden barrels about knee-high. They had a design burnt on to the wood – a little black fly, its wings open. I paid for three. The third barrel had a loose lid. It was empty except for a little baby in a blanket.'

There was a silence as Oscar licked his lips. Scarlet let go of Dalton's arm. Dalton hung his head, looked at his boots.

'Loades knows nothing, of course,' Oscar said with a dry chuckle. 'He had this outraged face on. White as candle wax. All confusion. "That wasn't there this afternoon! I swear!" All that stuff. But it doesn't look good for him, right? Smuggling's one thing. Slave trading? That's another. The senate would have his grapes for earrings and he knew it. In the end, I got the wine for nothing, the kid for nothing and a wallet full of chinkers into the bargain. As long as I kept my trap shut. Well – the kid had no identification. So I named him after the barrel.' Oscar made a little flapping sign with his hands. 'A little black fly with its wings open.' He cracked his knuckles. 'The baby was you,' he added, as if talking to an idiot, and winked at Dalton. There was a silence in which the airless room seemed to fall into complete stillness.

Scarlet cleared her throat. She was rotating the ring on her middle finger – the one with the red stone. 'But that's not the whole story?' she tried.

Dalton looked at Oscar. Oscar nodded at the box. 'When I unwrapped the little mite,' he said slowly, as if using the words for the first time, 'he had this with him.' And, as he spoke, Oscar opened the case.

There was a letter pushed into the bottom of the silver box. Resting on the letter was a pack of playing cards secured with a decorated band, a delicate silver chain looped through a dark ivory key, and a silver pistol with a crescent-moon design.

Oscar handed the tin to Dalton. 'I have to admit something,' he said with an absent-minded shrug, 'the letter was longer. But I lost it. Or burnt it. Can't remember.' He made a weak smile. 'I've often wondered whether to give it you one day. S'pose I was still deciding. Anyway,' he finished, 'you've forced my hand now, haven't you? It's yours. Take it.'

Dalton felt the weight of the silver box as he held it. It was a curious item – finely carved and decorated with intertwined vines and leaves. The room had fallen quiet. Scarlet leant close to look at the contents as Dalton flicked the band off the pack of cards and thumbed their edges. He fanned them in his hands, acutely aware of the familiar patterned design on their reverse sides: a weave of ivy leaves and stems; a repeating pattern of white on blue. He knew that pattern well; it adorned the back of his lucky Jack. He felt his mouth dry up and his chest squeeze as he counted them. Sure enough, the pack was a card short. He pulled his lucky Jack from his jacket pocket and placed it alongside the others. It was grubbier, creased and filthy from the river. But it was the missing card – of that there was no doubt. He looked at Oscar and the old man looked away.

Outside, Scarlet squinted in the brightness of the morning. The streets were busy and hot. Somewhere nearby, two dogs were issuing a series of bad-tempered barks at each other, and their owners hauled them apart. A horse passed them, its rider drinking from a jug of water. Traders shouted over each other down in the square.

Scarlet's eyes wandered the crowds. She pushed her hair back into her silk headscarf. 'You get more interesting all the time,' she said, and flashed Dalton a smile.

Despite himself, he grinned back. She was trying to cheer him up, he knew. Oscar had been as repulsive as he had expected – but she had stuck it out. 'What exactly is this?' he said to her, holding the case up between them.

'I've an idea,' she said enigmatically. 'Keep it safe. Don't wave it around, eh?'

'You've seen one before? This is the sentaway stuff?'

Scarlet laughed an empty laugh. 'Yes. I've seen a few. I've got one of my own.'

Dalton regarded her carefully. Most of what she said, he didn't understand. Perhaps something happened to you when you were sixteen – something which gifted you all this additional knowledge and understanding and grace. His heart beat hard against his ribs.

'What does it mean?' he said.

'It's a little box of special belongings,' she said. 'Your father or mother packed that carefully for you before you were hidden. But, in your case, something must have gone wrong.' Scarlet shrugged. 'And you ended up in a barrel.' She gave her grown-up laugh again, as if she were sharing a joke with an absent friend. 'As to what it means,' she said, 'it means two things.' She held up her fingers one at a time as if teaching a kid to count. 'It means you're a sentaway, that's for certain,' she said. 'And it means you're not Dalton Fly.'

TWENTY

They knew there was something wrong once they got into the grounds. Sal even stopped his poring over the map and folded it away, his attention drawn by the strange conference taking place ahead of them.

He'd guided them to the grand mansion on the higher edges of the Middle Circle without much trouble, and they'd found a way in through a gap in the iron fence. This was where the first of the names on the list – Knox – was hidden. As they made their way up through the city, they'd speculated as to how it might be best to hide a sentaway. 'In plain sight,' Scarlet had argued, and she seemed to know what she was talking about. In some cases, she said, even a sentaway's parents didn't know where they were – their entire welfare was in the hands of the marcher. 'It's about protection,' she explained. 'Because Mother is a senator, I'm a target.'

'For what?' said Sal.

'Use your imagination,' Scarlet said with a smirk, checking the map over his shoulder as they rested.

'Kidnap?'

'Right. Or worse.'

'For money,' Dalton said. 'Or for power. If someone captured you, they might have control over the senate.'

'Right,' Scarlet said again. 'These poison boys aren't so stupid after all! That's where marchers come in. They help protect sentaways.' And so marchers were a singular breed: tough, alert, clever and immensely well paid, Scarlet had said. Her respect for Marcher Gellis was clear.

Dalton wondered how long it would take the steely, determined woman he'd met after the shotpowder bomb to track down her escaped charge. As a sentaway, Scarlet explained, she'd been lucky to have such a capable marcher and to lead such a sheltered, hidden and privileged life. Most marchers turned their charges into students in private boarding schools, kitchen apprentices, governesses or servants. Sentaways like this dressed differently, lived secretly, adopted new families and friends, new ways of life and new homes until the danger was over.

'But you get to have parties in an Upper Circle

mansion?' Dalton asked mischievously.

Scarlet narrowed her eyes at him and shrugged. 'I'm sixteen now. When sentaways get older, they get more choice. A bit more control. And I'm lucky. Mine's a good marcher. She . . . understands me.'

Knox had landed on his feet as well, it seemed. No lowly life as a scullery boy for him. At the edges of the gardens, among the dark-leaved shrubs, the three companions waited, letting the last of the river water steam from their filthy clothes in the afternoon sun and watching the house where Knox was living his secret life. It was huge. Even from a distance they could see the glittering chandeliers through the windows of the ballroom, the maids scurrying along top-floor corridors with armfuls of fresh sheets for guests, and the horses of the house being exercised, led by well-dressed ground staff. If Knox was hidden here, Dalton had commented with a laugh, he might not want to leave, no matter what danger was descending upon him.

But the levity was short-lived. Sal had noticed something first, as the three of them were skirting the grounds looking for a way in. 'What's that?' he said, pointing.

A tall figure, dressed in a long riding coat and holding a cane, was pacing frantically up and down the gravelled pathways that linked the kitchens to the walled garden. A second figure, lithe and young, was with the first.

'That's a marcher,' Scarlet said. 'The stride, the posture. That's definitely a marcher. We're in the right place.'

'She doesn't look happy,' Dalton murmured, watching

the taller figure issue a series of urgent orders to the smaller.

A horse was being prepared, Dalton noticed. In a matter of moments, the smaller figure had mounted and galloped across the grounds towards the main drive, striking the beast ruthlessly in haste. Something was very wrong.

Suddenly, Scarlet broke into a run, heading straight for the stricken figure who now stood alone, leaning over the cane as if exhausted. Dalton gasped in alarm. What was she up to?

'What happened to stealth?' Sal spluttered, and the boys set off after her.

Scarlet was calling something as she ran. The marcher's attention was quickly with the three approaching figures, charging across the lawns in broad daylight, and her spare hand moved to the pistol under her coat. But she hesitated, and didn't draw. It was only then that Dalton realised, as he sprinted towards the house, that the two of them must know each other. Scarlet was waving. The marcher was running towards her. When the two of them met, they embraced, the tall marcher leaning over to scoop Scarlet into her long arms. Once the boys were with them, they were already talking, their words swift and urgent.

'These are my friends,' Scarlet was saying. 'They can be trusted. Marcher Watts,' she said by way of introduction, placing a hand on the woman's arm. Scarlet's face was pale as she spoke and clouded with sadness. Something had evidently already passed between them in the moments before the boys joined them. Something bad. 'She was my marcher once,' Scarlet explained, 'in Blackwater, when I was younger.'

Marcher Watts had dark blue eyes lined with kohl and a face creased with worry. 'You find me at a dreadful time,' she said, resuming her pacing. 'My charge, the boy Milo, is dead.' She looked away and above the boys, scanning the edges of the grounds as if expecting someone else. Dalton found his breath halt in his throat.

'Dead?' Sal said.

Watts grimaced. Her hair was short and stuck up in dark bunches and she ran her hands through it absently, fearfully, then leant her weight on the cane with the ivory handle. 'I must contact the boy's mother,' she said, distracted, looking back at the house now.

'Milo Knox,' Dalton said.

Watts regarded him evenly and pinched the bridge of her nose. 'You know him?' she said. 'You don't look like the sort of boys who would know him.'

Dalton looked at his mud-caked boots, the filth that had crusted at the knees of his trousers and his buttonless jacket. Sal was pushing his glasses back and up into his hair, irritated by the sweat coursing down his face. Dalton tried to wipe the grime from his hands. 'No offence taken,' he said. His stomach was a heavy knot of anger and frustration. They were too late. They had the map, they knew the plan – and they hadn't been quick enough to save the sentaway. Tench had got to him first.

'Marcher Watts,' Scarlet said. She was calmer now, straight-backed and grown-up. 'We think that someone might be trying to harm sentaways – to poison them. My friends here are poison boys. I think they can be useful to you.'

Watts couldn't hide her surprise. She bit her lip, looked back at the house and checked the perimeter again, thinking. Then she took a deep breath. 'In that case, you'd better come with me,' she said. 'We haven't got much time before the others arrive.'

They descended three steps to a stone-walled cellar. It was cool and shadowy, a dry storage room for fruit, vegetables and other kitchen supplies. Passing through this, they arrived at a short corridor and a chamber, which had been made up as a bedroom. A single bed, a table and chair and a chest for personal belongings had been added for the sentaway's comfort. On the floor at the foot of the bed, face up, lay the body of Milo Knox.

'I think I killed him,' said Marcher Watts, and put her face in her hands for a moment, composing herself. Dalton looked at the poor dead boy: pale, dark-haired, his face contorted and horribly blistered.

'Surely not!' protested Scarlet, her arm around her old marcher. 'How can you say that?'

Watts indicted an upturned clay bowl, cracked into a number of pieces, scattered on the floor near the table. A thick liquid that looked like some sort of tincture of herbs in water had pooled there beneath the broken bits. 'His nettle soup,' Watts said. 'I made it up for him last night. He complained – Milo always did – but I made him eat it. He was coming down with a fever. I wanted him strong and well rested. I thought it would help . . .'

Dalton looked at Sal. Sleepwell was peering at the green pool of nettles and herbs, rubbing his palms together in circles as he thought. 'Can we look at it?' he said, checking with Watts.

The woman nodded, taken aback. 'Of course.'

'Did you leave it standing by his bed?' Dalton asked. 'Did you leave the room, I mean?'

Watts blinked, then nodded. 'Yes. It was too hot. It stood for some time while Milo slept before breakfast.' The marcher frowned unhappily. 'Why do you ask?' Then she stopped and brought her hands to her mouth. 'Poison?' she asked.

Dalton took a few steps forward. He didn't want to be any closer to the body than he already was. But he knew he had to look. Sal was lifting the smashed shards of bowl and placing them carefully on the table. Dalton watched as his friend dropped to his knees and brought his face close to the liquid, drawing in air through his nose, assessing the evidence.

Dalton turned his attention to Milo Knox. He had been a handsome boy once. But, dead, he was hard to look at. His face was an ugly rash of red blisters – on his swollen lips, across his cheeks and at the edges of his eyes. They'd inflamed the skin so badly that his features were grotesquely contorted: his lips huge, his eyelids pushed closed, his nostrils swollen shut.

Dalton held his breath and crouched. He'd seen these symptoms before, and the memories weren't good ones. A young poison boy Oscar had taken on two autumns ago. Steeple, he was called. He was skinny and weak, and Sleepwell had befriended him, taken him on and become his protector. Steeple didn't last long. When they'd carried him away from the tasting at the senate a little before midnight one night, he'd looked just like Knox did now.

This was doll's eyes, no doubt. More than six or seven berries and the result was a rage of raw weals and blisters. It wasn't a poison often used. The berries were so bitter they were hard to conceal, easy to taste in water or tea. They only really worked when hidden in . . . Dalton grimaced. Medicines, soups and poultices. Bad smelling stuff. Just like Marcher Watts' nettle soup. Dalton placed a fingertip between Milo Knox's lips and pushed his teeth apart. Inside the unfortunate boy's mouth, the reaction had been even stronger. His tongue looked like a dead fish, his gums mottled deep red with the deadly rash.

'You could hide pretty much anything in this,' Sal was saying, pushing a suspicious finger through the dropped soup. 'It's strong-tasting and bright green, for Kite's sake . . .'

'Doll's eyes,' Dalton said.

Sal looked up from his work. 'Possible,' he nodded.

Dalton rose to standing and turned to Watts. 'He was poisoned by doll's eyes,' he said. 'Baneberry, some call it. It inflames the throat and mouth and stops the heart. There were seven or eight berries, by the look of the reaction, pressed into juice and slipped into the soup while you were out of the room.'

Even as he was speaking, Dalton's thoughts were with Pallis Tench. The man with the broken face was a shutter who knew what he was doing, he realised. So many of the foolish ones put strong-tasting, quick-acting poisons like this in pale wine or goat's cheese – easy to detect. But Tench was better than that. He'd chosen precisely the right poison for the opportunity, and he'd done it swiftly and mercilessly, only a few hours ago. He was chasing down the names on the list, and he was doing it quickly.

'Sleepwell,' Dalton said. He blinked away the image of Tench's vile face. They needed to move now. 'We need to be quick. Tench is one step ahead of us. Get the map out.'

Sal didn't need asking twice. He knew what his friend was thinking. Scarlet stepped over to help him unfold it, and the two of them examined it hastily.

'Who's dead next?' Dalton asked.

Sal ran a finger across the document, biting his lip. 'Here,' he said to Scarlet.

She leant in and nodded confirmation.

'Someone called Eppington,' Sal said. 'And Eden, too. Both names are in the same place.'

'Where?' Dalton said.

'St Eleanor's Preparatory School for Boarders,' Scarlet said with a wry smile. 'I know it well. I'll take you.'

TWENTY-ONE

There was a high iron fence around the grounds of St Eleanor's Preparatory and the dropping sun lit the fleur-de-lys that decorated its top. The city was preparing itself for evening: the streets less busy now; candlelight spilling from dice-houses and drinking dens; lamps popping and flickering on street corners as the day's light and warmth faded from the pale sky. The roofs had grown dark and houses stood silhouetted against the last of the sun's rays.

'Look,' said Scarlet. 'There're groundsmen. Two.'

The boys followed her extended arm. A pair of figures stood in the flagged yard beyond the fence. One was puffing at a pipe on the steps before the grand reception hall of the school, leaning over to deliver a hacking cough. The other had his back to them, hands in the pockets of a short riding jacket.

'Do they stay all night?' Sal asked.

'Don't know,' Scarlet said. 'It's years since I was here.'

'Why aren't you still?' Dalton asked. 'Are you too old now?'

Scarlet continued to monitor the two men in the yard and answered without looking at the boys. 'There was a problem,' she said flatly. 'I was asked to leave.'

Dalton saw Sal's mouth hang open and his long thin finger push his glasses back up his freckled nose. He knew what his friend would be thinking.

'Kite! What happened?' Sal asked, his face pale and his eyes wide. 'Did you get into a mighty scramble?'

Scarlet shot him a silencing glance, and Sal found himself suddenly compelled to study his boots.

Dalton smiled. 'So, you recognise these two?' he said, pointing at the men.

She nodded. 'One's Lungbutter. The other looks like it might be – yeah, it is – it's Saddlesore.'

'Why the names?' Dalton said, examining the front of St Eleanor's. It was a very grand-looking school – high windows with coloured, ironworked glass inlaid with little red and blue angels; a shadowy archway leading through to a large quad; and the sound of a fountain somewhere in the darkness beyond.

'Lungbutter is the fat-arse with the pipe. He coughs a

lot. Saddlesore – well, take a look.' She indicated the second man, who was crossing the yard to the main gate with a hunched, uncomfortable walk, both hands on the base of his back, a folded paper under one arm. 'He used to ride a lot,' she explained. 'It did him in.'

'Kite!' whistled Sal. 'It hurts just watching him.'

'We can get past him, surely,' Dalton said. 'He can hardly move.'

'Easy,' nodded Scarlet. 'Plus – he'll be asleep in no time.'

Scarlet was right. By the time the friends reached the main gate, Saddlesore was nodding over his copy of the *Advisor*, perched uncomfortably on the edge of a stool in his cramped hut. After a few moments, Scarlet indicated it was safe to proceed and carefully drew back the bolt. Saddlesore's head bobbed a little and he muttered something and licked his lips. Then he was under again, breathing lightly through his nose. His copy of the *Advisor* sagged from his grip and spilled on to his lap. The poison boys squeezed through and into the school grounds.

Scarlet was ahead of them, treading lightly and carefully as she crossed the yard towards the archway and the quad beyond. There was no sign of Lungbutter, though the smell of his pipe tobacco still sweetened the evening air. Sal began to follow. Dalton paused a moment outside Saddlesore's hut and, on impulse, pulled the paper gently from its resting place. Then he followed.

They gathered inside the archway where shadows had thickened. Somewhere above them was the clatter of plates and the splash of water. Kitchen staff cleaning up after supper, Dalton guessed. Scarlet was scanning the windows above them with a wistful look.

'Looking for your old room?' Dalton whispered.

Scarlet nodded. 'I used to lodge above the kitchens,' she said. 'That's where the fire broke out.'

'Oh, dear,' said Sal solemnly.

'Look at this,' Dalton said, figuring Scarlet might need the subject swiftly changing. He unfolded Saddlesore's copy of the *Advisor* and held it up so it caught the glow from the windows. 'Dying children,' he said, indicating a heading over a paragraph of tightly printed text. Scarlet leant in. Dalton could feel her breath on his shoulder as she read.

Scarlet whispered sections of the text aloud, knitting her brow in concentration. '"Further discoveries of children . . . tragic and unexplained death of Leyton Small . . . Another boy, Finlay Halfkey, is seriously ill. Doctors are hoping a treatment of mandrake root will lead to his recovery but there is declared to be little hope of survival . . . Both boys struck down by mysterious symptoms . . ." It's the same as the other story,' she said. 'This has got to be the work of Pallis Tench.'

'Check the map, Sal,' Dalton said. 'Do the names match up?'

Sal unfolded the map of the city and smoothed it out against his knee, leaning in close to examine it. 'Yes!' he said suddenly. 'Look – Small and Halfkey. One's in Skillet, here; the other's in Ivyhill, here. Looks like they were sentaways.'

'That confirms it, then,' Dalton said. 'Tench is after sentaways. He's picking them off one by one and killing them.'

'Not just Pallis Tench,' Scarlet added. 'Doone De Bello, too. He's after us all.'

'Not all,' corrected Sal. 'Just the names in black.'

'But why?' Dalton said, staring at the map of Highlions: the carefully drawn mazes of streets and alley-ways with each house marked, each well and fountain. And, inked in a different hand over Stretton's original map, the little silver crescents perched above schools and churches, mansions and theatres, opera houses, bear pits: a city full of secret sentaways – every one of them named; some red, and the unlucky few in black. Now, Dalton knew, he was one of these crescents. But he didn't even know his own name. Honeycut, Eden, Holt – could he be one of these people? Could his be one of the names on the list of the dead? He looked up. 'So these children are in danger because their parents are senators too?' he said.

Scarlet frowned. 'Not senators, necessarily. But these children must be valuable somehow. Their parents must have some power or influence – or there'd be no point threatening their kids, would there?'

'In that case, we need to get to the two here quickly,' Sal said, indicating their names. 'Eppington is the first. So, Scarlet – what's the best way in?'

'We'll go in through the lower dormitory windows. The girls won't be in bed yet; they'll be saying prayers.

Once we're in, we'll have to hide and wait for the bell. Then we can make our move. Follow me.'

There was still a little heat left in the amber sandstone of the school buildings. Dalton warmed his back against it as Scarlet planted a boot in his cupped palms and hoisted herself up to a ground-floor window. She ducked suddenly, and Dalton's grip wavered a little. Then she rose to standing again.

'Sorry,' she whispered. 'Someone in the dormitory corridors. Looks like Sister Amelia.' She checked again. 'Always hated Sister Amelia,' she added. 'Right. We're clear. If you just . . .' She paused. 'Kite!' she hissed.

'What?' said Dalton. He couldn't see.

Sal was looking up at Scarlet, the map for once forgotten. 'What?' he whispered.

Scarlet was pulling open the window with surprising ease. 'It's flogged,' she said. 'It's been forced, by the look of it. Someone's used a knife to break the lock.'

'Dreck!' Sal swore. 'A break-in.'

Scarlet shook her head. 'Probably not,' she said. 'One of the girls might have done it.'

'With a knife?' Sal said. 'What kind of pupils attend this school? Blood-thirsty bandits and lunatics?'

Scarlet looked down at him. 'Mostly,' she said.

'My arms hurt,' said Dalton. 'Let's get on with this, shall we?'

Scarlet made a little grunt of objection. 'What are you implying about my weight, poison boy?' she said with a rare grin. Then she hauled herself up and through the window.

The boys heard her feet hit the floor of the corridor inside. There was a moment of silence.

Sal looked at Dalton. 'I like her,' he said, folding his map carefully away and flattening his hair. 'What about you?'

Dalton's arms were burning from holding her up. Her legs had been pressed against him. He swallowed. 'No opinion,' he said.

Her face was at the window again. She looked comfortable, as if she was standing on something. 'You first, haircut,' she whispered.

Sal adjusted his glasses and looked blankly at his friend. Dalton folded his arms with mock patience. 'She means you, Sleepwell.'

'Wet yourself!' said Sal with an indignant gasp. He ran a hand through his enormous mop.

'You wet yourself.'

'Whenever you're ready,' said Scarlet. 'We haven't got all flogging night.'

Inside, the corridors were dark and quiet. They smelt of candle wax and dried roses. There was a musty, close quality to the air here, breathed in and out by sisters, schoolmasters and children a thousand times daily. The polished wooden flooring creaked a little under the friends' weight and they padded towards a wooden staircase with an elegant crimson carpet running up its centre. From above, the noise of chattering children and the scamper of feet drifted.

'It'll be lamps-out soon,' Scarlet whispered, 'and we'll have the place to ourselves. Apart from the patrols.'

'Patrols?' Sal said, scanning the corridors nervously.

'Only Sister Anna or Sister Bridget,' Scarlet said. 'Easily avoided.'

'Are we headed up?' Dalton asked.

'Yes, but . . .' Scarlet's response died on her lips. 'Some-one's coming. Follow me.'

Dalton hadn't heard it, but she was right – a purposeful tread was passing above them towards the top of the stairs. He looked up at the ceiling and followed its progress for a moment.

'In here.' Scarlet was holding a door ajar behind them, her eyes trained on the top of the stairs. Dalton followed her gaze. A pair of booted feet appeared and as they descended, a figure dropped into view.

'Dreck!' said Sal, and made a hurried run for Scarlet's position. Dalton followed. It was a cupboard choked with cleaning equipment. The three of them stood close together in the dark, the air hot and close and smelling of scrubbing soap. Scarlet pressed her eye to the gap she'd left between door and frame. The footsteps passed them, their steady pace unbroken.

'Sister Anna,' Scarlet turned and whispered. Dalton could feel her breath on his face. 'Still in a bad mood, it seems,' she added. 'Always hated Sister Anna, too.'

They remained in the darkness for a few moments

more. Dalton felt drowsy. *Sleep would be so sweet and warm*, he found himself thinking. The dull clang of a bell sounded nearby.

'Ah,' Scarlet's voice emerged from the blackness. 'Lamps-out.'

Upstairs was a wide corridor. Ahead, a pair of double doors stood open and beyond them was the low glow of an illuminated room. The doors that led off the passage-way were closed. They were grand: dark polished and panelled doors with brass frames mounted in their middles. Name tags had been slipped into each. The friends checked them as they crept forwards: Taylor. Marchmain. Spares.

'Here,' Sal said. He was ahead of them and had pulled up abruptly. 'Eppington.' He moved closer. 'The door's open.'

'Listen,' Scarlet said. Through the double doors came the sound of someone moving. 'The library,' Scarlet whispered, nodding ahead. 'Someone's in there.'

TWENTY-TWO

D alton moved forward, walking on the balls of his feet, trying to keep his breathing calm and steady.

'Could be Eppington,' Sal said at his shoulder.

'Could be,' Dalton nodded. He didn't want to talk about other possibilities – or even think about them. If Pallis Tench was already somewhere in the building, Eppington could already be dead. Or dying. Choking, maybe, or drowning, lungs flooding with blood. Dalton blinked the image clear of his imagination and paused at the doors. A library, as Scarlet had said, grand and candle-lit. A number of other corridors ran off it, each lined with closed bedroom doors. At its centre, in a recess between two tall bookshelves, a dark, hunched figure was squinting at a book in the low light. It wasn't Pallis Tench, that much was clear.

Dalton realised he'd been holding his breath, and slowly released it. Then he padded across the polished wood of the library floor. Sal and Scarlet followed. As they approached, the figure, a girl, looked up, startled. There was a moment's silence.

'Who are you?' she said. Her skin was so dark with dirt that her eyes and teeth seemed to hang suspended in the shadows between the rows of books. Her hair had been knotted in two bunches away from her face. She was small and compact, and stood like a boy with her bare feet apart and pointing outwards.

Dalton spoke first.

'We're looking for someone called Eppington,' he said.

'That's me. But I don't go by that name,' said the girl, putting down the book. 'I'm Luke.'

Dalton faltered a little. Sal blushed and looked at his map.

'But you're a girl,' said Scarlet, her eyebrows raised.

The girl amongst the books laughed at this — a brief and bitter laugh. 'Look around you, sister,' she said. 'We're the oppressed. The excluded. I choose not to be crushed by the male-dominated city-state. I denounce my girldom — and there's nothing you or anyone else can do to stop me.'

'Girldom,' Scarlet repeated, frowning.

'Yes!' burst the girl. She stamped a foot at this. 'Don't we have sense too?' she continued, throwing her hands in the air. 'Are we not flesh and blood and — brains? Yes — brains! We reason! And yet we suffer the ignominy of slavery!'

'The — what?' Dalton asked. She spoke so quickly, spat her words with force and speed as if they had been rehearsed a thousand times, it was difficult to keep up.

The girl shook her head slowly and took a weary breath. 'You wouldn't understand, pig-dog oppressor.'

'Listen,' Dalton said. 'We haven't got much time. We're looking for a — person called Eppington. Is that you?'

The girl nodded. 'That's me. But you must call me Luke. Gender is just a construct. And I for one,' here, the girl ground her fist into her palm, 'choose not to live my life as a slave to our city's expectations.'

Scarlet held out a hand of friendship. 'Well, we can certainly agree on that,' she said with a nervous smile. Luke shook, her scowl beginning to dissolve. Scarlet wiped the dirt from her palm down the thigh of her trousers. 'What have you been doing?' she said distaste-fully, indicating Luke's blackened skin.

'Reading,' she said.

'No. I mean, to get all of that black dust . . .'

'Oh,' said Luke with a grin. 'I like climbing in chim-neys. I could ask the same of you lot. You look as if someone tried to drown you in the river.'

Dalton raised his eyebrows. 'You're not going to believe this . . .' he began.

Sal checked his map again, his brows knit together in confusion. 'You're a chimney sweep?' he said. 'I didn't know sentaways could be chimney sweeps . . .' He peered closely at the map, unfolding it along its crumpled spine.

Luke had flinched as Sal spoke, Dalton noticed. Now her bluster had dissolved, and she was all fear and suspicion. She ran a hand across her cheek, leaving a pale smudge of clean skin beneath the rime of smoke. She was unsettled. It was the word 'sentaway' that had done it, Dalton decided.

Luke swallowed carefully, pursing her lips together. 'What's that you've got?' she said to Sal.

Sal gave his map a wave. 'A map,' he said weakly.

'I can see that,' Luke said, her voice level and guarded. 'Don't patronise me, pig-dog. What's on the map?'

Dalton took an uncertain step forward. 'Listen,' he said. 'Luke. We want you to come with us. To work with us. We know who you are: a sentaway – hidden here. Sal's map tells us where all the sentaways are. But it tells us something else too. Some sentaways are being targeted. Poisoned. We think you might be in danger.'

Luke gave the group a cold and fixed glare, biting her lower lip. She glanced about her, as if seeing the library for the first time. She was silent for some moments. She took a step backwards.

'It's true, Luke,' said Scarlet. 'I'm a sentaway too. But something's happening to people like me and you. My food was poisoned – an assassination attempt. Others have died; you must have read about it. It could happen to you next. I'm serious. You need to believe us.'

'I've seen the papers,' Luke said, thinking. 'So who are you? Where did you get the map?'

Before Dalton could reply, there was a noise from one of the corridors leading away from the library. The children tensed, united in the same state of hot and brittle fear. Dalton felt it tighten its grip around his neck. Scarlet, he could see in the half dark, had her hands over her mouth. The noise came again, quieter this time. It was hard to pin down its source. Luke's eyes were wide and fearful. Scarlet, gathering her composure, reached for her pistol in a slow, smooth movement.

'We can't stay here,' Dalton mouthed as quietly as he could.

Luke, watching him closely, nodded her understanding. She beckoned the three friends and moved across the open floor of the library, away from the source of the sound. There it was again: a footfall, light and measured. It was the sound of someone who didn't want to be heard, someone choosing their steps carefully. Dalton brought up the rear, throwing quick glances over his shoulder. Behind him, the empty library seemed to sleep in its cloak of shadows. A prickle of unease crept down his back like a spider.

Luke led them quickly back to her room. Once they were all inside, she turned the key in the lock. It was a small space, wood-panelled, with a bed, a desk and a large fireplace. A knee-high bookshelf was crammed with volumes; three lay open on the desk. On the bed, a small toy rabbit, once white, now grey and grubby, lay lifeless on its back. It had no eyes.

Luke faced the group, her hands on her hips. A wisp of her hair had worked its way free from its bunch. She blew at it, bringing her bottom lip upwards like a sulking child.

'Nice pistol,' she said to Scarlet. 'But you're over-reacting. It's probably Sister Anna.' She indicated the door and the library beyond with a soot-blackened thumb. 'She's caught me in there twice this month already. But let me tell you,' she continued, closing her hands into angry fists, 'I will not be discouraged from my studies by her or anyone else who peddles the tyranny of education. They try to shape my thinking – to crush my individuality – but they won't do it. We will rise, you mark my words, and shatter the chains with which . . . they bind us with!'

'Fine,' whispered Sal, approaching her with his hands raised. 'But can you lecture us just a bit more quietly? We don't know who's out there . . .'

'Oh, so it's like that, is it?' whispered Luke, nodding sarcastically. 'Silence the voice of the underclass. Silence the objections of the ill-used. The truth is too hard to hear, is it?'

'Luke,' said Dalton. 'You're a sentaway, not a chimney sweep. We're not here to oppress you.' The room fell silent a moment. Dalton felt the probing eyes of the group on him. He pushed on. 'This afternoon,' he said quietly, fixing Luke's gaze, 'a boy was poisoned and died. We were too late to save him. But we're not too late to save you. So stop the rebel speeches for a moment. I don't think it's

Sister Anna out there, Luke.' Dalton pointed to the door. 'I think it's someone else. And there's a good chance they're here to kill you.'

He felt Scarlet's shoulder touch his as she stepped up alongside him. 'He's right,' she said. Dalton felt a silly bubble of pride in his belly and tried to ignore it. 'You need to come with us. You want to strike a blow against the cowardly oppressor? Ditch your marcher. That's what I've done. You won't regret it.'

Luke looked at them each in turn. She fed her hair back into her bunches and crossed her soot-blackened arms. 'On one condition,' she said firmly.

Sal had moved across to the door of Luke's room and pressed his ear against the wood. He rolled his eyes. 'We haven't got time for this, Luke,' he whispered. 'We need to find a safe way out. We could be stagged in here.'

'What's your condition?' Scarlet asked.

'We break out a couple of friends of mine.'

Scarlet looked at Dalton. 'What do you think?' she said.

Dalton nodded. 'Right. Who are they?'

Luke grinned. 'Great!' she said. 'One's my sentaway friend. Name of Felix Eden. And the other's Hoppy.'

'Hoppy?' said Sal.

'Yeah,' said Luke, and scooped up the soft toy from the bed. The eyeless rabbit hung limply from her fist. 'Say hello to Hoppy. He's the blind champion of the exploited.'

Sal said, 'Hello, Hoppy.' Then he looked at the others, who regarded him silently. Scarlet was shaking her head in dismay. 'What?' he said.

'Check the corridor, Sleepwell,' said Dalton. He turned his attention to Luke. 'Where does this Felix sleep?'

Luke pointed at the ceiling. 'One up from here. We talk to each other through the chimneys. Our fireplaces connect.'

'Is that why . . .' Dalton made a gesture, indicating Luke's appearance.

For a moment, she looked as if she were blushing beneath her coating of dust and woodsmoke. 'Yeah,' she said. 'He doesn't like it. So I get to do all the climbing.'

'I prefer stairs,' said Scarlet, flexing her grip on her pistol in readiness.

Luke pointed. 'Along here.'

'It looks clear,' whispered Sal from the door. 'Let's go.'

TWENTY-THREE

I t was clear something was wrong as the group reached the top of the stairs. The corridor before them was dark and still, all doors closed, except one. The door to Felix's room stood wide open.

'What's he up to?' Luke whispered. 'Sister Anna will be furious if he's reading.'

'There's no light,' said Scarlet. She pushed Luke gently behind her and took a slow step forward, her weapon up.

Dalton saw the pistol bob and jump in her hand. 'You've used that before, I take it,' he whispered.

Scarlet scowled at him. 'Of course,' she said. She took a deep breath and steadied her grip. 'Just tired.'

As they drew closer, the air changed. It was hot and smelt of sweat. There was the sound of a muffled struggle. Scarlet moved quickly and Dalton followed. Together, they ducked into Felix's room. For a moment, in the gloom, nothing registered. Nothing except the boy on the bed, who seemed to be fighting himself, gripped by cramps. Scarlet threw back a curtain and the moon spilled in.

It was obvious Felix was nearly ghosted. The boy was trying to talk but he mouthed a jumble of silent croaks. He kept swinging his head left and right, pushing it hard against the damp, thin pillow of his bed, as if he was fighting against the spin of the room.

'Sleepwell,' said Dalton, trying to still his hammering pulse and think clearly, 'you need to see this.'

Dalton and Sal moved to the side of Felix's bed and leant over him. The boy fell quiet for a moment or two, his body limp and tangled in his sheets. He glistened with sweat. His clothes, a white shirt and underwear, clung to him. He blinked rapidly and tried to breathe.

Luke was just behind them and let out a gasp of horror. 'What's wrong with him?' she said, tugging at Dalton's arm. 'What is this? Do something!' She fell to her knees and held Felix's hand, smiling into his unseeing eyes.

Dalton froze. He didn't know what to do. This wasn't like the afternoon – Milo Knox's ugly mask of swollen blisters was easy to read. Dalton's head was empty, suddenly. Memorising symptoms and their causes had never been his strong point. Where to start?

'Sleepwell,' he said. 'What do you think?'

Felix was moaning and muttering now – odd little gasps of sound. He kept shutting his eyes tight, then opening them wide, his mouth contorted into a weird wet grin, full of spit.

Start somewhere. Work fast. Sal was leaning close to the boy's face, trying to make sense of his slurred speech. Felix's hot breath was clouding his glasses. 'He's not making any sense,' Sal whispered. 'Perhaps he's confused. Or we're dealing with something that distorts speech.'

Dalton put an arm around Luke's small shoulders and moved her away from the bed. He placed a hand on the boy's chest. Felix seemed to be a year or two younger than him. *Eleven? Twelve?* His ribcage was tiny, Dalton thought, his skin like paper drawn over his brittle bones. Underneath, his heart was sprinting – galloping. And the way the boy kept shutting and opening his eyes, the throwing of his head from side to side, the mad grimace – it wasn't cassava. *No sickness, either,* Dalton thought, so it wasn't John Crow or snakeroot. Monkshood would stop the heart, not speed it up like that. Not belladonna either, since the pupils were regular.

Sal's gaze was fierce and focussed. Dalton could see his friend working his way through the possibilities, just as he was. Scarlet handed Dalton a jug of water from the table beside the bed. He sniffed it and dipped his lips briefly against the surface. It was clean. Water was one of the hardest things to poison. Wine or beer was far easier – its flavour and colour could hide so much. He dropped the rim to Felix's lips and tried to pour a little in, but the boy's mouth seemed furred up, as if it were constricted. He was struggling to draw a ragged breath through his swollen throat. The water splashed his face and Felix blinked it from his eyes. He fell still suddenly, spat his mouth clear and tried to raise his head.

Dalton leant in. 'Felix,' he said as gently as he could. 'What happened?'

Then, for a moment, Felix seemed all right.

His breathing steadied. Luke sobbed and hugged him. Felix blinked his pale-grey eyes over her shoulder. He seemed comically serious for a boy about to die. Luke lowered him back on to his wet pillow.

'What happened?' she said, her face close to his.

Felix licked his lips to speak. It took all his effort. 'Monster got me,' he said.

Luke started crying again. Sal had rolled up the sleeves of Felix's nightshirt.

'Look for a wound,' Dalton said. 'Has he been needled?'

Sal pulled the bed sheets clear of the boy, disentangling them from his legs. A needle was a thin blade that could be dipped in poison. A victim could be stabbed in any part of the body where there was a bulk of muscle – usually the top of the arms or the backside. Some needles were so thin it was like being stung – a pinprick, nothing more. Until an hour or two later, when your arse had turned yellow and you couldn't breathe.

Felix had to work even harder to talk this time. He fought for breath. 'Nasty monster got me in the leg,' he said, and this time he held Luke's arm tight in his fingers, squeezing hard, squeezing with the last of his strength.

Then Felix let out a screech, threw his head back and kicked hard. He beat the jug away, sending a splash of water across the floor. He was trying to curl up. His belly was boiling. In a moment he fell still. The room was silent, except for Luke sobbing. Scarlet drew her away.

Felix was dead.

Confused speech, Dalton thought. *Vomiting, and visions or hallucinations.* 'Looks like it might be clotbur,' he said almost to himself. 'Sleepwell – help me check for wounds.'

Carefully, Sal and Dalton straightened Felix up and rolled him on to his back. Both boys checked his thighs.

'Here,' Sal said.

The left leg was punctured deep. A bruise blurred the pale skin, turning yellow. *Definitely clotbur, then. Pallis Tench again – but not doll's eyes this time.* Clotbur was swift and deadly. No need to hide it in food; a needle to the leg was an efficient, brutal way to get the job done. This was a skilled and heartless shutter. Sal pulled the sheets up to the dead boy's chest. Felix looked as if he was sleeping off a fever – skin white and drenched in sweat. Except his jaw had slewed sideways and he'd ground his teeth into pieces.

'Luke,' Scarlet was saying quietly behind them. 'We have to go. It's too late for Felix. But not for you.'

'I have to tell his marcher,' Luke said. 'Marcher Underwood needs to know about this.'

'No,' Scarlet said firmly. Gellis was chasing them; Watts

knew what was happening. It would be too complicated. 'We can't involve any more marchers. They'll find him soon enough. If you want to come with us, Luke, you have to come now.'

'That noise downstairs . . .' Luke started. Her voice broke and she closed her eyes to stop the tears.

'Exactly,' Dalton said, seizing his chance. 'You could be next.'

'Quiet!' Sal hissed suddenly.

Someone was climbing the stairs. The tread was soft and regular, the wood yielding with a slight creak at each step. Scarlet made a leap across the room and shut the door quickly and quietly. She turned to face the group. 'The window,' she said.

Dalton was at it in a moment, pushing both curtains clear and scrabbling at the frame. He heaved it upwards. The cool air of the night chilled the room. 'Luke,' he said. 'Can you jump? You need to go first.' The girl blinked rapidly at him, twisting her toy rabbit in her hands. She looked like a child, freshly woken from a bad dream.

'I'll follow,' Sal said. 'Come on. We can cross the yard here . . .'

He was pointing out across the dark flagged quad, but his words of encouragement died in his throat. The footsteps were gathering pace at the top of the stairs, less careful now, more urgent.

Scarlet turned to face the door and levelled her pistol. 'Go,' she hissed over her shoulder. This time, Dalton noticed, her arm was as steady as iron.

Luke was at the window now, her legs over the sill, looking downwards doubtfully. 'Kite!' she said quietly as she took the measure of the drop. She threw the rabbit first, then she vanished after it. Sal was out next, swinging his legs over, holding his breath and jumping. Dalton heard the two of them land heavily on the flags beneath and heard Sal blowing hard as he made it to his feet.

'Sentaways first,' he said to Scarlet, and he pulled out the gun she'd given him. It was still wet from the river, and he'd already fired it. It was next to useless and Scarlet knew it.

Along the corridor the steps came.

'Are you mad?' said Scarlet. She frowned at him.

Dalton prised the pistol from her fingers and they swapped weapons. 'I know what I'm doing,' he said, boldly, though he hadn't a clue. 'Go!'

She held his gaze for a moment and looked as if she were about to speak. But she didn't. The next moment, she was gone, pushing off from the window ledge and dropping into the darkness.

The door opened at the precise moment Dalton heard her land. With just the moon for light, it was hard at first to pick out details. The bulk of the figure at the doorway moved forward. There was a pale flash of a blade in one huge hand – not a needle, a wide, steel blade. Then, as the figure stepped forward, its face was washed with moonlight.

It was Tench. His good eye was clean, like a peeled egg. It blinked. The moon played across the trenches torn through his skin. His scars glowed like veins of light. His breathing was animal and his face shuddered as he spoke.

'The boy in the boat at Midwater,' he said, bringing his knife up, tightening his grip. It was terrible looking. A skull was emblazoned in silver on its handle. The blade was wet; he'd dipped it in something. This, then, was the end intended for Eppington – another poisoned blade. Dalton could see Tench's jaw working as he ground his teeth. He pointed coolly at the pistol Dalton was holding. 'Give me the silver-butt.' He held out an expectant palm, unmoving, and added, 'or I'll rip your stomach out.'

Dalton noticed the pistol in his own hand for the first time. It was shaking wildly.

He began a shuffle in the direction of the window. 'Stand still!' he said to Tench, and his voice cracked. His arm burned with the effort as he made his slow retreat.

Pallis Tench took a step forward – confident, casual. With his spare hand, he thumbed the lid of a hip flask and knocked back a mouthful of something. Fever-tea, Dalton realised. He could smell it.

'Boy,' Tench said, replacing the flask in his belt and sighing with pleasure as the drink did its work, 'it's very simple. Give me the pistol or I tear you to pieces.' He grinned. 'And I want my map back.'

'Stand still!' Dalton tried again, his breath coming in cracked gasps. He cursed to himself. Sal had the map – and he was already outside. Tench was a monster. The man had the strength to rend him into bloody bits with his bare hands.

'Give me the map, boy,' Tench said once more, trying a different tack, 'and I'll let you go.' He made a smile, except only half his face responded. It came out as a ravaged leer.

Dalton cocked the pistol with his thumb. His palm was sweating so hard the handle seemed to wriggle in his slippy grip.

'For the last time,' said Pallis Tench, passing his knife from one hand to the other, 'put down the pistol and give me the map.'

Dalton considered what the knife might feel like; found himself thinking for a strange moment about where the tip of the blade stopped. Did they go through bones, or just skin and flesh? This one looked as if it would pass through anything. And Dalton noticed it had a fuller – Oscar's name for the channel running along its length. If a blade was dipped, gluey poisons would gather in the fuller, then stay in the wound as the knife was drawn out. *Nasty*, Oscar had warned him. *Don't go near them.*

Dalton's raised arm was wavering, hot with pain. Tench was getting close. He didn't seem remotely frightened of the pistol. But there was still just enough space between them for Dalton to reach the window.

Something in his eyes must have spelt out his intention, because Pallis Tench said through gritted teeth, 'Don't do it, boy.'

Dalton wiped his forehead clear of sweat. 'Get flogged,' he said.

He turned and threw himself at the window. He heard Tench bellow. Something sliced his ankle. Then, with a scramble he was out and falling. He struck the flags below painfully and rolled twice. The silver-butt went skittering across the stone. He was on his back. His ankle roared with pain. There was blood. Above, he got the impression of Tench readying himself to jump, to follow. Dalton had just time enough to touch his lucky Jack.

'Vivas Gannet,' he mouthed. No breath came out — it had all been knocked from him in the fall. He made it to his feet, scooping up Scarlet's pistol. One of his boots was full of blood now, and his foot slid inside it. His ankle throbbed. He was wounded.

But not wounded enough to stop him running.

TWENTY-FOUR

'It's bad,' said Sal, examining Dalton's ankle. 'You don't want to look at this.'

'Gannet!' spat Dalton through the pain. He'd kept a hand over his eyes as Sal had eased his boot off. Luke had flinched away as the blood spilled out, pooling in the cobbled alleyway where they were hiding. 'How bad, Sleepwell? Has my foot fallen off?'

Sal snorted, leaning closer. 'No. It's a deep wound though. Actually, that might be your bone I can see there. Anyone want to see Flyboy's ankle bone?' He looked up, gauging the success of his offer. Scarlet had turned her back. She was tugging at her shirt, tearing at the material to make an improvised bandage. Luke had one hand across her mouth and gripped her blind rabbit tightly around the throat with the other.

'The blade had been dipped, Sleepwell,' Dalton said through gritted teeth. 'I can feel it. If the cut doesn't kill me, the poison will.'

Scarlet handed a long piece of torn material to Sal, who nodded his thanks.

'Let's get it bandaged,' said Sal. 'If the blade's dipped, you'll be able to describe the symptoms soon enough, and I'll know what to do.' He began winding his fingers, moving with steady skill. Dalton squeezed his eyes shut and swore quietly.

'So the question is,' Sal said as Dalton hobbled to his feet, 'who next?' He pulled the map from his pocket, wiped his bloodied hands and began to flatten it out carefully on a low wall.

'The sequence is the key,' Dalton winced. 'But I can't remember who's next. What did De Bello say?'

The children leant over, shoulders together.

'De Bello?' said Luke. She was better now – her face still smeared with streaks of soot and tears, but her mouth set firm and her shoulders thrown back. 'You mean the House of De Bello?'

Dalton nodded.

Luke knit her brows. 'They run the Palace of Justice,' she said, and asked again, aghast, 'De Bello is behind this? He's the one killing sentaways?'

'Looks that way,' said Scarlet. 'But why?' She pressed

her thumb against her teeth, thinking. 'We're valuable. Or a threat. Or,' she said, raising a finger, 'our parents are. It's not something we've done. It's who we are.'

'So – he wants you dead because of something in your background,' Sal said. 'That's why you're on the list.'

Luke looked along the alleyway where the gang had convened. It was almost entirely swallowed by shadow, running along the back of the opera house, east of the river. It smelt of piss and dust. Other than a solitary Street-watch patrol, it had been a still night. Sal had chosen the spot well – a quiet district of the Middle Circle where Tench couldn't find them and no one would be looking.

Luke wiped her eyes. 'It doesn't surprise me,' she spat. 'Corrupt pig-dogs. Not just with the systematic oppression of the common citizen, eh? Oh, no. De Bello simply removes those who—'

'That's the question, Luke,' Dalton interrupted. 'Why these particular victims? And why the names in black first? Is it to do with your parents, like Scarlet says?'

'My mother is Loyola Dropmore,' Scarlet explained, rotating the ring on her finger. 'A high-born senator. Are your parents senators, Luke?'

Luke's face quickly darkened. 'No,' she said, her lip curling. 'But they might as well be. My father owns the *Advisor* – the newspaper. I don't like to talk about him,' said Luke, 'ever.' There was an awkward pause. Luke cleared her throat. 'What other names are in black?' she asked with exaggerated brightness.

Sal began pointing them out. 'Here,' he said. 'And here.

Milo Knox – he's the boy who got ghosted earlier today. Felix Eden is here. There's you; and here's someone called Holt, and someone called Honeycut. We overheard De Bello discussing these names before we stole the map,' Sal explained, 'and they had a sequence in mind. Scarlet. Then Milo Knox, then you; Felix after that. The other two – it's hard to remember.'

'Honeycut,' said Scarlet. She was knotting her fingers together. She'd been thinking something over for a few moments now. 'Listen,' she said, biting her lip. 'There's someone on this list I know.'

The group looked at her. 'Who?' said Sal.

Scarlet cleared her throat. 'Edward Honeycut,' she said. 'He's a friend of mine.' She pressed the tip of her finger against the underlined name on the map.

Dalton felt his spirits sink. He knew that name: the boy at the party before the shotpowder bomb, the one who'd called him *barrow boy*.

'You didn't mention this before,' Dalton said, his voice cold. He watched her run a hand across her headscarf.

'No,' she said. 'There wasn't time. Like you said – we had to get to the top of the list first . . .'

Dalton scowled. 'Not that we were quick enough.' His ankle throbbed forcefully and he shifted his weight with a wince.

'Fly,' said Sal. 'Leave it. We got Luke, didn't we?'

Luke smiled. 'Thanks,' she said.

'So it's this Honeycut next?' Sal said.

'No,' said Dalton. 'We can't keep doing this one at a

time. Tench is too quick for us. There are four of us now. Let's split up.'

Luke clenched a fist. 'Emancipation for the down-trodden!' she declared, a gleam of anger in her eyes. 'Only we can liberate these suffering prisoners of misfortune!'

'Whatever you say, Luke,' said Sal. He turned to Dalton. 'Flyboy, don't make me go with her.'

'Get flogged, pig-dog,' said Luke with a dark scowl. 'Don't make me go with him,' she added, folding her arms around the blind rabbit.

Dalton checked the position of the moon. It was high – the night was clear and cool. Somewhere, Pallis Tench was on the move, seeking his next target. Tench's words came back to him as he checked the mouth of the alley. *Put down the pistol and give me the map.* It was difficult to read such a broken face, but Tench seemed desperate – furious. With the map, they had the advantage. But they would have to move quickly to make it count. Tench could have much of it by memory. Somewhere out in the alleyways and galleries of the city, he might be picking his way towards his next victim, choosing a poison to fit the time and place. Dalton tried to blink away the grisly memories of the day, but the images wouldn't leave him. Now, two more faces joined the bloodied mask of Bennie Jinks in his imagination – the lifeless faces of the ghosted sent-aways he had failed to save. Milo Knox with his blistered tongue and swollen face. Felix Eden coughing out his dying words.

'Dalton,' said Scarlet. 'Come on.'

Dalton ground his teeth against the pain in his ankle. If the blade was dipped, he'd need Sleepwell to identify the poison. But it might not take effect for hours, and only the Mapmaker's youngest could make swift sense of the city in the middle of the night. That meant Sal with Luke. Dalton cleared his throat. 'Sleepwell,' he said. 'There's no choice. You'll have to go with Luke and take the map so you can find this Holt quickly. Where does it say to look?'

Sal indicated a Middle Circle street in Jacksonbridge.

'Right. When you've found him, stay where you are. Scarlet – we'll get Honeycut, then join the others.' He checked the sky once more. 'We'll all need to be quick,' he said. 'It's getting late.'

It was close to midnight when they reached their destination. 'He's always here,' Scarlet had explained as they'd walked – making slow progress as Dalton tested his throbbing ankle. 'Especially late at night.' But she'd been silent on any details. Dalton had probed a little, but Scarlet had stayed mute on the subject. 'A friend,' was all she would say. Dalton wasn't convinced. They'd been leaning close together over the dice at the party and, in his memory at least, their fingertips were touching. And, Dalton realised, on the night they first met, hadn't she called him Edward? Had she been expecting a visit from Honeycut when he'd stumbled through her balcony doors, doused in Bennie's blood? Dalton swallowed back a bitter feeling.

They were in the shadow of a grand archway set back

from a wide and well-to-do street in the Upper Circle. They hovered for a moment below an ornate sign on which curling gold lettering spelt out, 'The Ivyhall Steam-rooms' and, below it, 'Pools and private quarters for gentlemen'.

'Dreck!' Dalton swore. 'How are we going to get you in here?'

Scarlet grinned. 'Disguise,' she said, and gave him a wink. She tugged at the heavy doors, hefted them open a crack and slipped in. Dalton had never been in the steam baths before. No one he knew had ever been in the steam baths. Only the city's wealthiest could afford to idle away their nights splashing in pools or sitting naked on hot tiles, pouring with sweat. Edward was clearly a very rich young man.

The corridor ahead was elegant, the floor inlaid with tiles, the crimson walls rising high to an arched ceiling. Lamps glowed in little ironwork baskets. Dalton looked at his jacket, his undershirt, his bloodied boots. His spirits sank. 'We're flogged if anyone sees us,' he whispered, taking a few uncertain paces forward.

'We need to ditch these clothes,' said Scarlet.

Ahead, a fat man with a bald head was leaning over a ledger at a huge desk. Robes hung from hooks on the walls around him. Towels were piled on low benches. There were cubicles, each candlelit. The man rose, grunting, and moved away, his belly swaying in front of him. Scarlet crept forward. A stairwell, blue with the reflected surface of the pools below, dropped downwards. Steam drifted up. The man descended, carrying a tray of unguents in bottles.

Scarlet began to undress hastily, pulling her jacket off and balling it up. 'Look away,' she said, undoing her belt.

It was the second time she'd asked him to do that. Dalton saw her suddenly, stepping out of the bath with just a robe around her, steam rising from her wet hair, the little silver hoops in her ears and her pulse visible at her wrist. Now she was checking the stairs, which dropped down to the steam halls. She looked back at him.

'I'm waiting,' she said.

Dalton blinked. 'Sorry.'

His voice came out as a squeak and he cursed himself for blushing. He turned his back to Scarlet and began to take his jacket and shirt off. His fingers weren't working very well. The buttons seemed suddenly small and slippery. He felt sweat prickle his scalp. He pulled his torn boot gently off. The bandage was fat with blood. He closed his eyes and tried to concentrate, cursing the pain and trying to keep his balance, but his mind kept returning to Scarlet in her bath, shrouded in steam, the water beading on her shoulders. He'd only ever undressed near boys before. Oscar didn't use poisongirls. As far as he knew, no one did.

'I'm done,' she said. 'Hurry up.' Scarlet was in a cotton robe. It was thin and white. She held another out for him.

Dalton swallowed. 'Look away,' he said, but no sound came out.

Scarlet laughed. 'Get on with it.'

Dalton crammed his clothes in the dark space beneath the desk, pausing to pull out his lucky Jack and flatten it against his leg before dropping it into the pocket of his robe. He felt an idiot in his new clothes with his wincing limp and his ugly bandage exposed. But there was no going back. They moved down the stairs to the pools below.

TWENTY-FIVE

T he steam was thicker here, hot clouds obscuring their view. Fresh sweat broke out immediately on Dalton's face and shoulders. Scarlet pushed the wet hair from her eyes. Someone moved slowly through a pool nearby, sloshing and spitting as he swam. Ahead was a second pool, and a series of curtained chambers off it. Figures lolled at the pool's edge, reclining in robes. Fat men lowered themselves naked into the hot water. Scarlet had to stop and gather herself, Dalton noticed. She looked pale and revolted. The man from upstairs, his bald head glistening, was collecting towels and lighting candles with a taper. The scented air was heavy.

Dalton and Scarlet padded towards the second pool and circled it, one behind the other. Soon, they were back where they began.

'There's no sentaway here,' Dalton said in a low voice. 'What do we do?'

'Sit,' Scarlet said, wiping her eyes and shrugging. 'And watch. He's always here.'

'Why?'

Scarlet rolled her eyes. 'I don't know, do I? It's what men do.'

'Men? How old is he?' Dalton looked at his battered ankle.

'Seventeen,' said Scarlet.

Dalton cursed him silently.

'Keep your eyes open,' she continued. 'He's tall. He has black hair. Bangles. Black fingernails.'

Dalton ran through a mental inventory of insults for the new sentaway as they took their places on the benches and sat in the steam, pouring with sweat. He wished he'd never agreed to this. His shoulder touched hers and she shifted position, moving away from him.

'What about his marcher?' Dalton said. He felt light-headed in the heat.

'Oh, I don't think Marcher Ashover has much control over Edward any more. He lets him come here, for a start. And when Edward's eighteen, his legally binding relationship with his marcher comes to an end. He says he's going to relieve him of his duties.' Scarlet spoke like a proud younger sister, blinded with admiration. Dalton suppressed a scowl.

He decided to examine the pools to clear his mind, to try and fight back the nausea. The occupants were all old: greying men, men with wobbling paunches, swimming in lazy circles on their backs. There were no young men here. His eyes rested on the four curtained chambers across the second pool. What had the sign said outside? 'Pools and private quarters'? He remembered again the glistening head of the bald attendant as he descended the stairs, and the tray in his hand – oils in bottles. Oils for treatments, massages.

'Maybe your rich boy is in one of those,' he whispered, nodding towards the chambers. The curtains were drawn across curved archways. Outside each were compact wooden shelves with dishes of salt, candles, clothes folded in piles.

'Why don't you take a look?' said Scarlet. Her mood had darkened.

Dalton got unsteadily to his feet. He felt dizzy. It was hard to swallow. He made a slow and mazy route around the pools, snuck a glance through the gaps of the curtains, and returned.

'Fat men getting back-punishment from other fat men,' he said. 'That's what it looks like to me.'

'What, in all of them?'

'Well, no,' Dalton admitted. He tried to swallow. 'In the first two, though. I couldn't see in the third and fourth ones.' They both stared at the remaining cubicles for a moment. 'So, perhaps your Edward's in there. Getting his punishment.'

As they watched, one of the first curtains was drawn back, and they saw beyond for a moment: the white soles of a pair of feet – a man lying on his front, a towel over his head. Jars of salts and crystals; a bottle of dark wine and a single flicker. An attendant with a long wet fringe in a darker robe moved through the steam towards the stairs, carrying a tray of preparations. When he returned a few moments later, he brought with him towels, and swept open the curtain of the chamber next door, swapping places with the assistant there.

'If he's taking a break from getting his back stamped on – we might be able to speak to him,' Dalton observed.

'We'll have to be quick,' Scarlet said. Another curtain was opened. 'They swap places regularly by the look of things.'

They settled themselves at the pool's edge nearest the fourth chamber. Closer to the private rooms, they could see the items left on the wooden shelves: hand-made boots, cotton shirts with pearl buttons, silver charms on chains.

'What are you going to tell him?' Dalton asked. 'I mean, when we get in?'

'Leave that to me,' Scarlet said.

As she spoke, the curtain next to them was drawn back and a heavy-set, bearded man emerged, drawing it shut behind him with one arm, the other supporting a tray with an empty wine bottle and hand towels. He padded along the poolside and away through the steam.

'Here we go,' Scarlet said under her breath, and the two

of them raised themselves up, checking they hadn't been noticed. Scarlet pulled back the curtain to the fourth chamber, Dalton wiped the sweat from his eyes again, fought down a wave of sickness, and they went in.

The figure lying face down on the treatment table was tall, thin and tanned, naked except for a white towel around his waist. One braceletted arm dangled over the nearside of the table, and in the swinging palm was a drained wine flicker. His fingernails were painted black. Rather than turning to see who had entered, the young man raised his drowsy head, brushed his hair from his eyes and propped a chin on his other palm, staring at the candles arrayed along a shelf on the far wall.

'I must get back soon, Luca,' he said. He had a low voice, but it was one of those voices, Dalton thought, with a permanent whine of complaint hidden in it, just like at the party. 'Just finish my shoulders and neck with the lavender oil.'

Dalton pulled a face at Scarlet but she wasn't looking.

'Edward,' she said almost reverently, one hand extended as if she were waking a prince.

He turned his head, his eyebrows raised quizzically. 'Scarlet!' he said. 'Darling!' A broad smile illuminated his face.

Dalton felt his insides curdle inexplicably; his ribs hurt and his stomach knotted. This was why Scarlet wanted to see Edward. Not because he was in danger. Not because he needed rescuing. Because she was in love with him. Dalton wished again they hadn't come.

Edward was talking. 'I was just thinking about you!' he was saying, and Scarlet was beaming at him, her face open and alive. 'What are you doing here?'

'I'm here to rescue you,' said Scarlet.

Edward began laughing, but quickly realised she was serious and fell silent, his dark eyes intent.

'You need to come with us,' Scarlet said.

It was only then, at the use of 'us', that Edward looked at Dalton for the first time. His face expressed nothing and his attention lasted no more than a moment. He turned again to Scarlet, sitting up now, putting down his wine flicker and taking her hands in his. 'Who's the boy?' he said to her gently, his eyes not leaving hers.

'His name is . . . Fly, or something,' Scarlet said. 'He's a poison boy, would you believe.'

Edward regarded Dalton once more. Dalton found himself trying to smile, and hated himself for it. 'A food-taster?' Edward said to Scarlet. He held her hands close to his chest and spoke quietly, dipping his head and looking at her through his long dark fringe. 'Darling, I've spoken to you before about how important it is to choose companions with care. Especially in these difficult times.'

Scarlet pushed out her lower lip. 'Don't start that again, Edward. I know what I'm doing. Anyway, he's been interesting.'

'What's going on, Scarlet? Have you escaped your marcher again? And dragged him in to help?'

'I'm still here, you know,' Dalton said, his hands in fists in the pockets of his robe. 'I'm standing here, listening.'

He'd found it hard to speak. His tongue felt thick. This wasn't just the steam and the heat and the exhaustion, he realised. These feelings – they were Tench's poison starting to work. He needed to get back to Sleepwell.

'He's got a lucky playing card,' Scarlet was saying with a nod to him. 'It's sweet.'

'Gannet!' burst Dalton. 'Can we just go? We're here for a reason.'

Scarlet looked at him as if for the first time, then turned to Edward, who was arching an eyebrow at this curious intruder. 'We have to go,' she implored. 'Sentaways across the city are dying. Being poisoned. You can help us.'

Edward grinned and licked his lips. 'Of course,' he said. His eyes blazed eagerly. 'I've been reading about it. Here.' He reached for a damp, folded copy of the *Advisor* on a table alongside his bed. 'Is this anything to do with you, Scarlet?' He extended a painted black fingernail, indicating a column of dense print.

'Yes,' she said. 'But a lot has happened since then. We need to go.'

Dalton brought his eye to the gap in the curtain and tried to see through the hot mists that drifted over the surface of the pools. A figure was approaching, bearing towels. 'There's someone coming,' he whispered.

'Luca,' said Edward, hopping down from his bed and tightening the towel around his waist. 'Hide. In the curtains. Quick.' Edward pulled Scarlet by the shoulders and positioned her. 'Stand here with your boy,' he said and, a moment later, he was flinging the heavy cloth back to conceal them both and speaking to the approaching attendant. 'Luca,' he said. 'Time is against me. I must go, sadly.'

Dalton suddenly found himself crushed against Scarlet, wrapped in a cotton curtain. His body was against hers, his head pressed against her shoulder.

Luca was inside the cubicle now; Dalton could hear his wet feet on the tiles. 'I'll just refresh these,' he was saying. There was the tinkle of little bottles. 'A last drink, sir?' he asked. Edward declined. It sounded as if he was dressing hurriedly.

Dalton felt about to burst, pressed against a girl in the steam. Scarlet was frightened into complete stillness, but he was aware of her heart thumping. Her hair was tickling his face. When she blinked, her eyelashes brushed against his cheek. Dizziness crept over him. The room began a slow spin. Tench's poison was starting to move through his blood.

Suddenly, the curtain was flung back. Edward was dressed, red-faced and sweating in a cream suit. 'Hope you're enjoying that, poison boy,' he said with a sour grin. 'It's as close as you'll ever get to having a girlfriend. Right. What's the plan?'

TWENTY-SIX

'This,' said Sal with a smile, 'is Isis Holt.'

They were in a cramped room together, standing almost shoulder to shoulder. Edward was looking about him, his face a picture of distaste, Scarlet's arm linked in his. Isis Holt was a nervous-looking skinny boy of fifteen or so, Dalton guessed, and he was blinking at the gathered group through a straw-blond fringe.

'My room's not very big, I'm afraid,' he said and wiped his nose with the back of his hand. He had a scattering of freckles on his pale skin, and moon-like eyes.

'But it's better than Oscar's house,' Sal said, a hand on his shoulder.

Isis Holt, as Sal and Luke had explained, was a sentaway whose marcher had disguised him as a stagehand at the Black Swan – the second best theatre in Jacksonbridge. Dalton didn't fancy seeing third best if the Black Swan represented second. It was a crumbling wreck.

For a year now, Isis had been building stage sets, sweeping up after performances and helping drunken actors with their costumes. In return for gruelling days and nights of work, he got to sleep in the servants' quarters in the roof of the theatre, as far away from the paying public as possible. His room was a box, furnished with a bed and a battered chest for personal effects. There was a single grimy window the size of a theatre programme. The wind moaned in the eaves and through the thatch. It smelt of bird dreck.

'Nice place you've got here, Isis,' Edward said.

Scarlet dug a shoulder into his ribs.

Dalton wasn't feeling any better after a painful walk back through the city streets. 'This is Edward,' he said, indicating Scarlet's companion. No one seemed eager to talk.

Sal dropped to the bed. It creaked unhappily. 'I'm flogged,' he said, elbows on his knees. 'What I'd give for some sleep.'

Dalton felt his poisoned wound continue its cold, hard roar of pain. There wasn't time for resting. There were other sentaways to protect, names in red as well as names in black. He ran his hand across his forehead. He needed to take control of this.

'Listen,' he said. He had to fight back a prickle of feverish heat on his face. 'Everyone listen.' He squeezed himself forward to the bed. 'Sleepwell, show everyone the map.'

Sal unfolded it and flattened it out.

'This,' Dalton said, 'is a map we stole from the Senate Hall on Midwater last night.'

Edward raised his eyebrows. 'You've been a busy boy,' he said. 'How in Kite's name did you get in?'

'The storm drains,' Scarlet said.

Edward looked at Scarlet, then at Dalton. 'Impressive,' he said. 'Just you two? Or did you take the walking fringe along for the ride?'

Sal was scanning the map again, his chin on his palm, his glasses propped on his forehead pushing back the mass of his hair.

'He means you,' Dalton said.

'The important thing about this map,' Sal said, oblivious, 'is that it has names on it. Names of sentaways. Your names. Isis – you're there.'

Isis made knots of his fingers, examining the white knuckles. He didn't seem keen to check for confirmation. 'What does it mean?' he said.

'We're not sure,' said Sal. 'Edward Honeycut is you, I guess,' he added, regarding Edward and prodding the map.

'Of the House of Honeycut,' said Edward, eyeing the room. Dalton looked blank. 'You haven't heard of the House of Honeycut? Where have you been, barrow boy? Trapped in a gutter somewhere?'

Sal held up the document for Edward and he snatched at it, irritated.

His manner soon changed. 'My name's in black ink,' he said. 'So's Scarlet's. What is this?' He turned the map over in his hands, his movements anxious. 'This was on Midwater? A map with my name on it?'

Dalton nodded. 'Not just your name,' he said. 'The names of others too.'

Edward continued his close examination, speaking the names softly under his breath, 'Dropmore, Honeycut, Eden, Knox . . .' He looked up, his eyes sharp, as if seeing the assembled group for the first time. 'This is you lot,' he said.

'Apart from the dead ones,' said Sal, 'yes.'

'I'm guessing Eppington is the chimney sweep with the pet rabbit,' Edward said.

'It's Luke, actually,' she said with a sneer. 'And this is Hoppy. Don't think you can judge us, imperialist pig-dog.'

'Those with black names are all dead or dying,' Dalton said, stepping in quickly. 'We found Milo Knox this afternoon. Felix Eden died this evening. And Scarlet's house was attacked too.'

Edward put a protective arm around Scarlet's shoulder. She had told him all about the shotpowder bomb, the poisoned food and the escape from Marcher Gellis on their journey from the steam halls.

Dalton had been forced to endure Edward's whispered words of support, spoken with his face dipped close to hers. He'd sneered at their stupid names for each other, and tried not to be sick. 'Isis,' he said, 'you're on it as well.'

'Why?' the boy said, rubbing his hands together unhappily. Dalton noticed how frail and small he seemed next to the tall, broad-shouldered Honeycut. 'What have I done?'

'It's not what you've done,' Sal said, explaining their thinking so far. 'It seems to be who you are. These names are all sentaways with powerful parents. De Bello seems to be targeting the children of senators or other important people.'

Edward tapped his chin with his forefinger. 'The House of Honeycut has a long association with the Dropmores and the Highlions senate,' he said airily. 'We're influential. That's why I'm a sentaway. Father is convinced I could be targeted.'

Sal pointed. 'Right. That proves it.'

'But we're all targets,' Dalton added. 'We could all end up dead.'

'Not exactly all of us,' Edward cut in. 'I don't see your name on this, poison boy.' He tossed the map back on to the bed. 'I'm missing where you fit in to all of this. Are you a sentaway?'

'No,' said Dalton.

'Yes,' said Scarlet. There was an uncomfortable pause. 'He is. He just doesn't believe it yet.'

Edward arched his eyebrows. Dalton looked at the group. Luke's face was fogged with grime and her hair had come free of its bunches again. Little clouds of soot broke away from her shoulders as she moved to tie it back. Edward waited for his answer, his eyes sharp. The new boy, Isis Holt, studied him silently, biting the nail of his thumb.

'Show them the box,' said Scarlet.

Dalton tried swallowing again, and pulled the box from his jacket pocket – palm-sized, silver and rattling with its mysterious contents.

'Scut and feathers!' swore Edward Honeycut. His eyes were wide. 'Where did you lift that from?'

'I didn't steal it,' Dalton said wearily. He felt his voice waver at its edges. 'My employer says it came with me when he adopted me. I was just a little kid. I can't remember how I came to have it. Or who my parents are.'

'But that's a buckle box,' said Edward. 'I've got one. My father gave it to me. Mine's silver too.'

Scarlet nodded. 'I have one as well.'

'What's a buckle box?' said Luke. 'I don't have one.'

Edward gave her a stare. 'It's a private pocket for your belongings,' he said. 'You attach it to your belt under your coat. Personal stuff. Papers or letters, usually.' He held out an open palm. Dalton handed it over. 'It's a nice one,' Edward said with a whistle, turning it in his hands. 'My brother had one like this. And a few of the boys at school. I've not seen one like this for a while.' He looked at Dalton. 'What's in it, poison boy?'

Dalton felt the heat rise in his face. 'Just – stuff,' he said. 'I don't understand it.'

The group gathered around the bed and Edward snapped open the box and tipped its contents across the map of the city. Out fell the strange tokens that he'd scarcely had time to think about since his visit to Oscar that morning: the letter folded into thirds, its edges battered; the playing cards; the pistol; the coil of silver chain with its mysterious dark key.

The room seemed to be holding its breath. Honeycut leant over the map and, with the painted nail of an outstretched finger, disentangled the items. He picked up the letter, unfolded it slowly, then looked at Dalton. Dalton shrugged.

Edward read silently for a moment, then cleared his throat. His voice had softened. He spoke just above a whisper. '"G. A."' he began. '"It saddens me beyond words to contact you in such circumstances and with such news. I have been dishonest with you and, I confess, shame and anger have prevented me righting my original wrongs. I can only ask for your understanding and, perhaps in time, your forgiveness. In short, the issue stands thus: the movement of the child is a matter of utmost urgency. It is to you that I entrust the responsibility of care. It goes without saying that the identity of the child must remain an unuttered secret forever. Provision has been made for the settling of all appropriate accounts. The arrangements for transport are as discussed. Only your brother could be trusted to begin the—" Where's the rest?'

'Lost,' Dalton said. His heart thumped heavily, as if made of lead. He tried to blink the spinning room back to stillness.

Edward checked the back of the sheet, returned to the

top and read again. 'Well, well,' he said. 'What an interesting little keepsake you have here, poison boy. Kite knows what it means.'

'What about the other stuff?' Sal said. 'What are these other things?'

Dalton cleared his throat. 'I've never seen any of them before.'

Edward rolled the ivory key between thumb and forefinger. 'Very nice piece of work. Decorated. Needs a clean, though.'

Luke spoke up, her voice tentative. 'So,' she said. 'Who exactly are you?'

Dalton looked at the ceiling. There was a moment of silence. The wind moaned in the eaves again. 'I don't know,' he said.

'So, have you got a marcher somewhere?' Isis Holt asked. He blushed under the group's gaze. 'Just wondered,' he added softly.

'Yes,' said Scarlet after a moment's pause. 'But he's dead.'

'It's true. Someone's been following me around. They caught up with me recently but . . .' Dalton stopped, struggling to find the right words, fighting back a weary anger.

'The undertaker!' breathed Sal.

'Listen,' Dalton said as firmly as he could. 'None of that matters. We need to rescue the rest of the names on the map, or they could die.' Bennie's face kept swimming back up into his imagination – bloodless, his white skin pulled close over his skull, his tongue blue-black. And Felix Eden's broken teeth.

Edward smacked his lips. 'Well,' he said. 'I'm for it. Anything's better than dying of boredom with the city's dullest marcher.'

'I'm in,' Luke said.

'And me,' said Isis Holt with a firm smile. He squared his shoulders and thrust his hands into his pockets.

Sal grinned at him. 'Right,' he said. 'We start tomorrow. Now, let's sleep. Please.'

'I'm having the bed,' said Edward, reclining. 'Being the only man in the room has its advantages.'

'Ha!' spat Luke. 'Typical!'

Isis settled himself cross-legged and Luke joined him, bristling with anger, her back against the wall, her arms around her knees. Scarlet sat on the edge of the bed and stretched, cat-like.

'Sleepwell,' said Dalton. 'I'm feeling ill.'

Sal, who had been making a pillow of his jacket and stretching himself out on the floorboards, stopped his work and sprang to his feet. 'Tench's poison!' He stared at Dalton's bandaged ankle, grinding his teeth rhythmically, thinking. 'Oscar's hospital,' he said with a firm finality. 'I can get whatever it is you need. But we need to go now. Describe the symptoms as we walk. Dizziness? Sickness? What about your breathing?'

Dalton waved away the questions. 'Something else too,' he added, and tapped his buckle box. 'There's someone we know who might be interested in this letter.'

Sal crammed his glasses into his hair. 'You mean Eyesdown,' he said.

'The river's only a short walk from Oscar's.'

'One thing at a time, Flyboy!' Sal rubbed his hands together, exasperated. 'If you're getting gutted, the last thing you need is a chat with that lunatic. What is it you want to know?'

Dalton put the silver box into his jacket pocket. The tips of his fingers were itching. Exhaustion seemed to grip him by the bones. 'Who I am,' he said.

TWENTY-SEVEN

F rancis Eyesdown was climbing the stairs up from the shadows under the bridge, sweating hard.

'Warm night for a hat,' Sal said as they approached. The moon was like a white wedge of melon, high and clear. The low river glittered in its light.

Eyesdown was wearing a heavy hunting hat with lined earflaps. 'Funny,' he said. 'Very funny.' He took it off and wiped his forehead with the back of his hand. His bald head was wet. 'It's all I could find,' he said, putting the hat back on again. Then he added, 'Kite! Have you two slept since I last saw you? You look like dreck.'

Dalton felt an aching in his legs. His ankle was hot with

infection. He had to lean against the stone balustrade of the bridge. His fingers wouldn't keep still, he noticed; they jumped and jittered. 'Francis,' he said.

'Yeah, I know,' said Eyesdown, setting off across the Laceway at a stride. 'You need my help. What's new? Follow me.'

Dalton took a moment to gather his strength. Sal, he noticed, was bent over with his hands on his knees, eyes tight shut and grimacing as he swallowed. He looked up. 'I'm flogged,' he said.

'Me too,' said Dalton. 'Come on.'

Eyesdown was piloting a crooked course back towards Jacksonbridge. The dust of the streets and galleries was still warm and broke in clouds around their boots, raising a stink. On nights like this, the city air was thick with sweat and tobacco and the competing scents of spices, pollen and stale beer. The river, away to their left as they walked, had dropped low with a lack of rain. The claggy mud steamed off the last of the day's heat in the moonlight.

'Where are we going?' Dalton asked.

'Kite almighty, Flyboy. Have you sparrow piss for brains? Tomorrow's Duke Elber's funeral. I've got to make my preparations. Get the best spots. The stories I'll be able to catch will make me a fortune. It'll be pies and wine again, boys.' Eyesdown sighed. 'Pies and wine,' he repeated softly. 'The crowds will be gathering early. The whole of Sixteen Fountains will be thronged by sunrise. They're pulling Elber through on the back of this mighty carriage of roses in the afternoon. Twenty horses, they say.

A cortege of plumed fancy boys; the senators leading the procession. Imagine the tales that'll be told. Might dip a few pockets too, boys – plenty of letters and bone to be had.'

'We need you to look at something,' Dalton said, fighting off a tiredness which sucked at his steps like the river mud below them. He pulled the silver box from his pocket.

Sal touched his arm. 'Fly,' he said, nodding ahead. They were at the edge of Greengoose now, near the Sixteen Fountains and the route the Duke's procession would be taking the following day. There were small groups of Streetwatch guards at checkpoints against the walls of the library ahead, working late; another group in the centre of the square gathered around the trunk of an old oak, sharing a pipe. Three of them were looping rope across the mouth of one street to shut it off. Sal called Eyesdown back and the boys drew away from the main street and paused a moment, considering their options.

'I haven't got time for this!' Eyesdown grumbled. 'Time is talk and talk is money.'

Dalton showed him the silver box. Flogged as it was, its surface gleamed in the glow of the moon, as if it were made of pearl. Eyesdown gawped. A sequence of emotions seemed to chase each other across his face: shock, fear, excitement. He took off his hat, kneaded it between his thumbs, put it back on again.

'Dreck!' he said in a dry voice. 'Where did you get this? Get out of the street. Move.' He ushered Dalton and Sal back the way they had come, checking the Streetwatch patrols in the square.

Sal indicated an upward flight of steps leading to the back of a series of shops and, in the deeper gloom of the alleyway, Eyesdown lifted the little silver case from Dalton's hands and turned it carefully in his own. 'A buckle box,' he said. He blinked rapidly. 'With an inlaid keyhole, too. Kite! Where did you get this?'

Eyesdown seemed to register their clothes properly for the first time: boots plastered in mud, trousers torn at the knees, jackets black with dust and dreck. 'The black cloud that follows Sleepwell and Fly wherever they go,' he said. 'It's not about to rain on you again, is it?'

Dalton nodded, wincing against the pain of his poisoned wound. 'Perhaps,' he said, then touched the Jack in his shirt pocket. 'Perhaps not. Eyesdown, tell us what you know about these things – buckle boxes.'

Eyesdown took a deep breath. 'Wallets or cases, usually silver, attached to a belt about here,' he touched his hip, 'near the buckle. Worn underneath your shirt or riding coat so it can't be seen.'

'For what?' said Sal. The moonlight played on the lenses of his spectacles as he wiped them clean and propped them on the tip of his nose.

'Secrets. Can I open it?'

Dalton nodded and watched as the other boy prised its lid off.

Eyesdown whistled to himself and sifted the items within with the tip of a finger. 'A pistol. Playing cards.

Nice silver chain with a key on it – strange. Oh – and a letter!' His face was bright and eager. 'Can I read it?'

Dalton rubbed his eyes. 'That's why we're here.'

Eyesdown checked the sky, looking for the position of the moon and principal stars. A cloud passed over and the alleyway dropped briefly into darkness, submerged. 'You want a valuation. Well, I've not got long,' he said, handing the buckle box back to Dalton and unfolding the letter. 'Only one sheet,' he said. 'The rest is missing?' Dalton and Sal nodded in confirmation. 'Pity,' said Eyesdown, and he began to read.

The change in him was immediate. The colour fell from his face. His brow buckled. He wiped a trickle of sweat from his temples. Dalton could see a little muscle twitching in his jaw.

Eyesdown finished reading. His hands were trembling as he lowered the sheet of paper. He ran his tongue over his lips. 'You need to listen carefully,' he said. He spoke slowly and deliberately, the way Oscar used to when he didn't want the boys to know he'd been drinking. 'Kite almighty!' Eyesdown said, gathering himself. His eyes were darting backwards and forwards through the shadows as if he were looking for something valuable and lost.

'What is it?' ventured Sal.

'This letter is addressed to G. A.' said Eyesdown. He was whispering now. 'That's Gabriel Applefell. The senator.'

Dalton blinked. *Applefell. Wasn't that the undertaker's name?* Dalton glanced at Sal. Something in his friend's gaze told him he was thinking the same thing.

'Applefell?' said Sal slowly.

'You know – Gabriel Applefell, for Kite's sake. The senator – the man with the cape and sceptre. It's written to him.' Dalton bit his knuckles, trying to remember the undertaker's precise words. Sal's eyes were wide behind his glasses.

'But there's a million "G. A."s walking the city streets every day, isn't there?' Dalton tried.

Eyesdown scoffed. 'Wake up, horse-arse!' he said. 'Only a few have buckle boxes. Especially in silver. Fewer have locked boxes. And fewer again receive a letter about a sentaway that mentions their brother.'

'Brother?' Dalton said, struggling to keep up. 'There are two Applefells?'

Eyesdown silenced him with a raised hand and peered at the letter again. 'Here,' he said, 'the last line: "Only your brother could be trusted to . . ." It ends there. But it seems pretty clear. The younger Applefell is the senator – G. A. – and I happen to know that the older Applefell – the brother mentioned here – left the city some years ago, though there's a rumour he's back.' Dalton thought about telling Eyesdown what he knew – that Marcher Applefell had indeed been back to Highlions; that he now lay in a cellar in Midwater with a hole in his face. He decided against it. It was too complicated. 'If I'm right,' Eyesdown continued, his voice slowing as he reached his conclusion, 'this letter is from Elber. Dead Duke Elber.' Eyesdown ran a hand across his mouth.

Dalton was fighting a falling feeling.

'Now there's an old story that not many people know about. You two won't know it, being a pair of pointless p-boys. No offence. But I read of it a couple of times a few years ago now.'

'Go on,' said Sal.

'I never believed it. But,' Eyesdown raised the letter. It looked like a little white flag in the dark. 'I might do now. The story goes that the Duke wasn't childless, boys.' Eyesdown waited a moment; waited for it all to sink in, then carried on in a hissing little whisper. 'He had a kid. A number of years ago now. It was all covered up.'

'Why?' said Sal. 'Why cover it up?'

Eyesdown gave Sal a sympathetic look. 'This is a bastard kid we're talking about here,' he explained. 'The child of some sort of secret affair. I saw it mentioned first in a note sent by a senator's wife that I took from a locked desk in the chambers. Who'd written it?' Eyesdown shook his head. 'I can't remember. I might still have it. I'd taken a mighty risk stealing it and I couldn't sell it on, I remember that much.'

'But how does the letter confirm any of this?' Dalton said, indicating the buckle box. His heart felt as if it were being crushed in a huge fist.

Eyesdown unfolded the letter again, scanned it quickly and, when he found the section he was looking for, whispered, 'Listen to this: "The movement of the child is a matter of utmost urgency. It is to you that I entrust the responsibility of care. It goes without saying that the identity of the child must remain an unuttered secret forever. Provision has been made for the settling of all appropriate accounts. The arrangements for transport are as discussed."' Eyesdown turned the sheet over in illustration. 'Its meaning is clear enough. I know my letters, boys. Trust me. This is an original. It's the note Elber packed in a buckle box to send away with his bastard kid. He hasn't had a chamberlain or advisor write this. He's written it himself. This is the Duke's own hand, boys – the Duke's own hand.' Eyesdown pursed his lips and made a low, long whistle. 'The story is true,' he whispered to himself, distracted. Then he wiped his face and looked at the two poison boys. 'Where in Kite's name did you get this?' he asked. 'This is huge.'

Dalton felt as if he were going to be sick. He felt Sal's hand gripping him tight on his shoulder. He thought for a moment he'd forgotten how to breathe, but then he managed a great ragged intake of night air. Sal lowered him until he was sitting, back against the alley wall. Dalton felt a great dull ache behind his eyes and the hot throb of poison in his blood. 'Why huge?' he managed.

Eyesdown was staring at the letter as he answered. 'Think on, Flyboy. Upon the death of a duke, a successor must be announced within the span of three days. Elber has no children. So Gabriel Applefell begins the search for the next Duke. It's been in all the papers. They've been asking for any potential heirs to make themselves known.' Dalton recalled the hawkers on the Laceway bellowing headlines. Eyesdown was, as ever, right. 'Applefell must announce an accession tomorrow at midnight, following the funeral. Who's next in line, boys?' Eyesdown looked up from reading and pointed a finger at them. 'Whoever owns this buckle box and this letter, that's who.' He paused a moment before finishing in a whisper, 'So I ask again – where did you get them?'

Sal looked at Dalton. Dalton watched the shadow of cloud passing the moon, waiting for his vision to sharpen again. 'I think it's mine,' he said.

Eyesdown stared. 'Scut and feathers!' he swore. Then he seemed to gather his wits. 'Flyboy,' he said, his hands on his temples. He spoke slowly and quietly. 'You're the Duke's heir.'

Dalton found he couldn't respond. He licked his dry lips and concentrated on not being sick.

'Francis,' Sal said. 'Can you confirm this? I mean – if I come back again tomorrow, can you be more certain it's true? Check some letters or something? Look for other sources?'

Eyesdown nodded vigorously. 'Yeah. Yeah. I can do that.' He dropped to a crouch and spoke with a calm certainty. 'Fly,' he said, 'you need to make yourself known to the senate before midnight tomorrow.'

'Why?' Sal asked. 'Why then?'

Eyesdown shook his head. 'You may still have your hair you two, but the poison took your brains, didn't it?' He spoke slowly, with mock patience. 'Because, if you don't, then Applefell won't know you exist. And if Applefell doesn't know you exist, he'll just select the next in line for accession.' Eyesdown dipped his head, meeting Dalton's gaze. He spoke with cold clarity. 'Rumour is there's been a complication. Don't know the details yet – still working on it. But it hasn't gone to plan for Applefell. The story goes he's not been able to line up the successor he'd hoped for. He's running out of options, so they say.'

'Anyone asking for heirs in the city's papers must be getting desperate,' Sal noted.

Eyedown nodded. 'Right. So unless things change – and change pretty quickly – by tomorrow night the new Duke will be –' Eyesdown paused, a cold grin spreading across his face – 'Doone De Bello.'

TWENTY-EIGHT

The floorboards of Isis Holt's attic room were hard and they creaked as sleeping figures shifted. Luke Eppington snored, her head dipping and rising. Sal's shoulders moved slightly as he breathed. Outside, the slumbering city was still.

Dalton couldn't sleep. He could still taste the sour, herbal tincture – the antidote to Tench's dipped knife that Sal had made for him. He could remember Sal uncorking a bottle and forcing him to drink, but his recollection of where they had been, or for how long, was hazy and indistinct. Half-memories of their conversation surfaced: Sal unloading an armful of bottles on to a table and speaking rapidly. 'The way you describe it,' his friend had said, 'it sounds as if it could be something like jessamine.'

'I know it,' Dalton had said. Heartbreak grass, it was called sometimes. He'd begun to feel the dizziness and nausea almost immediately but, as the night had worn on, it had been the sensation of his throat clotting up, the difficulty breathing. That and the strange lights that crowded at the edges of his vision – little explosions of green that prickled and spun.

'You'll need to check your pulse,' Sal whispered, breaking a mandrake root into dusty pieces. 'It'll get sluggish. You'll find it hard to swallow and speak. Breathing's really difficult. Eventually you'll pass out and never wake up.' His friend flashed him a Blackjack Gannet grin. 'But we can avoid that,' he said.

'Mandrake,' Dalton said. 'I hate mandrake.'

Sal wrinkled his nose. 'Well, you'll need to take it regularly. Give it a try,' he'd said, offering him a sip.

Dalton kept his eyes shut and breathed in and out slowly through his nose. Sal's antidote was doing its work. He could feel his chest open a little, his heart pick up, the throbbing of his ankle ease a little and his energy gather. But night thoughts still plagued him.

Sometimes, he used to imagine he could remember his parents. But he'd been deceiving himself, he realised. There was nothing in his memory to confirm Eyesdown's amazing story: no recollection of senate corridors in marble; no wet nurse leaning over his basket. Just the opening page of a letter addressed to Gabriel Applefell.

What he knew of the man he could recount in a moment: a tall figure in a gown whose likeness was sketched in the *Circle* or the *Advisor*; a man with a down-turned mouth and dark eyes. And what he knew of Duke Elber amounted to no more. The endless clanging of funeral bells was the first and last he knew of the man who could be his father.

Eyesdown's final remarks also haunted him. Three days, Eyesdown had said, between the passing of one Duke and the coronation of the next. The tolling of the bells on the night Bennie had died – the night Elber had died – that was two days ago now. If Doone De Bello was to succeed as Duke of Highlions, it would be tomorrow night. Unless someone emerged to challenge him.

He knew he must have fallen asleep because a sound woke him. He was too fogged in sleep to open his eyes and search out the source of it. It had been a single footstep, the kind carefully placed. His lids seemed glued together, as if with Bennie's blood. But then they opened and Dalton found himself staring into blackness.

Someone was moving in the room.

The footsteps were careful and small and seemed to last a moment or two – then they dissolved into silence. Dalton fought his fatigue. But at some point, he fell asleep again.

Then it was morning. Sal Sleepwell was cursing loudly – shouting almost. This wasn't dreaming any more. This was real. Dalton brought a hand to his face; wiped his eyes.

'The map,' Sal said. He was moving around the room, stepping over sleeping figures, his boots bringing up dust. Luke was awake now – Dalton heard her voice mutter something. 'The map,' Sal said again. 'Flyboy. The map.' Sal was in his face now, leaning over him. 'Fly,' said Sal, a tight anxiety in his voice, 'I've lost the flogging map.'

Dalton sat up, suddenly awake. 'What?' he managed. 'Where was it?'

Scarlet was awake too, sitting up at the end of the bed. 'What's happening?'

'It's got to be here somewhere,' Dalton said, blinking away a flurry of lights in his eyes. 'We need it.'

Sal was checking the desk and chair, rattling the drawer and bashing its contents about. Something suddenly made Dalton reach for his breast pocket, the breath trapped in his throat; but his lucky Jack was safe. The buckle box was safe. The bottle of antidote was safe.

'It was in your pocket, Sleepwell,' he said stupidly.

'I know that, horse-arse,' said Sal sharply, scattering Isis Holt's belongings across the face of the desk. 'It isn't now.'

'Wet yourself,' Dalton said, grimacing against the pain in his ankle.

'No joke, Flyboy,' Sal spat. 'The map is gone.'

Luke was up on her feet now, searching. 'There's nowhere for it to go,' she said. 'It's here somewhere.' She stopped suddenly. 'Unless it's been stolen.'

Dalton looked at her. *The footsteps in the night. Had they been a dream?* He sat up straight. 'That's possible,' he said. 'I couldn't sleep. I might have heard something.'

'Might?' said Sal. He pushed a hand through his hair. 'What good is "might"? Did you or didn't you?'

'I don't know,' Dalton said. 'I thought I heard someone awake in the room. Moving about.'

Sal covered his glasses with his cupped hands. 'Great,' he said. 'Just great.'

Edward shifted his position in bed. He'd thrown a sheet over himself but his feet emerged at the end, resting on Scarlet's lap. He pushed himself up on to his elbows. 'What's all this?' he said groggily, licking his teeth.

'The map's gone,' Sal said. 'It might have been stolen.'

'Maybe the Earl of Honeycut took it,' said Luke. 'Being an imperialist pig-dog and everything.'

Edward wiped his eyes. 'Trap it, chimney-girl. I've just woken up. What's going on?'

'Could anyone else have got into the room?' Dalton tried, getting to his feet. 'Isis?'

The blond-haired boy was awake now too. 'I don't know,' he said. 'It's possible.'

'There,' said Edward. 'The kid says it's possible.'

'Did you see them?' Sal asked.

Dalton shook his head. 'It was too dark. I only heard them.' Dalton tried to call up that footfall again, tried to picture its owner. It could have been someone from the theatre. *An actor searching Holt's room? That wasn't likely.* Dalton looked about him. It was someone still in the room, he realised suddenly. His stomach lurched.

'Let's all look for it,' he said, pushing the thought aside. He brushed the dust from his elbows and knees and straightened his filthy clothes. 'Come on. It's not gone far.'

Edward swung his legs out of bed. Luke stripped the sheet. 'Hey!' Edward objected. 'It's nothing to do with me.'

Luke folded her blind rabbit in her arms. Her chin jutted out when she was angry. 'Look,' she said. 'Isis says no one could get in. Who benefits from stealing the map? The ruling classes, that's who – oppressing the young and the lost, denying them their freedoms . . .'

Edward rolled his eyes. 'Kite!' he said, turning to the room. 'Is she always like this?'

'You could always turn out your pockets and prove her wrong,' said Dalton, and instantly regretted it.

Edward pointed a finger. 'Trap it, poison boy, or I'll make you eat every badly chosen word.'

Scarlet dropped her gaze. The room fell silent.

Dalton cursed himself inwardly. Scarlet wouldn't look at him. He cleared his throat. 'We need that map,' he said foolishly, and began a search of his own, testing the strength of his ankle as he hobbled around the room. Slowly, one by one, the others joined in. For a time, the group worked methodically without speaking, turning the room over.

Then Sal threw has hands up. 'It's gone,' he said. He pressed his face against the grimy pane of the window. Dalton could read his friend's exasperation in the shape of his shoulders.

'This is all pointless,' Luke said gloomily, studying her boots. 'What are we hoping to achieve here?'

No one answered.

Eventually, Edward returned to the bed. 'Wake me when there's a plan,' he said with a mirthless grin and threw himself on to his back. Isis Holt shuffled, embarrassed. Scarlet let out a long, slow sigh.

'We've got trouble,' said Sal suddenly. 'Big trouble.' He turned from the window. 'Look. We better move quick.'

'What is it?' said Luke.

'Marchers,' Sal said.

He was right. Dalton wiped the pane and saw, in the crowded streets below, a horse-drawn carriage with a number of figures milling about it. One of them was Marcher Gellis, dismounting and arching her back like a cat. The others looked like Dropmore guards with short brass-buttoned coats and big belt-holsters worn across their chests. That usually meant repeaters. They were gathering at the edge of the square before the Black Swan theatre, looking up at the building and speaking together. A gust of warm wind tugged at the marchers' hair.

'It's Gellis,' Dalton said. This was bad. If the marchers got them now, there'd be no way they'd unravel the mystery of De Bello's map and list; no way they'd rescue anymore sentaways. Scarlet blanched. 'Kite!' she spat. 'How's she found me? How is that possible? Were we followed?'

Edward sat up. 'Kitten,' he said, 'calm down.'

Dalton grimaced. 'We need to go now,' he said, imagining the endless interviews and countless questions Gellis would subject them to if they were caught. They wouldn't see daylight for weeks. 'And split up. We'll meet under the Laceway. There's a little room there — Eyesdown's place. He'll keep us safe.' As preposterous as the idea of trusting Eyesdown seemed, at least the boy worked above the law, Dalton figured, and wasn't likely to let them down.

The room became a whirl of movement. Edward pulling his boots on and complaining; Luke discussing the quickest way to the bridge with anyone who'd listen; Sal still fruitlessly searching for the lost map; Scarlet cursing her marcher with fiery venom. Dalton remained at the window and watched the figures make their preparations in the square below, heads close as they whispered a final conference. Then they fanned out; four — no, five — of them. Two heading for the front of the theatre; Gellis disappearing into the crowds down a back alley; and two others approaching the artists' entrance. There wasn't going to be an easy way to evade capture.

'Quick!' he said. 'They're coming in. Isis, what's the best way out?'

The thin boy with the freckled face looked lost. 'The stairs take us down backstage,' he stammered.

'Let's go, then,' announced Edward, striding for the door. He turned to face the room, one hand clasping the handle. 'Kitten, are you coming?'

Scarlet looked flustered for a moment, pushing her hair back out of her eyes and tying her headscarf tight. She looked at Dalton, and her expression seemed like an apology. 'I'm going,' she said, indicating Edward.

Dalton felt as if his tongue was glued to the roof of his

mouth. He tried to look unconcerned. 'Go,' he said with a shrug. Then, as she turned, couldn't help adding, 'Good luck.'

Edward's face darkened and he ducked through the door. With a brief and unreadable backward glance, Scarlet followed.

'Isis, you take them,' Sal said. 'You know the best way out. See you under the bridge. Laceway, remember?'

The boy made a nervous little bow. 'Right,' he said, and scampered after them.

Sal and Dalton exchanged glances, planning. They were getting used to being hunted. Dalton checked the window again. 'That leaves us three,' he said. 'Let's try a different route. If it all gets flogged – head for the bridge.'

TWENTY-NINE

O utside, they could still hear the clattering footsteps of the others as they hammered downstairs
in haste. Sal checked the corridor. It led across to
the far wall of the building, a series of doors on either
side. They hurried along it and followed, for the next few
moments, a maze of low-ceilinged passageways linking
the service areas and stock rooms of the theatre's roof
space. There didn't seem to be a way out. Twice, Sal had to
turn around and head back the way he'd come. Eventually,
they found a set of stairs that took them closer to street
level. They descended carefully, peering ahead into the
space that opened up.

Resin lamps and deep red carpets – the upper storey of the theatre. A 'staff only' sign at the foot of the stairs they had just descended. The corridor, studded at intervals with watercolour paintings of actors in costume, was deserted. Along one side was a set of recessed, curtained openings. Sal ducked his head through and stole a glance. 'Look at this!' he whispered.

Beyond the curtains, a series of balconies commanded a sweeping view of the stage from a dizzying height. The vast open space of the theatre was much more impressive than Isis Holt's dusty back room had suggested. Its domed roof looked as if it were fashioned in ivory and gold. In the deep blue shadows below, an orchestra pit and the empty stage slumbered and, before them, rows and rows of cushioned chairs.

Luke picked up a pair of binoculars from a brass holder and focussed them, gazing around her with a cold grin of contempt. 'A mighty pointless playground for the carefree rich, if ever I saw one.'

Sal put a finger to his lips and ducked, beckoning the others on to their knees. Two figures were picking their way down towards the stage, barely discernable in the gloom. Sal tugged the binoculars from Luke's hand and pointed them down into the darkness. 'Marchers' lackeys,' he said. 'They've got pistols.'

'Look!' Luke hissed. The boys followed the direction of her startled gaze. Sal focussed the binoculars. Another figure was scurrying softly between the seats, hunched in a careful crouch. It was Scarlet Dropmore, watching the progress of the two men towards the stage, waiting for them to pass so she could slip away. 'Where's fat-pockets, the scumbag boyfriend?' said Luke.

Sal chuckled softly, following Scarlet's progress with the binoculars pressed hard against the lenses of his glasses. 'You really hate him, don't you?'

'Only in the sense that I'd like to see him squeal as the righteous underclass tear him limb from limb,' Luke said.

'Fine words, coming from a rich girl,' Sal said. Luke drew breath indignantly, ready to reply.

'Trap it, both of you,' Dalton hissed. He was watching the progress of the two guards. They were close to the stage now. Scarlet needed more time and more space to make good her escape. And, if Edward was still backstage with Isis, they'd need help too. He had a sudden thought. 'Sleepwell,' he said. 'You two go. I'll make a distraction.'

'What? Wet yourself.'

'Give me the binoculars,' Dalton persisted. 'You two go.'

Sal regarded him solemnly. 'How will this help exactly?'

It was a good point. Dalton wasn't sure what he was doing or why. But he wanted Scarlet safely away – along with Sleepwell and Luke. This, at least, was a way to do it. 'I'm going to throw these,' he said patiently, raising the eyeglasses, 'and you're going to run.'

'That's a lunatic plan, if ever I heard one, p-boy,' Luke said, regaining her bluster. Then she grinned. 'But, since it involves trashing the trinkets of the rich, I'm all for it.'

Dalton nodded his thanks. 'So, go.'

Reluctantly, Sal Sleepwell lifted himself to his feet and patted his friend on the shoulder. 'See you at Eyesdown's,' he said. And then they were gone, and Dalton was alone on the balcony.

He looked at his feeble missile, then down at the stage below. He knew the spot where he wanted them to land, and he could envisage the spinning arc they would take as they fell. He made one final check of Scarlet's position, steadied himself and his grip, then flung the binoculars high into the open space of the theatre. There was a moment of cool empty silence as they spun downward. Then they hit the stage and skittered along the wooden boards in shattered pieces.

One of the marchers' men let out a hoarse shout and spun around. The other pointed his pistol upward. Dalton could tell they couldn't see him. They spun left and right, scanning the high balconies to try and locate the source of the object. Then Scarlet broke for it, and Dalton was aware of her slight figure darting through the darkness, away from the stage, towards the theatre entrance.

One of the guards held up a hand. 'Don't shoot,' he barked. The other paused. Then they both broke into a run, following the girl.

Dalton allowed himself a smile of satisfaction, waited a moment or two to be sure Scarlet was safe, then took a seat. He had time, he figured, to rest and check his ankle. It had been as insistent as ever with its hot, dull throb. He slipped his boot off and pulled carefully at the edges of the bloody bandage. His skin had turned a deep blue, he noticed with alarm, and the veins beneath were like little black spider webs. *Best to leave it.* He pulled his boot back on and uncorked Sal's slim bottle of antidote. Gritting his teeth against the sourness, he took a swig and forced it down, then laboured to his feet, feeling the mandrake start to work.

He pushed the curtain back, checked for guards and crept out. Ahead, he was sure, beyond the curve of the corridor, would be another set of stairs, perhaps dropping down into the foyer. Surely Gellis and her men would be gone by now, and everyone safely away. He was comforting himself with this thought, and had gone only a matter of steps, when he became aware of a light footfall approaching from around the corner ahead. He'd just passed the last of the curtained balconies. With a prickle of fear, he took a swift step backwards, ready to dart into safety. But before he could, a figure appeared ahead.

It was Scarlet Dropmore.

He was staggered. His shock must have been evident on his face.

'What's up?' she whispered, padding cautiously forward. She halted some distance from him and cocked her head.

Dalton found his voice. 'Why are you still here?' he said. 'Where are the others?'

'All out and away,' she said. 'Was that you? The distraction back there?'

Dalton nodded. 'For your benefit,' he said. He cleared his throat. 'The idea,' he explained slowly, still shaking his head in disbelief, 'was that you'd run off.'

'Oh.'

Dalton tried his question again. 'So – why are you here? Outside is that way.' He pointed unnecessarily.

'I know,' she said. She put her hands in her pockets. 'I came to rescue you.'

Dalton swallowed back a laugh. She was serious, he could tell. 'I don't need rescuing,' he said, trying not to sound indignant. The palms of his hands prickled with energy.

'Poison boy,' said Scarlet with a wry smile, 'ever since you broke into my room you've needed rescuing from one thing or another.'

He hated her cool certainty. She couldn't possibly be right. 'Name me one thing,' he said.

Scarlet thought. 'My room, of course,' she said, raising a finger, 'though we've covered that one already. In addition: my house; Midwater; the steam halls; and here. That's five rescues so far.'

'Listen, lackbrain,' Dalton said. 'I'm trying to rescue you. But you keep coming back.'

Scarlet shrugged. 'If it makes you feel better thinking it,' she said. Then she studied her hands. 'Listen,' she said. 'I wanted to ask. What did you find out about the letter?'

Dalton felt for the buckle box in his pocket. Eyesdown's story came rushing back suddenly, flooding his head again. The big, dead weight of it all made his shoulders sag.

'Kite,' said Scarlet, reading his face. 'That bad?'

Dalton managed a nod, wishing he was just an orphaned food-taster of no consequence, a kid without a care. But those days were over. He could never un-read the letter to Gabriel Applefell, or bring bursting back into life Bennie Jinks or Milo Knox or Felix Eden. Those boys were dead and gone, and everything only ever went forward – forward into trouble and chaos. He had to tell someone, he realised. Dropmore was as good a person as any. He licked his dry lips.

'Duke Elber was my father,' he said.

Scarlet brought her hands up and touched her temples, staring at him intently, her lips parted in shock. 'How do you know?' she said hoarsely.

'A friend told me. He knows these things. I think I believe him.'

Scarlet ran a hand across her headscarf, thinking. 'This is madness,' she said. 'I mean – the minute I saw the buckle box, I knew you were a sentaway, and a high-born sentaway at that. But . . .' She inflated her cheeks and let out a long, exasperated sigh. 'Duke Elber?' she said. Then her eyes narrowed as a thought came to her. She opened her mouth to speak.

But the sound never came. Someone else talked in her place – a cold, firm voice from the corridor behind her.

'Scarlet,' it said. The voice of Marcher Gellis; Dalton recognised it instantly. His heart jumped as she appeared, a pistol raised high, her long riding cloak rising in a dark wave behind her as she walked calmly towards them. Her eyes were like steel. Her jaw was tight. 'You're both coming with me,' she said. 'I don't want any more foolishness.'

Gellis couldn't see Scarlet's face yet, though the marcher was drawing closer. Scarlet fixed Dalton with fire in her eyes. She mouthed one word slowly, deliberately: 'Run.' Then she turned to face her captor, her arms raised compliantly. 'Marcher Gellis,' she said, aloud now. 'How nice to see you again.'

Dalton knew this was his moment. The woman wouldn't shoot him, he figured. Though her guards might. There was no more time. He broke suddenly into a hobbling run, back the way he had come, towards the stairs, and, as he did so, he heard the drum of Scarlet's boots follow.

'Scarlet!' Gellis shouted, her voice like a knife. 'Scarlet! Poison boy!'

Then a volley of curses followed and, in an instant, her men were thundering after them. Dalton leapt up the stairs, legs aching, and made for Holt's room, Scarlet at his shoulder.

Neither of them looked back.

THIRTY

Down in the shadows of Eyesdown's room, a rag-tag assembly had gathered. Outside, the sun was climbing and it was hot and clammy. The low river stank. Francis Eyesdown, unused to his place being suddenly invaded, was forcing a smile through gritted teeth, his bald head glistening in the low light of his flogged resin lamps. Luke was brushing soot from her clothes and tucking her blind rabbit into the pocket of her trousers. Isis Holt drifted at the edges of the group like a silent ghost.

Edward was stooping, shifting from foot to foot, his features dark and brooding. He hadn't been happy when

Dalton and Scarlet had arrived together. Though she stood at his side now, he'd berated her in a low, insistent whisper as Sal had introduced people. 'And I'd remind you,' he finished, biting his painted nails, 'that he's just a barrow boy with no place to go. So please stop embarrassing yourself.'

Scarlet, Dalton had noticed, had hidden a smile behind her hand as he finished his speech.

'Listen, everyone,' said Francis Eyesdown irritably. 'You're standing on my letters. Just all of you stay still, right?' He wiped his forehead. 'There's a system here,' he scowled, indicating the slewed piles of folded documents arranged around their feet. 'I don't want it flogged up.' Eyesdown turned to Dalton. 'Flyboy, I've got everything you asked for. Let's do this quickly.'

'Do what?' Edward said, wiping his hands on his coat. 'Kite, this place is filthy.'

There was an uncomfortable silence. Dalton searched for the right words and came up with nothing. Sal had asked Eyesdown for confirmation, and it looked as if the boy had got it. Dalton swallowed hard, dreading what was coming.

'Well, if you're not going to tell them,' Eyesdown said, holding up a handful of letters tied with string, 'I will.' He cleared his throat. The group looked at him.

Edward lifted a boot and shifted a letter or two underfoot. 'Can we just get on with it, bullet-head?' he said.

Eyesdown glowered. 'These letters are all we need to confirm the story,' he said. 'I spent the small hours searching my stuff to gather these together.'

'Story?' Edward said. 'What is this?'

'A tale of exploitation and misrule, I should expect,' Luke said flatly.

Eyesdown glanced at Dalton, unsure of himself.

'They're always like this,' Dalton said. 'Ignore them.'

Eyesdown ran a palm across his bald head and began. 'These letters tell the story of Duke Elber's bastard son,' he said, and waited, biting his lip as the room fell silent. Nobody moved.

It was Luke who spoke first, her voice a careful whisper. 'Wait,' she said. 'You're saying Duke Elber had a son?'

Isis Holt looked at the gathered assembly with pale, fearful eyes. 'That's not possible,' he whispered.

Eyesdown nodded. 'It is,' he said. 'And you know what? I'm not saying anything I haven't heard before. This is an old, old story. And, if you steal letters from the right people—'

'Which you do, I assume,' Edward put in.

'I do . . . and this is what they tell me.' Eyesdown pulled them clear of their string and fanned them in his hands. 'Letters written by chamberlains, advisors, marchers. All of them half-speaking of this secret baby.' The boy's gaze was fierce with excitement. He looked at each of them in turn. 'I've been saving them up. Someday, I figured, these letters'd keep me in pies and wine for the rest of my life. Then horse-arse here came along −' Eyesdown jerked a thumb in Dalton's direction. He cleared his throat for emphasis −'and he had something with him that changed

248

everything: the buckle box. Tell 'em, p-boy,' he said.

Dalton felt all eyes on him. A gang of children in a cellar full of stolen letters, all looking to him for some sort of explanation. Only Sleepwell, his downward gaze avoiding the room, knew the whole story. Dalton wished a hundred pointless things that couldn't possibly be true, and then, resigned, he started to tell the tale: the barrel story; the undertaker and his last words; Oscar keeping the buckle box secret all those years. It was like the story of someone else's life.

Four days ago, he'd been just a poison boy. Then he'd woken up nearly drowned in spit and blood – and the boy who'd woken up was someone else. And now he had to learn to live that other person's life.

'So,' he finished, his voice wavering, 'it seems the letter is to Gabriel Applefell, advisor to the Duke. And the child it was sent with –' he could barely believe it as he spoke – 'was me.'

For a moment, no one said anything. They looked each other over – checked each other's response. Isis Holt seemed washed white with exhaustion. Sal had to grip his shoulder. Edward's head dropped. Dalton eased the cork from the bottle of antidote and forced down a dose, shuddering against the bitterness.

Luke let out a long slow breath. 'Well,' she said. 'Looks like your days as a poison boy are numbered.' Her blackened face was broken by a grin and she added with a wink, 'Your Worshipfulness.'

Sleepwell smiled broadly for the first time that morning,

letting out a slow sigh of relief. Dalton allowed himself a grin. Perhaps Luke was with them. But the others . . .

'This is complicated,' said Edward. The older boy was ahead of them, figuring out consequences and possibilities, his forehead creased in concentration.

Eyesdown, tying his bundle of letters together again, nodded in acknowledgement. 'Well, that's the problem,' he said. 'Upon the death of a Duke or Duchess, the senate has three days to appoint a successor. There's the funeral first, then the senate gathers at the Palace of Justice on Midwater and an heir is announced. And tonight at about midnight, time's up.'

Edward winced. 'So, given the old man didn't have any children – present company excepted of course – who do we get?'

'Does it matter?' said Luke. 'They're all the same.'

Eyesdown held up a hand. 'Gabriel Applefell, the senator, has been dealing with this. In the event of no immediate heir, he's the one who has to assess the possible successors. But the word is, he's having trouble tracking some of them down.'

Dalton drew breath sharply, rocked on his heels by the swiftness of his realisation. There in the shadows of Eyesdown's room, it was as if a bright light suddenly burst into life and in that rush, it all made sense.

'Scut and feathers!' Edward swore to himself, reaching the same point at the same moment. He was looking at his hands, palms up, as if watching a puzzle slip into shape in his grasp.

'What?' said Luke, regarding them suspiciously. 'What?'

'The poisoned sentaways . . .' Dalton breathed. 'They're the Duke's heirs.' The map with the names in black. De Bello had lined up Duke Elber's potential heirs, listed them and poisoned them. Milo Knox, the high-born kid hidden in the kitchens. Felix Eden at St Eleanor's. The dead children in the copy of the *Advisor*. There was a sequence in which they had to die because there was a sequence in which they stood to inherit the throne. With Knox and Eden, Eppington, Dropmore and Honeycut all dead or absent, De Bello had calculated he was next in line. But De Bello was wrong, Dalton thought grimly. He'd seen his plans hijacked by a nobody poison boy, who'd gathered around him a ragged group of survivors. And, to cap it all, this poison boy held a trump card: he was himself the Duke's true heir.

The silence in the room was broken. It was Luke. 'So correct me if I'm wrong, citizens. But this means that unless we do something, De Bello becomes Duke tonight.'

Eyesdown gave her a nod. Dalton tried to focus on the evening ahead. Through the streets of Highlions, Duke Elber's funeral cortege would process. Then, on Midwater, with the last light of the day dwindling, the senate would gather. And unless he was there to prevent it, Doone De Bello would be sworn in as Duke Elber's heir. Doone knew what he was doing. Having Tench kill sentaways, or even just keep them away from Midwater till after the ceremony, would mean he could have his way. As far as

Applefell was concerned, the new ruler had to be in place in three days. If potential heirs had vanished – there was nothing he could do but work with what he had. And once De Bello had been sworn in, it wouldn't matter if other heirs reappeared. The deed would be done. And all-out war would surely follow, as the Houses of Highlions rose up against each other. Dalton wiped his eyes. His fingers were shaking, he noticed – he had to bury his hands in his pockets to hide his fear. There was much more at stake than he had first thought.

Sleepwell's eyes were wide and his gaze was steely. He too was thinking it all through. He ran a hand through the wild ruck of his hair. 'We need to get into Midwater again,' he said.

Isis Holt stood a little taller now, but when he spoke he seemed to be swallowing back a stammer. 'Is that possible?' he said.

'You've done it once already, haven't you?' Edward said, looking at Dalton.

'Boys,' Eyesdown said, raising his palms outward, a mirthless grin splitting his face. 'You've got to be mad. The security will be mighty. Whatever you did before, it'll be ten times harder now. The whole senate gathers tonight. There'll be Streetwatch crawling everywhere.'

'And there's only one bridge,' Luke said. 'Unless you fancy swimming.'

'You could do with a wash,' Edward said with a wry smile.

'Trap it, fat-pockets.'

Eyesdown made a little cough and shook his head hopelessly. He was pulling on his battered coat and yanking his hunting hat from one of the pockets. 'Listen,' he said. 'It's been a pleasure hosting this little gathering. But there's letters and bone that need lifting and they'll be lining the streets for Elber's funeral, so if you don't mind . . .' He raised an expectant eyebrow.

Dalton nodded. 'Right,' he said. 'Except we could do with your help, Eyesdown.'

The boy shrugged his coat on and rolled his eyes. 'Kite,' he muttered to himself. 'Haven't I suffered enough? I've solved the mystery of your birth, haven't I? And I really don't want to be around when Dalton Fly's little black cloud of trouble starts raining again. If you're going to ask me to help get you on to Midwater, the answer's no. Kite! You're all mad!'

'Help me get on to Midwater,' Dalton said.

'Less of the "me", Flyboy,' Sleepwell said, elbowing him. He flashed Eyesdown a winning grin. 'We need a way to get two of us in.'

'Three,' said Edward. There was a stunned silence. 'What?' he asked. 'The alternative is kicking about the steam halls, waiting for my marcher to grow a personality.'

'This is impossible,' Isis Holt said.

'Count me in, citizens,' said Luke brightly. 'I'll come along, if I can be useful.'

Dalton felt a rush of gratitude push tears to his eyes. He blinked them back, smiling at the assembly.

Eventually, Eyesdown found enough wits to speak. 'It

seems you have a little crew, Your Holiness,' he said, tipping his head to one side and delivering Dalton a sarcastic smile. 'Well, all right then. But if I miss good thieving time on account of a bunch of dreckwits with a death wish, I'll be less than pleased.'

THIRTY-ONE

D alton had never seen the city like this. Highlions was thronged, buzzing with chatter and movement, each street lined with gathered hordes awaiting the procession. The crowds were thick and it was easy to hide. Dalton and Sal exchanged relieved glances as they prepared for the passing of the Duke's carriage. Here, immersed in the ebb and flow of the anonymous crowd, there was little chance they might be recognised. Streetwatch guards gathered in pairs and threes at junctions, heavily armed, but their attention was on the ceremony. Dalton was relieved to see there was no sign of Gellis or any other marchers. The last thing they needed now was any sort of delay.

Duke Elber's funeral cortege had begun its journey through the streets of the Lower Circle an hour or so earlier. It was just as Eyesdown had described: an open carriage carrying a coffin, pulled with slow reverence by a team of twenty black and blinkered horses with glinting reins. Ahead of them, their heads bowed low, walked the senators in ranks of four, led by Gabriel Applefell.

Dalton watched the solemn figure as he passed. He wore his fine robes of state: a great ankle-length cloak over a dark, silver-buttoned jacket with a red sash. His expression was blank. This, then, was the undertaker's younger brother. Dalton hadn't seen his own marcher for very long – caught only glimpses of him before he was killed – so it was difficult to establish any immediate similarities. They had the same bearing, though – the same determined stride. He imagined how Applefell might respond if he saw the letter in the buckle box, a letter written fourteen years ago and meant for him. Perhaps Dalton would have the chance to place it in his possession before midnight. Perhaps.

Walking in the first rank of senators was the beautiful Loyola Dropmore. Dalton watched Scarlet's mother pass: a fiery-eyed woman with high cheekbones, pale skin and dark hair wound under a headscarf, her hands clasped behind her back and her solemn gaze downward. She looked fearsome. Strangest of all was the sight of Elber's coffin passing. Polished, wooden, edged in gold, its lid was open but, from where he stood, Dalton could see nothing of what lay within. It seemed so impossible that the lifeless figure resting inside could be his father.

Sal placed an arm around his shoulders and pulled him close. 'It's time we went,' he said quietly.

Dalton uncorked his antidote and swallowed back another sour mouthful of the brew. His breathing was slow and sticky, his chest tight and his body weary. Earlier, he'd found once more that he couldn't watch as Sal changed the dressings on his wound; but he'd seen his friend's eyes widen in anxiety as he checked it over. It felt worse that it looked, Dalton reckoned. If he was still alive tomorrow, he promised himself, he'd find Oscar and ask for help. He blinked away a cloud of spinning green lights. Sal's antidote could only do so much against the deepening influence of the jessamine. Just that morning, Dalton had found himself misjudging distances as he climbed steps, stumbling foolishly. *More mandrake*, he kept telling himself. Half the bottle was gone now.

'Hey. Slow down on that,' Sal said, indicating the bottle Dalton had slipped back into his jacket pocket. 'There's only enough for a few days.'

Dalton tried to smile. Scarlet was looking at him oddly, a shadow of unspoken concern clouding her expression. Edward looked away, biting his nails.

'Let's go,' Dalton said, and the companions left the crowded streets and made their way through quieter ones, towards the river and the bridge to Midwater West.

*

'Boys,' said Eyesdown, 'this whole endeavour is impossible.' He was squinting through a flogged telescope, his gaze fixed on the bridge. They were further up the city now, leaning against a wall that followed the river's edge down the hill towards the Lower Circle. The group had assembled themselves in a line, elbow to elbow, all occupied in studying the island in the middle of the river.

Dalton raised a hand, his palm open. 'Let me look.'

Eyesdown handed him the telescope, took off his hunting hat and wiped the sweat from his forehead. 'There's no way in,' he said. 'The walls are huge. The gates are locked and guarded.'

Dalton brought the bridge into view, held his breath and focussed the jumpy image. The bridge was wide enough for two carriages to pass each other. The river kneaded and eddied at its arches, a deep and swiftly moving thing, foam-topped and glistening in the sun. At the island's southernmost point, Dalton could see the arched exit at the bottom of the chute, the point at which the slipway had spat them out in the skiff. It was some way above the water. There was no way they could swim to it and climb up the steep tracks back to the cellar where Marcher Applefell had died. And the storm drain just beneath the bridge – the entrance where they had first gained access – was gated now. De Bello had seen to it that his island fortress was well protected. He wanted nobody but the Highlions senate present as the bells tolled midnight.

Edward leant in close and nudged Dalton, pointing out

the new metal grille. 'Looks like you won't be able to repeat your trick,' he said. 'They've blocked the drains. But what about the quay?'

Dalton brought the telescope down and cradled it a moment, blinking away a mist of disorientating lights. 'What quay?' he said, handing over the eyeglass.

Edward took a turn. 'There's a quay on the north side of the island,' he explained as he focussed. 'A little landing platform. Just for one boat. There's a set of steps carved into the cliff face that take you up on to the island . . .'

Luke held her hands over her eyes, shading them from the morning sun. 'I see it,' she said.

'The current's too strong,' Sal said. 'If you were to swim to that, you'd need to jump in upstream and let the river carry you down towards it.'

Edward grunted his agreement. 'I can't tell where the steps go,' he said. 'But if they lead to a gate . . .'

'They'd have to,' Eyesdown said with a snort of laughter. 'There's no way you're climbing those walls.'

Dalton looked them over. Eyesdown was right. They towered, sheer and smooth, over the cliff face and the river below.

'The Skeltonyards are in there,' Eyesdown added, wiping his eyes. 'Those walls are built to keep prisoners in. As well as lackbrains, like you lot, out.'

'Wait!' Sal Sleepwell said, standing erect suddenly and bringing both hands up over his eyebrows. 'Pass me the telescope.'

Edward handed it over. 'What have you seen?'

Sal pushed his glasses up on to his forehead and squinted into the eyepiece. 'The bridge,' he said.

Everyone looked. Isis Holt, fidgeting, spoke first. 'What is it?' he said.

Edward grinned as he picked out the movement below. 'A delivery.'

They could all see it now. A horse and cart, rattling along the bridge towards the gates, the driver hunched over the chains. And in the back of the cart . . .

'Barrels,' Sal said with a smile, adjusting the focus. 'Resin or wine.' The group watched in unbroken silence as the cart rattled across the causeway and pulled up at the gate. The driver hopped down and approached the Street-watch guards. 'He's got papers,' Sal reported, tracking the figures carefully. 'They know him.'

A moment later, one of the guards thumped a fist against the gate and it opened, revealing a tantalising glimpse of the courtyard within. The driver mounted again and the horse snorted and moved forward.

'Go on,' said Luke, making a leering scowl of disgust at the opening gates. 'Drink your wine while the city tears itself apart, why don't you?'

Dalton watched. The cart had dark lettering along its side — branded on to the wood. An idea suddenly occurred to him. 'Sal,' he said, 'what does it say down the side of the cart?'

'What?' Sal refocussed and leant forward. 'Difficult to see . . .' he began, and steadied himself, placing both elbows on the coping stones of the wall. 'Wait. Got it.

Griffin Brothers, Wine Merchants, Ivyhill.'

The barrels in the courtyard, Dalton remembered. There must be regular deliveries. That's why the guards knew the driver.

Eyesdown was laughing. He slapped Dalton on the back with an open palm and grinned. 'Your Worshipfulness!' he said. 'Perhaps your luck's about to change.'

Dalton shrugged, confused. 'What do you mean?'

'I know the Griffin brothers,' Eyesdown said with a wink. 'I managed to recover some lost letters for them last year. Saved them a deal of embarrassment. So, as it happens, they owe me a favour or two.'

Dalton looked again at Midwater, its great grey roofs basking in the warmth of the morning, its high, impenetrable walls sun-topped, and found himself gathering a series of ridiculous thoughts. 'Are those barrels big enough to hide something inside?' he wondered aloud, watching the cart, emptied of its load, make its way back across the bridge.

'Depends,' Sal said, handing Eyesdown his telescope. 'What have you got in mind?'

Dalton shrugged. 'Me and you?' he said.

Edward began to laugh.

THIRTY-TWO

T
he sun was dropping now, and the afternoon sky beginning to deepen in colour. Soon, the lamps and lanterns would be lit and the day would draw to a close.

'It's time,' said Nathan Griffin, squinting down over the city from the streets of the Upper Circle. He was a gruff man with a dense beard and a high forehead, a serious and silent tradesman with big calloused hands. 'You boys will need to hide yourselves,' he said, and ran a hand along the flanks of his horse. The animal stamped and whinnied. Griffin pulled himself up to the driver's seat, then turned to check on Dalton and Sal.

Eyesdown watched the poison boys making their last preparations. He nodded his thanks to the driver of the cart. Griffin grimaced in return. Dalton had detected the man's reluctance the moment they had met just a few hours ago, and found himself again wondering what debt must bind a wine merchant to take such a dangerous course of action. Whatever it was, Eyesdown had made it clear that after this, they were even.

The plan was a simple one. Griffin was to return to Midwater with a second consignment of wine. Three barrels of the first delivery were suspected faulty and needed to be replaced. New paperwork was prepared and the cart filled with barrels of wine and others of lantern oil. Two barrels, however, would be ventilated by holes in their lids – and inside, two poison boys would be huddled. These would be left in the courtyard against the wall of the Senate Hall. From there, Dalton and Sal would make their way to the Palace of Justice and arrive before the appointed hour.

As the horse and cart were crossing the bridge, upstream Edward would be waiting in the water with Scarlet, Luke and Isis, clinging to the banks of the river. Dalton didn't envy them; having been swept through the city in the vast and eddying water once, he had no appetite for repeating the experience. The four of them would be steering themselves towards the little quay, and hoping they could gain access to it without being pummelled against the rocks. Then they would begin the climb up the stairwell carved into the cliff face, and hope there was a point of access somewhere. From there, they'd move on to the Palace of Justice, bedraggled and weary, to face their foe for the final time. As Sal had said with a sarcastic smile, 'What could possibly go wrong?'

Sal talked Dalton through his cache one more time. It was split across two shoulder bags, one each, and wrapped in muslin. 'There's oleander and mandragora,' Sal said, indicating a packet of seeds and dried leaves in waxed paper. 'There's a little foxglove, if it comes to it. Emergencies only, though.'

They both knew how fierce and terrible digitalis could be if used in the wrong way.

'There's a little bit of belladonna,' Sal continued, tapping a small corked jar, 'and some John Crow, just in case.'

Dalton packed it away again and pulled the bag tight around his shoulder. Who knew whether any of it would find a use?

Whether it would or not, Sal had spent the early afternoon raiding Oscar's hospital. 'This is our advantage,' he had said, his eyes bright. 'It makes sense to be ready to use it.'

Dalton, on the other hand, was beginning to find thinking, planning and preparing close to impossible. His brain swam and his eyes fizzed with dancing lights. His balance was off and his ankle throbbed with a hot insistence. He threw back another mouthful of the mandrake and felt his senses sharpen again and his pulse pick up. Sal had prepared a fresh batch and it was stronger and quicker but he needed it every hour now.

'Boys,' Griffin growled from the driver's bench, shaking the bridle of the horse. 'Time to move. Get in.'

Sal lowered his legs into his barrel and dropped to a crouch. He flattened his wild hair and adjusted his glasses. 'Flyboy,' he said, his face a picture of concern.

Dalton shook himself into action, blinking away a blur of green. 'Ready,' he said. There was just enough room to huddle down in his barrel. Holding a crouching position was exquisitely painful. He shifted his weight, pressing his body against the stained and pungent wood. The silver buckle box dug into his hip and he pulled it free, jamming it between his feet. The last thing he saw was Eyesdown tipping his ridiculous hat at him and then dropping the lid into place.

The breathing holes allowed three sharp shafts of light to illuminate his cramped hiding place. With a jolt, they were moving. It was hot and dry and Dalton felt the sweat break out on his scalp and under his arms immediately. He tried to press back Oscar's image and voice, but in the darkness the old and ruined man was all Dalton could think about. The story came back again like a forgotten song: 'Once, I found a little boy in a barrel. I was trading spice and pollen in the cellars under Downholland. It was late in the year. The days were short and cold.' How many times had he heard those words slurred and stuttered, Oscar's favourite tale? *Well*, Dalton thought to himself, *a lifetime after the first barrel, here is the second. Perhaps this story will outshine the other.*

Soon, there was a change in the sound of the cart. The clatter of the wheels on city streets became duller. They were on the bridge now. Dalton's eyes had grown used to the light. He prised open the little silver box. There, glinting in the gloom, was the silver chain and the dull grey key. There was the deck of cards and the tiny silver pistol with the ivory grip. And there was the letter. Dalton took the chain in both hands, lowered his head and dropped it carefully around his neck. He pulled his lucky Jack, dog-eared and blackened with river grime, from his jacket pocket and added it to the back of the pack to which it belonged. He slipped the full deck into his inside pocket. He didn't need the Jack any more. It was just one of fifty-two others. Blackjack Gannet couldn't help him now; Gannet protected poison boys and orphans. And he wasn't sure he was either any more.

The light through the barrel's ventilation holes was dimming. Dalton pushed the pistol into the belt of his trousers and folded the letter back into the buckle box in the near darkness. These were his things. He was going to carry them with him. When he stepped out of this barrel into Midwater, he was going to be Dalton Elber, the invisible Duke.

Soon, Dalton felt the cart draw to a stop. Nearby, he heard Griffin's grunt of exertion as he lowered himself down. Then voices; impossible, though, to pick out their owners or hear the exchange of words. The conversation seemed to go on a long time. *Too long*, Dalton thought. Was there a problem? Perhaps the guards had become suspicious. They could be eyeing the barrels now, weighing up the possibility of a search. The roll of the river was audible. The voices remained low.

And then, the creak and scrape of the huge gates being drawn back. They were in.

Dalton heaved a sigh of relief and braced himself against the wood, trying to avoid being thrown back and forth as Griffin steered the horse and cart through the gates and on to Midwater West. As he crouched, tense and sweating, the sound of the wheels changed again – from cobbles to smoother stone – a gentle hissing sound. The horse's hooves clattered and echoed. They must be passing through the yard. Dalton remembered the pile of barrels stacked outside the Senate Hall on the night he'd first entered Midwater. They didn't seem to be stopping, though. There must have been a change of plan. Perhaps that's what the conversation at the gate was about.

Dalton nudged an elbow against the lid of his barrel and pushed it upwards. A crack of cool air opened up. They were still moving. What was going on? Cautiously, he pressed the crown of his head against the lid and raised it further. His barrel was one of the outermost ones; he could see the buildings passing. The streets were deserted.

Then they moved out into a huge tree-lined square. The pattering echoes of the horse dulled as they moved into open space. Dalton drew breath, watching the scene unfurl. The Palace of Justice was vast: a mighty marble building with six huge columns, three either side of an archway inside which a pair of enormous doors stood open. Golden light thrown from lamps of the entrance hall patterned the rise of steps, making them glow amber against the grey of the moonlit stone. Great black windows punctuated the façade, and turrets and towers rose to stand like silent sentries against the purple-black of the sky. A blade of yellow moon made the eyes of the stone lions, six stately beasts carved reclining in marble, glitter.

This, Dalton knew, would be where the senate would gather at midnight. Francis Eyesdown had worked his way through every letter, note, rumour and report he could lay his hands on as the companions had prepared for their assault on Midwater. He'd filched pockets, intercepted secret missives, called in favours and bribed informants to ensure access to every communication sent and received across Highlions in the last two days. And every one confirmed the same arrangements. Inside the Palace, beyond the entrance hall and past the courtrooms and council offices, was the Senate Chamber. It would be there that Gabriel Applefell would be drawing around him the sniping, jealous senators of the city and announcing Elber's successor. It would be there that Doone De Bello would be ready to sweep the robes of state around his shoulders and take up his position as heir.

And it was there, Dalton realised, that Griffin's cart was heading.

THIRTY-THREE

He ducked back down into darkness, and used a probing finger through one of the ventilation holes to pull the lid back into position. Perhaps the guards had requested that the barrels be taken straight to the Palace. Either that, Dalton thought, or Griffin was about to turn them in.

Waiting, helpless and flogged by cramps in the pitch dark, was a torturous horror. But eventually, Griffin's cart jerked to a stop. Dalton could hear the horse whinny and stamp and the wine merchant talk to it in a soothing voice before he dismounted. It wasn't long before Dalton felt his barrel suddenly move — lurching upwards and then swaying from side to side. He was being carried down some stairs. After a short time, his barrel came to rest. Dalton was alert now, blinking away the spinning blur of lights and shaking his head clear. There was the sound of a heavy door closing – being dropped closed, as if it was a trapdoor above cellar steps – and a bolt being drawn across it. Wherever they were, they were locked in.

How long before they could emerge from their hiding places? Dalton wondered if he could take another hour of squatting in the cramped darkness – or if he'd have to burst out, straighten his legs, cool off, drink mandrake and breathe clean air. The pain he felt – his knuckles and knees, shins and feet, bloodied elbows and swollen, poisoned ankle – was next to unbearable. He distracted himself by imagining his companions, led by Edward and Scarlet, heaving themselves, exhausted, from the water of the city's river and beginning the arduous climb up the slippery steps. They'd be suffering too.

And he visualised the remainder of the night; playing it out in his mind, picturing the possibilities – the triumphs and disasters, the victories and humiliations that could be waiting in the Palace of Justice for him. Pallis Tench's shattered face sneered at him in the darkness. Doone De Bello's disdain drifted like the dying smoke of a flogged lamp.

Then came the wax-faced Duke – his dead father – speaking riddles he couldn't decipher, and the fierce and fire-breathing Senator Dropmore fanning a deck of cards. Dropmore and a deck of cards, blurring and sharpening, like a half-dream. For a moment, Dalton thought he could smell mint and soap. The senator had become Scarlet now, close to him like she had been in the steam halls, leaning in and breathing against his cheek.

'Choose a card, poison boy,' she was saying, her voice husky and warm. Dalton tried to shake his head clear. He was dreaming. A card had fallen free from the pack somehow. Had he chosen it?

'The King of Spades,' said Scarlet. 'A dark stranger is your protector.' She smiled, her teeth white and smooth and close to his. 'Pick another, poison boy.'

Dalton found himself plucking at something in the dark, trying to choose a card from a deck that was nothing but a fevered dream. He saw her on the night they had met, the steam rising from the copper bath, the wet skin, the black hair stuck in ringlets to her shoulders; Scarlet Dropmore, barefoot, bright points of light dancing about her. He felt his heart slow then surge. He could see the pulse push at her wet wrist. She reached for the pendant at her throat and held it for a moment in the palm of her left hand.

'I'm Dalton Fly,' he remembered saying, 'one of Oscar's boys. There's more of us. We can help you if you're ever in trouble.'

'Thanks,' she whispered, fanning the deck. 'But if there's someone in trouble here, it's probably you.'

Then, for a moment, she was very close.

Soap and mint, warm breath. His arms found her shape in the blackness. He felt her hair brush against his cheek and her voice close by his ear, but then she pulled away. He thought he could still see her, trailing green stars, but it was getting darker now.

'Dropmore,' he managed to say. His tongue felt hot. He could hardly tell if anything was real. The jessamine was tightening its grip, leeching into his brains and stirring up whirling visions, knotting itself around the chambers of his heart and lungs and crushing them. He was going mad. Scarlet was gone. She was away in the river, swimming across to an island quay and climbing the slippery steps up to Midwater. She wasn't in the barrel with him. He'd been dreaming.

'Flyboy,' came a whisper. Dalton knew that voice. It *was* real. It was Sleepwell. 'Flyboy,' it said again, cautious and low. 'Ready?'

Dalton was awake now. He ran a hand across his face. The mad stream of spinning pictures wasn't real. 'Ready,' he said, and he nudged the lid of his barrel open with the tip of his elbow. It popped free.

The first thing he saw when he raised his head carefully over the lip of the barrel was his friend's hair, upstanding like the wild crown of some exotic tree. Then came Sal's spectacles, reflecting a pale glow of moonlight – moonlight that was dropping into some sort of cellar from a window somewhere above them.

'Fly,' Sal said, as the rest of his face rose into view. 'I swear, if I ever go near another flogging barrel – shoot me.'

Dalton looked about him. A wine cellar, illuminated

from three windows high up against its stone ceiling. Their barrels had been left amongst a group of others. Some lay on their sides, branded with strange and unfamiliar names in foreign languages. Against a nearby wall, ranks of dusty bottles lay aging. The air was dry and cool. They were under the Palace of Justice.

Dalton couldn't believe his luck. Instead of having to plot some lunatic way into the lair of his enemies, he'd been brought into its heart in secret and dropped off. He thought for a moment about tapping his lucky Jack and mouthing a familiar 'Vivas Gannet'. But that wasn't him any more. Instead, he rose to standing, his joints thundering pain, and leant against the lip of his barrel until his senses straightened. He took a long, deep draught of the mandrake mixture and forced it down. He waited as his chest opened a little, his heart woke up with a skittering gallop and his breathing steadied. Then he corked the bottle and pocketed it.

Beside him, Sal was out of his barrel and dropping the lid back into place as silently as he could. 'Flyboy,' he whispered. 'Perhaps our luck's changing. Do you know where we are?'

Dalton nodded. 'Let's take a look around,' he said.

He stepped out of his prison and reached inside a final time to scoop up his belongings. He shouldered his bag of poisons and poultices. The silver chain with the key swung between his collar bones, the key tapping his chest like the tip of a cold finger. He took the pistol with the ivory grip from his belt and thumbed the cap back before

273

replacing it. He wondered briefly if he was ready to use it. If he'd ever be ready to use it.

Sal was ahead of him, making slow and careful progress through the cellar. Above them, the Palace of Justice was still and quiet, a sleeping giant. Where was everybody?

Sal turned and beckoned, his boots kicking up little clouds of cellar dust. 'Look at this,' he whispered.

Dalton moved forward, feeling his ankle numb a little as the mandrake potion began to work. Sal was indicating a door with a brass handle. It was open a crack, and from beyond it came the kind of deep warm light thrown by resin lamps. There was more than just a cellar below the staterooms of the Palace, it seemed. The boys paused a step before the door. Sal was flexing his fingers, steadying his breathing. He was frightened; Dalton could see it in his friend's wide eyes and pale lips. Dalton felt it too. The whole insane endeavour was like plucking a final card from a deck, pinning everything on a single outcome. If they were caught now – by Tench or De Bello or one of the Streetwatch – it would mean death. *Hopefully swift*, Dalton thought with a grim smile. He nodded to his friend and Sal hooked a trembling finger around the edge of the door and pulled it open.

Beyond was a furnished room. The same high windows lined its outer wall and three low lamp-flames flapped and guttered on a central table. Flickers and bottles were arranged among decanters and cut-glass serving jugs. Dalton scanned the exits. If this was the place the staff prepared wine for serving, there was surely a way up to the staterooms from here. There were two doors, both open, but neither enough to see what lay behind them.

'Sleepwell,' Dalton whispered.

Sal was staring at the wine, his attention captured. He was biting a thumbnail, blinking rapidly as he thought.

'Sleepwell,' Dalton tried again. 'What is it?'

Sal turned to his friend. He lifted his spectacles and wiped his eyes. 'Who will be drinking this wine, do you think?' he said. 'Later tonight, I mean?'

Dalton shrugged. 'I don't know. Who cares?' There was a knot of fear in his belly. He considered the two doors for a moment and chose one. 'Follow me,' he said, burning with fear. They entered a corridor and found another door, this one open wide. It looked promising. Dalton imagined steps climbing upwards into shadow – a way out of the cellars and into the Palace.

He made his way forward, Sal following behind. What he saw as he approached the room made him falter: a flickering wash of firelight. He slowed as he reached the door, beset by doubt. A lit fire meant people.

For a moment, the room seemed empty and he stepped in. Then his blood turned to iron and he froze.

THIRTY-FOUR

'D alton Fly, at last!' said a voice.

A familiar, battered and slurred voice. A voice that made Dalton's heart drop like a bucket down a well.

'I've been expecting you,' Pallis Tench continued, steepling his fingers and leering over them at the two terrified poison boys. He was sitting in a high-backed chair with carved armrests, legs thrown out in front of him, head tipped so he could stare at them down what was left of his nose. A fire burnt in a stone hearth beside him, and on a table within easy reach stood his pitcher of fever-tea and a flicker. His spoons and sugar were there, too, and a low candle for dissolving and mixing. He'd been taking a drink, waiting for them.

The last time Dalton had seen Tench had been in the half-light of a dead boy's bedroom at St Eleanor's school. He'd been shocking enough to look on then; now, in the sharp yellow light of the lamp that blazed on the table beside his drink, he was hideous.

'And you've brought your friend with the hair,' Tench went on, licking his lips and rising from his chair. His gnarled face seemed to shudder and tremble when he moved, the ploughed lines of scar tissue reflecting the firelight oddly.

Dalton flinched. This was impossible. How did Tench know they were coming? Sal nudged Dalton and held his hands open, palms up, his face blanched with fear. He didn't need to speak; his question was the same. They had entered Midwater in secret. No one could possibly know precisely where they would be and when – could they?

It was Sal who got there quicker, his eyes suddenly widening. 'The map,' he said softly. It took a moment for Dalton to catch up. His thinking was muddled and muddy, slowed by jessamine and exhaustion – but he got there in a tumble of mental connections. The map had gone missing last night. It hadn't been an accident or carelessness or coincidence. Someone had stolen it – someone in the room where they had all slept. And whoever had taken the map had done it for Tench. The conversation at the gates, Griffin's horse and cart adjusting its route – it was all set up. They hadn't been lucky, getting dropped off in the cellars beneath the Palace; they'd been tricked. They'd walked into a trap.

And that meant one of his companions was working for the other side.

How else could Tench know where and when to expect them?

'I realised I could search the city for you,' Tench said, pulling from the inside pocket of his jacket the map and unfolding it casually, 'or I could wait for you to come to me.'

There it was in his hands, the very document they had stolen from him. A directionless fury rose in Dalton's belly, broiling and burning. Someone had betrayed them.

Tench sensed his anger and grinned. 'No, I won't be telling you who's been helping me out,' he said, 'but it was simple, really –' and here he stepped back and fed the map slowly into the fire, tipping and rotating it to ensure the flames caught – 'all I had to do was add the name of my informant to the list in black and wait for you to collect them.'

Dalton felt an uneasy fear bristle at the top of his shoulders. The list of names had been doctored. Dropmore, Knox, Eppington, Eden, Honeycut . . . It had been cleverly done. And whoever the spy was had been an impressive actor. A cheat, a beguiler, a trickster – a black-hearted, greedy, selfish—

'Who was it?' Sal said. His voice was small and cold; he spoke as much to himself as anyone else. Dalton stared at Tench, trying to deal with the hammer-blow of this betrayal. *Honeycut,* he found himself thinking. *Honeycut, with his painted nails and expensive jewellery and his lackbrain pet names for Scarlet. It had to be him.*

Tench wiped his hands and watched the remainder of the map curl and blacken in the hearth. 'You have something I am going to take from you, poison boy,' Tench said to the flames. Then he held out a hand, regarding Dalton with empty eyes. 'You've been keeping yourself alive with a clever little potion. My special concoction should have killed you within hours. You're strong – I'll give you that. But I want your antidote. I'm a collector of clever little potions, poison boy. A fan of them. It's my specialism. My line of work.'

Dalton sneered, sick to bitterness of being tricked. Sick with running, hiding, escaping, evading – sick with sticking to the shadows. It curdled in him. 'Get flogged,' he said.

Tench issued a short laugh. He drew a pistol, a repeater with a long muzzle, and raised it slowly. 'Do it,' he said, 'or I shoot your friend.' And he pointed it at the space between Sal's terrified eyes.

Dalton clenched his fists. He couldn't reach for his buckle-box pistol in time. And, even if he could, was he brave and foolish enough to use it? Some childish instinct in him was nearly strong enough to make him lift a hand and tap the lucky Jack in his jacket pocket. But that was a comfort for children and fools. His options had curled themselves up into ash like the burnt map. Tench had him stagged. Slowly, he raised an unsteady hand. Tench's one good eye followed his movement. Dalton put his hand into his coat pocket. Tench thumbed back the catch on the cannon barrel with a steely grin. Sal drew in a thin and ragged breath, wheezing. Out came the bottle of antidote. Tench lowered the pistol.

'Here,' Dalton said through his teeth and placed it on the table beside the pitcher of fever-tea, just a little way from where Tench stood with his back to the fire. That was all he could do. And yet, by placing it there, a stride away from the man . . . perhaps there was a chance . . .

Dalton Fly had never kicked someone in the face before. Tench had to stoop to reach the bottle and, as he did so, his broken features gleamed with greed. For just a moment, his merciless concentration slackened. The pistol wasn't aimed at Sal now. Dalton brought his leg up with as fierce a speed as he could, and struck Tench hard.

There was a dull splitting sound: the sound of the big man's nose breaking. He roared and fell, and his pistol slipped from his grip. He knocked the table over and his spoons and sugar scattered.

Then there was a mad whirl of movement. Dalton hurled himself on to Tench's back and pummelled him wildly, fists hammering his head and neck. Despite his attacker, Tench raised himself up, a furious giant of an opponent, and threw Dalton clear of him. Dalton crashed against a chair and struck his head against the frame. Tench beat Sal across the face with a fearsome fist and the poison boy went down.

For a moment, Tench seemed to be concerned with his

lost weapon and stooped to seek it out. Dalton scrambled to yank the little silver pistol from his belt. His hot and trembling hands kept slipping on the smooth ivory grip and his head spun. Stupidly, he found he was holding it in his left hand – but he raised it and fired nevertheless.

The pistol still worked, even after years dormant in a buckle box. He knew that immediately because a cloud of spray, like a red balloon, burst from Tench's shoulder. The hulking man bellowed and fell to his knees, stunned by the jolt of the bullet. There was a ragged hole torn in his coat. A black circle pumped blood, dark like lantern oil.

Tench hurled a table at Dalton with a guttural roar and the heavy wooden top clattered into his knees, skinning them. A lantern tipped over, splashing hot oil. In a moment, Tench was above him and kicking him mercilessly, throwing his body into repeated, furious, aimless blows. Dalton buried his head in his hands.

Sal must have done something to stop Tench, for the big man dropped again, his face down close to Dalton's, his breath hot and animal, his breathing wild. He'd been struck by something across the back of the head.

Tench held Dalton's face in the huge palm of a single hand and squeezed, his fingers finding the points of weakness – the eyeballs, the mouth. Dalton bit down as hard as he could. Skin broke. It smelt as if blood was everywhere, its harsh iron stench and its stickiness on everything. Dalton could taste it again: a sharp cloying nastiness at the back of his throat, just like the night Bennie Jinks got gutted. Tench pulled back with a wounded roar. Dalton couldn't see for a moment. Then, as he struggled to open his bruised eyelids, he was struck in the face twice with violent and precise punches.

There was a moment of strange half silence in which only the sound of a silver plate spinning lazily to a stop could be heard. That, and Pallis Tench's breathing, tearing and flapping like a flag in a storm. Dalton opened his eyes. Tench dominated the room, a great bleeding beast, rising up to its full height, its monstrous face a mask of blood. In his hand was the bottle of antidote.

'Without this,' he said, 'you die nasty.' He breathed hard, his chest rising and falling, sweat drenching his shirt. He winced with pain. His coat was black with blood. He recovered his flicker and took a deep swig of fever-tea, then smacked his broken lips. 'And tonight, kid,' he continued with a twisted smile, 'you're going to die nasty.'

That was the last thing Dalton remembered before Tench started kicking him again.

THIRTY-FIVE

Someone was shaking him awake. Dalton tried to open his eyes. One of them was too swollen, but the other seemed to respond. He became aware of the room around him again: the dying warmth of the fire, its light flickering around the edges of his vision, blurring with the spinning green he saw there permanently now. He was on his back. Underneath him he could feel his shoulder bag, its contents crushed. And there was something leaning over him – something grotesque. It took a confusing moment to place it. He was looking through his one good eye at a filthy stuffed toy being waved in his face. It was Hoppy, the blind champion of the exploited.

'Hey, Your High-Mightiness,' said Luke. 'You still alive?' She withdrew the rabbit with a shrug. 'He wanted to say hello,' she explained.

Dalton couldn't help but smile. His lip spilt again as he did so and he groaned as it bled freely; but he'd never been so relieved to see one of his friends. He struggled up on to his elbows, leaning there for a moment and waiting for the dizziness to subside.

Luke looked unholy – a witch dipped in tar. Only her blinking eyes weren't black. Her skin, her clothes, the skewed bunches of her hair were all caked in soot. Her teeth and tongue were grey with chimney grit when she grinned.

'Scut!' Dalton swore. 'What happened to you?'

Luke ran a hand across Dalton's forehead, pushing his matted hair clear of a swollen and bloody bruise. She winced as she examined it. 'I was going to ask you the same question,' she said.

'Tench was waiting for us,' Dalton said. 'He knew we were coming. Someone betrayed us. And he's got my antidote.'

Luke paused a moment, taking in the news. 'Kite!' she said simply, and blinked her big eyes in her soot-black face. 'Who?'

Dalton shrugged and groaned, a fist of pain in his back.

'And he took the antidote?' Luke said. 'The green stuff Sal gave you, right?' She bit her lip. 'I'm guessing that's bad.'

Dalton took a moment to assess his body. His lungs felt

like a pair of burst balloons; his ribs, more bruise than bone. His throat was tight. He couldn't see properly, even through the eye that would open. And the room shifted and spun, blurring and flexing as if it were an image in a shattered mirror.

'It's bad,' he confirmed. 'I think I'm going to die here.' Strangely, it felt almost comical. There was nothing left to do but laugh.

Luke raised a stern eyebrow. 'No, you're not, Your Most Worshipfulness. I'm going to get you out.'

'Where's Sal?' Dalton said, trying to sit up.

'I'll explain later. Let's get moving.'

Dalton shook his head. 'Tench locked me in.' It took a moment for his muddled thinking to clarify. Luke was covered in soot. 'No . . .' he exclaimed. 'Not the flogging chimneys! Please.'

She held out both hands, encouraging him to his feet. 'You'll love it,' she said. 'Besides, Your Dukeness, have you any better ideas?'

She was lithe and speedy. After ducking beneath the fireplace, she lifted herself upward with nothing but a whispered scuff of her boots on the chimney's interior wall. Dalton was a dizzy and clattering buffoon by comparison. He lifted himself clear of the grate on which the map had been burnt, and scrambled partway into the sooty blackness before slipping and pitching back down into warm ash.

How long had he been unconscious? he wondered,

rubbing the dirt from his hands. The logs had burnt very low. Tench must have kicked his lights out and left him for a number of hours. Did that make it midnight? Was De Bello already Duke?

Above Dalton, Luke's disembodied voice echoed from the dark column. 'Try again,' she whispered. 'Feel for my feet. My toes are on the climbing stones; that's where your hands should be. When you're in fully, brace yourself against the inside with your back. The higher you get, the easier it is. You'll be able to rest your ankle. You won't fall.'

Dalton heaved and sweated and cursed his way upward until he was a couple of metres above the fireplace. The chimney was thin. A dry, gritty ash was everywhere and within moments Dalton's clothes and hair and eyes were thick with it. But it was possible, he soon discovered, to wedge both feet on the lip of a climbing stone and lean against his bag on the chimney wall, holding himself upright.

He began to climb, feeling for Luke's boots above him and listening to her whispered instructions. The close, dry darkness was full of horrors. Nameless things brushed against his cheeks; insects or curtains of soot seemed to creep upon his neck.

'Your Excellency,' Luke said quietly, her face down-turned in the foul blackness.

Dalton manoeuvred himself into a contorted resting place, his legs trembling with exertion and his ankle ringing aloud in pain. 'What?'

'Above us here,' she said, 'we reach a ground-floor

room. Can you see the light?'

Dalton couldn't see anything. He'd been climbing blind, his good eye squeezed shut against imagined spiders, flies and countless other fantasies and spinning visions. It was becoming difficult to separate reality from the sequence of contorted pictures that fizzed in the green lights. 'I see it,' Dalton lied, embarrassed.

Luke laughed. 'It's difficult,' she said. 'But you can feel the change of air on your face when you pass a vent and then open your eyes, as long as you look downwards and not up.' She shifted position and her voice dropped. 'There's a vent just above us, and this one will take us out into one of the staterooms.'

They made slow progress upwards. Then there was a faint stirring of the air and the smell of flowers. Luke had gone, he realised, dropped silently through a vent and into a room somewhere nearby. With his eyes closed, Dalton found it almost impossible to feel for the passageway which would allow him to follow.

Then her voice came again, unnervingly close, like an unexpected whisper in his ear. 'When you're in the room,' she said slowly, 'move with care. This ash won't fall from you unless you jump or stamp or run.'

'Luke,' said Dalton through a grimace, 'I won't be doing any running any time soon.' As he whispered into the pitch, his hands located a short horizontal passageway. It wasn't a climbing stone, he realised with relief. It was a way out.

'Pull yourself through,' Luke said.

Dalton emerged as elegantly as he'd gone in, dropping into the mouth of a huge stone fireplace, his arse in the air, head and shoulders in the iron grate; kindling scratching his battered face. Luke hauled him up. His bag had torn against the hot stones and Sal's collection of poisons lay scattered at his feet.

For a moment he had to lean against the blackened stone of the fireplace and wait for his senses to return. The room spun so crazily it was impossible to register – but gradually it slowed and steadied: a plushly decorated place, with wall hangings, a desk in dark wood, lounging chairs and a fine deep-red rug under his boots. He gulped the scented air. A full-length window was open and a long dark curtain caught the light night-wind and undulated slowly. The scent of jasmine was drifting in from outside.

Dalton swallowed hard. He was never going in a chimney again, he decided. That had been horrible. He found a sudden new respect for Luke's bravery and calm. 'How did you find me?' he said eventually, leaning over, his palms on his skinned kneecaps.

'Sal,' she replied. 'He saw Tench lock you in. He was all for breaking the door down with an antique chair. Then we turned up.'

'You found a way in, then. How was the river?'

Luke rolled her eyes and plucked at her filthy clothes. *Just wonderful*, her expression said.

Dalton managed a smile, his teeth black with grime. 'Where's Sal now? And the others?'

'Edward and Scarlet went looking for the debating

chamber. Isis went with them. The Palace is empty. I don't know what time it is, but the senate aren't here yet. I forgot to listen for the church bells.'

Dalton thought for a moment. Which were closest? Angels, across the river, was a district full of churches. And Downholland. Outside, they'd be able to hear the bells. With that and the position of the moon, they could soon work out how much time they had left. Perhaps all was not lost. Yet.

'Edward said he'd meet us out in the gardens. That's where Sal will be waiting. There are some big white glass doors that open out on to the lawn just here,' Luke continued, indicating the curtains. 'Across the gardens, we can access the main ground-floor rooms. And from there, with luck, the debating chamber.'

'You seem to know your way around.'

'I've been searching for a way to get you out. I used this fireplace. All the rooms along here are private quarters, by the looks of things.'

Dalton took a moment to study his surroundings again. She was right. They were in a suite of rooms; an open door at the far side led to a bedroom, a heavy wardrobe standing next to an unmade bed. The desk across from them had recently been used; scattered papers littered its top. There was a metal pitcher and a flicker. A jacket hung loosely from the back of the chair. Dalton blinked. Pitcher; flicker; jacket.

'Yeah,' Luke said, following his gaze with a scowl. 'A plush little palace for a pampered prince, eh? If the money spent in here on furnishings alone was divided amongst the poor—'

'This is Pallis Tench's room,' Dalton cut in. He took a few unsteady steps across the carpet to check the jacket. There was a ragged little bullet hole in the left shoulder, circled with dried blood. Tench's jacket. A sudden lurch of terror made his head spin. He had to regain his balance again by placing both hands on the desk. Tench could be nearby. Asleep next door. Or hiding.

'There's no one here, Your Frightendness,' Luke whispered with a reassuring smile. 'I checked before I came down.'

Dalton released a sigh of relief, scanning the room with his one good eye. She was right: the rooms looked as if they had been left some time ago. There had been no sign of a fire in the grate. The ink on the papers was long dry, and the fever-tea had hardened and crystallised along the rim of Tench's flicker . . .

'The fever-tea,' Dalton said, and a dark and terrible possibility blossomed suddenly. Tench had a hip flask. Dalton had seen it the night he'd been cut: the big man had flicked back the lid and swallowed from it before lunging forward with that terrible dipped blade winking in the moonlight. If Tench was a fever-tea addict – and everything Dalton had seen suggested that he was – a hip flask wouldn't be enough to get him through until dawn. After all, he'd seen Oscar enslaved to this stuff all his life. He knew how much, how often and how strong men like Tench needed their mix. He'd be back to refill his flask.

Dalton reached out for the pitcher. It was broad bottomed but thinned quickly to a delicate neck with a lid and lever. Dalton lifted it. Heavy. Nearly full. He sniffed the lid. There was the scent of his childhood; the aniseed smell of pollen smugglers and bandits smoking from china pipes in the kitchen below his bedroom long into the night. The brawling and shouting; the rattle of coughing laughter.

This particular dose of fever-tea was a strong one. If Dalton knew anything, he knew this: Pallis Tench would be drinking from this pitcher tonight.

'Luke,' said Dalton quietly, indicating the fireplace. 'Get me my bag.'

THIRTY-SIX

From the garden outside Tench's room, there was a good view of the Palace square. The garden was walled, and a flight of steep steps gave access to a little walkway along the top of the wall. From there, Dalton watched the senators and their personal assistants arrive. The night air was still and the tolling of church bells drifted over from the city as the coaches drew in. It was eleven. Carriage after carriage emerged at the far side of the square and hissed across it on their iron-rimmed wheels.

First to arrive, Dalton saw, was Gabriel Applefell, who paused at the top step of his carriage to look out across the streets and gardens of Midwater before he descended. The tall man in the cape was tasting the night air. It was an important night for the principal senator, a night which held difficult work for him.

Next came Senator Dropmore. She moved swiftly, shutting the door of her carriage behind her, patting the flanks of her horses and crossing the remainder of the square with strong, deliberate strides. Her riding coat flapped behind her as a whirling eddy of night air gathered it up. She looked like Scarlet, Dalton thought. *Pick a card, poison boy*, said a voice near his ear. He blinked away the unnerving pictures that swirled in his imaginings and wished he had a little of his antidote with him. He'd checked Tench's room without expecting to find anything, and he'd been right. The visions and dreams were gathering more feverishly now. His throat felt tight and sore, as if he were wearing some sort of leash.

More carriages pulled up, dropped off their passengers, then pulled around in a circle to make the journey back along the square to the gates and the bridge. A fat man with a brace of scurrying servants made his way up the steps. A senator with a broad-brimmed hat, his assistants bearing bags of documents and papers, followed. A man with two sleek greyhounds arrived and they scampered and skittered at his heels. Then came an old gentleman, stooped and shuffling, a younger woman with short cropped hair, tall and upright and holding his arm, guiding him up past the stone lions with the amber-coloured eyes.

'A procession of the city's rich,' Luke scoffed from her hiding place along the wall from Dalton.

Dalton found it hard to respond. He hadn't much left in the way of ordered thinking. In fact, he was having trouble staying in control of his breathing. And he was tired: nauseous and dizzy with fatigue. He tried to feel for the collar about his neck — the cold iron thumb pressed on his Adam's apple. *Tonight, you're going to die ugly.* Dalton started coughing. *Pick a card, poison boy,* someone said.

He was going to be sick.

'Hey,' Luke said. 'What's wrong?'

Someone was dragging him across the lawn. Sal was talking. Then Dalton found himself on his back beneath a stand of trees. The moon, a yellow circle halved, seemed to be darting among the leaves like a lantern pitching on the end of a rope. But then he realised it was the breeze stirring the branches. A night bird was calling. Dogs were barking. Another street fight had broken out somewhere in the Lower Circle; pistol fire rattled and clapped. Sleepwell was crouching next to him, bent over and grinding two stones together.

'Kite almighty, Flyboy!' Sal said as he saw his friend wake. 'You gave me a scare back there. But you're going to be all right. I'm working a little bit of magic for you here . . .' Sal returned to his work, talking quickly, fuelled by fear and desperation. 'This is Tench's garden. It's full of stuff: oleander, plenty of digitalis, jimson weed, belladonna — probably the berries that ghosted Jinks.'

He worked the stones together. He was making something, grinding leaves and stems. It smelt sharp and nasty. Sal leant in close and examined it, dipped the tip of his little finger in, tasted, grimaced and heaved, added something and resumed his work. 'That's disgusting,' he said, wiping his mouth with the back of his hand. 'But it should work. I've checked your ankle, by the way.' He looked up, breathing hard. 'Terrible. I've put on a poultice. You owe me.'

Dalton felt the skin around his neck. There was blood there, sticky and drying. He must have been scrabbling at his imaginary leash with his fingernails. The jessamine had been tightening its grip, slowly squeezing the sense of out him; but his breathing was more regular now. His vision was clear and sharp. 'I feel better,' he managed, though his voice sounded twisted and broken.

Sal nodded. 'You will,' he said. 'I've given you some jimson and a bit of mandrake. This place is as good as Oscar's hospital, if you know what to look for.'

'Where's Luke?' Dalton began, trying to work out what had happened.

'Keeping watch, up on the wall,' Sal said. 'Scarlet and Edward said they'd meet us here.'

'I was watching the carriages come in,' Dalton remembered. A thought jolted him upright. 'What time is it?'

Sal continued grinding, sweat breaking on his forehead and steaming his glasses. 'I've just heard the bell for the half hour from Downholland church,' he said. 'We haven't got long until midnight.' He tested his mixture again and spat it out. 'If we're going to do anything, Flyboy,' he said through a grimace, 'we need to do it now. Eat this.' He offered up a sticky green glue of mashed leaves. It looked like the pummelled dreck of some unfortunate animal.

Dalton knew better than to ask what it was, or to negotiate. His ankle was glowing with intense pain – deeper than before, as if his bones were melting. He knew he was going to die without medicine, knew it with a cold calm certainty, and yet fear seemed beyond him now. He scooped the mixture up with a cupped hand and pressed it into his mouth, chewing hard, trying not to be sick. When he swallowed, a great bitter ball dropped into his gullet like a stone. It was vile.

It seemed to open up his veins and rush through his blood. He could breathe deep and hard until his lungs prickled with energy. Fatigue seemed to drop away.

'How is it?' said Sal, watching his friend. 'Nice?'

'Wet yourself,' said Dalton.

Then a noise sent a flurry of fear up his back. His scalp ran with sweat and his instincts were suddenly sharp. There was someone in the garden with them. Sal froze. Dalton shifted position, squinting through the undergrowth. There was a small, slight figure picking its way across the lawns. Dalton felt his mouth fall open.

It was Isis Holt.

Perhaps it was Sal's mixture that had fired his senses into life once more; perhaps it was just the fact that he could reason like a normal person again at last. But he knew, all of a sudden, that it had been Isis Holt who'd stolen the map, Isis Holt who'd guided them into the jaws of Pallis Tench and left them there to die, Isis flogging Holt that was finding a way out of trouble before it all exploded.

'Scut and feathers!' Dalton swore. He made it to standing and moved forward. The black look on his face must have made his feelings plain.

Sal cocked his head. 'Fly?' he said, his eyes narrowing. 'What's wrong?'

'It was him,' Dalton said, wincing against the pain in his ankle and breaking into a run through the whipping branches of the undergrowth and out on to the moonlit lawn.

The boy jumped, startled at Dalton's sudden appearance. Then he grinned and raised his eyebrows in relief. 'Dalton,' he said, his voice a thin tremble. 'Edward and Scarlet are on their way. We've found the debating chamber.' He was speaking quickly, his fists tight balls against his thighs. 'You'll need to be quick. There's less than half an hour before midnight. Follow me. I'll show you.' He half turned, back towards the silhouette of the main building, expecting Dalton to follow.

Dalton held his ground, watching the fair-haired boy. Holt was an impressive actor, that much was clear. But, despite the performance, Dalton knew he had it right. Holt was the only one who could have taken the map that night. Light on his feet, slippery, silent. A sudden burst of colourful memory surfaced. De Bello and Tench, the night they'd first seen them on Midwater, poring over the map

297

in the Senate Hall. De Bello had read out the list of names. 'Dropmore, Knox, Eden, Eppington, Honeycut,' he'd said. Then there'd been a pause and Tench had added, 'And, of course, our friend Holt.'

Dalton rubbed his eyes, thinking. Holt's name was on that list as a back-up plan. A spy and a safety device in one. If the map was ever lost or stolen, Tench would know and Holt could simply bring the thieves to him. It was clever, very clever.

'Our friend Holt,' Dalton said in a low, calm voice. It was a strange relief just to speak it aloud.

Holt smiled, though his eyes had gone glassy now. Sal emerged from the bushes and on to the lawn. Holt raised a hand. 'Sal,' he said. 'I was just saying—'

'Spare yourself the bother, Holt,' Dalton said, a dark bitterness under his tongue. 'You're working for De Bello, right? You stole the map back. You told him how we were getting on to Midwater tonight. And then it was just a case of the guards on the gate re-directing the cart. You made sure we were taken right into the cellars. You arranged for them to drop us there. That's why Tench was waiting for us.'

'I don't know what you're talking about,' said Isis Holt, running a finger under his shirt collar.

'You're no sentaway,' Dalton said. 'You're an actor. How much did they offer you, Holt?'

Isis tried to smile. His face slackened and he licked his lips. He looked about him for a moment, assessing the contours of the dark bushes and trees. He sighed. The Isis Holt Dalton knew, the quiet boy, the shy creature, frightened of everything, suddenly slipped away, as if the person before them had shrugged off a coat and let it fall at his feet.

'You got me,' he said, and shrugged. 'What can I say? I needed the bone.' He opened out his hands, palms upward, and offered them a confident smile. 'See it from my point of view,' he said. 'I thought you were just some jumped-up dreckwit out to cause trouble. That's the story they told me.' He looked out across the lawns to the garden wall. The night breeze ruffled his hair. He was very different now: older – strong and bold. 'Turns out you're not,' he finished. He winked. 'Good luck, Flyboy,' he said. 'And you, Sleepwell.'

And, with that, he began a slow walk across the grass towards the wall where Luke was keeping watch. He had his hands in his pockets. Dalton watched him go. He felt hollowed out – empty and cheated.

'How did you know?' said Sal.

Dalton sighed. 'I didn't,' he said. 'Not really.' He looked up at the moon. Little flags of ragged cloud flitted across its thin face. 'We haven't got much time,' he said.

Sal pulled his shoulder bag on and waved at Luke. She raised a hand in return and began to move along the walkway back to the steps and down to the lawn.

Then Dalton saw something move inside the ground-floor rooms of the Palace.

A broad black bulk against the burning lights of Tench's quarters, a figure at the desk, beyond the desk now, crossing to the doors. Dalton felt his heart charge and his stomach shudder. He couldn't move. In a moment, Tench was out and on to the lawn, his pistol raised and his face a scrambled mask of fury.

'Poison boy!' he bellowed. His voice was like the wounded roar of some terrible animal. 'Poison boy!' It came again, the big man striding across the lawn. His arm was like iron, straight and true and unshakable. The pistol was cocked. Tench's finger was white on the trigger.

'Piss and daggers!' said Sal.

Tench pointed the pistol at Dalton's chest, and fired.

THIRTY-SEVEN

There was a crack and a cloud of shotpowder. The air fizzed. Dalton was struck, thrown backwards – swept off his feet and dumped on to the grass. Fear and shock disorientated him. He couldn't breathe. The stink of the hot bullet prickled at his eyes and nose. Burnt paper; scorched skin. Someone – Luke or Sal or both – was screaming. Hoarse, sobbing cries.

Tench was over him, and Dalton stared, dumbfounded, as he raised the gun again. The huge, towering monster was going to finish the job. Two shots in a big repeater pistol like that one – and this shot would spill the brains from his skull.

'You little bastard,' Tench growled through a grotesque smile. 'I'll . . .'

But his sentence was never finished.

His face washed suddenly pale and he shuddered, gripping his stomach. 'Kite!' he cursed, and doubled over. His eyes widened as a wave of pain surged up from his belly. He looked shocked, as if slapped. His good eye watered. 'Kite!' he said again.

He looked at Dalton and, in the moonlight, Dalton saw the monster's mind working through the glaze of that one eye. Then Tench rocked for a moment, and straightened with a vicious scream. 'You little bastard!' he bawled, his voice as shattered and broken as his face. He cocked the pistol with a trembling thumb, his good eye fiery black with desperate determination. Then his legs wouldn't hold him and he fell to his knees across Dalton's chest.

Dalton's heart and stomach heaved. Tench squatted right over him, pushing the muzzle of the pistol into the space between his eyebrows. His breath was a foul, sugary glue. He'd been drinking his fever-tea. Dalton could see each rut and track torn by the teeth of the dogs across Tench's face. He closed his eyes, waiting to die, wincing as Tench ground the pistol against his forehead.

Then the belladonna came to finish Tench: the poison Dalton had dropped into the fever-tea less than an hour earlier. It had been a ferocious dose, five times what Bennie Jinks had suffered. The big man uttered a strangled shout and coughed a great black gout of blood, just as that little boy had. His arms weakened and the pistol dropped from his grip. Tench twitched oddly and fell on to his side, freeing the crushed poison boy. He gave another hollow shout and a rictus wrenched at his muscles. His mouth foamed red and black. He writhed on the grass, a blurred shape jerking and kicking.

Dalton wiped his eyes clear of tears and began to push himself away. Somehow, he knew, he'd been shot – but he wasn't dead. He could see the torn hole in his jacket, a bullet hole just over his heart. He could smell the sharp heat of it. But there was no blood. His heart was still drumming and galloping with terror. It made no sense.

Pallis Tench seemed to be fighting himself now, trying to pull his own clothes off, straining at them with knotted fingers. Even in the distorting moonlight, Dalton could see his face turning blue, one big purple bruise as his veins exploded.

Dalton pushed himself further clear of the dying man. Sal was at his side now, and Luke; Sal trying not to cry, Luke's black face streaked with shocked tears. It was impossible to ignore the twitching of the dying man on the grass, his insides coming out in coughs, compelling and terrible.

The three friends cowered together, their breathing unified in ragged gasps as they watched Tench finally fall still and close his one good eye for the last time. His fingers were great haggard talons. His spine was frozen in an arch. His face was a slick of blood.

Luke turned her attention to Dalton. 'He shot you,' she said, blinking. Her fingers found the bullet's entry hole and she stared in wonder at it. 'So, are Dukes unkillable or something?'

Dalton propped himself up. He pushed a hand under his jacket, pressed it against his heart and held it there. He could feel the thud of his body working. He brought his hand out and examined it. It came out dry.

Sal stared at him. 'Impossible,' he whispered.

Then Dalton felt for his jacket pocket; the inside pocket. *The pack of playing cards*, he thought suddenly. He'd crammed them there in the dark as his barrel crossed the bridge on the back of Griffin's cart. They'd become entangled with the torn lining of his jacket and he pulled them free. There was the crushed pellet of the pistol bullet, embedded in the playing cards like a little metal eyeball. The cards were smashed and blackened, a perfect hole punched in each.

'Kite almighty,' Sal said with a low whistle.

Dalton fanned them and the bullet fell out, still hot. Every card had been punctured: the first twenty or so almost obliterated by the impact of the bullet, the others that followed in various stages of blackened damage. The final few, those that had slowed its progress to a stop, were almost pristine apart from a small, perfectly circular hole with burnt edges the size of a sooty fingerprint. Then there was the final card in the pack – the one at the bottom. It looked older than the rest – considerably more dog-eared. But it was entirely untouched by Tench's bullet.

'It's a good job there are fifty-two cards in a pack, ohfortunate-one,' Luke said, a grin of wonder splitting her face. 'Any less, and you'd be a dead boy.'

'What's the last card?' Sal asked. Dalton looked at the pattern on its reverse side, the pattern that had been so familiar to him as a child: interwoven nets of ivy leaves and stems. He flipped it.

The access to the Palace of Justice was easy enough from the gardens. Dalton and Sal pulled themselves up to the broad window ledge and slipped in. Sal leant out and dropped a hand down to Luke, hauling her up after him.

They were in a wide corridor, lined down its centre with a carpet of red, trimmed with gold. The walls were richly decorated in a tangle of deep green. Oil paintings hung high in the shadows; half faces and pale eyes peered down at them. Display cases in dark polished wood were illuminated in stripes by bright bars of moon. At each window, an urn stood, tumbling with waxy-leaved plants and scrambling ivy.

Luke's dark scowl seemed a permanent fixture now, but her fury had spent itself. Her soot-black face was creased with exhaustion. 'Pig-dogs,' was all she could manage, glowering darkly at the wealth around her.

'Look!' said Sal with a smile, nodding down the corridor.

Edward Honeycut, a hand raised in greeting, was picking his way towards them. At his shoulder was Scarlet Dropmore, a broad smile illuminating her features. The two of them were still wet, their clothes clinging to them and streaked in river dreck. Edward's hair had clotted in muddy bunches. Scarlet's boots studded a wet pattern on the floor.

Scarlet hugged Luke and Sal in turn, tears of relief in her eyes. Then she nodded at Dalton, twisting her fingers together, rotating her ring with the stone. 'Hello,' she said, frowning at his ash-blackened appearance. Then her eyes widened as she saw the ragged bullet hole in his jacket. 'Have you been shot?' she said. She wasn't entirely serious. There was a little light dancing in her eyes and the start of a smile.

'Sort of,' Dalton said. 'Pallis Tench is dead.'

Scarlet fell silent, her face pale. 'Kite!' she whispered. 'Are you all right?' She cleared her throat, raised her gaze to the rest of the group. 'Is everyone all right?'

'Just great,' Luke said, and jerked a dirty thumb in Dalton's direction. 'His Holiness is bulletproof.'

Sal grinned. Scarlet swallowed back a laugh. Dalton, too, felt a sudden rush of relief, of companionship. For a fleeting moment at least, it seemed as if anything were possible. He had his friends around him.

'We need to get moving,' Edward said, watching the shadows. 'We've found the debating chamber but the place is crawling with Streetwatch and senators. Kite knows how we'll get in.'

'Which way?' Dalton said.

Edward cocked his head back the way they had come. The corridor made a sharp turn into the darkness of the building. Little wall-mounted resin lamps cast weak pools of golden light, penetrating only the edges of the gloom. 'That way,' he said. He regarded Dalton briefly. 'We lost the kid – Holt. Seen him?'

Dalton swallowed hard. 'Yes,' he said. 'But he's not important now.'

There was a silence. Edward looked from Dalton to Sal, then scratched the stubble on his chin. 'Care to elaborate?' he said, his forehead creased.

'Some other time,' Dalton said. 'We need to get going.'

The group padded cautiously forward, Edward ahead, Dalton at his heels. Sal's foul paste seemed to have revived him a little. His vision had straightened itself, lost the buckle and blur of before. The green stars had gone.

They made steady progress deeper into the mazy heart of the Palace. At the top of a broad sweep of stairs, the corridor ended at a pair of decorated wooden doors with gleaming brass handles. Two lamps either side hissed on their high brackets.

'Through here,' Edward said, his voice low, 'is an antechamber. Then, beyond it, the debating chamber.'

'How many Streetwatch?' Sal said.

Scarlet shrugged. 'Hard to say. They were all gathering half an hour ago; there was a big meeting. They were getting their positions assigned.'

Dalton thought for a moment. 'So, is there another way in?'

Edward nodded, and spoke at a whisper. 'The debating chamber is huge; it drops down in levels, all lined with seats. There are four ways in, one on each wall of the

307

room. They all have antechambers,' he indicated the door before them, 'like waiting rooms. There's robes and ceremonial stuff.'

'Were the Streetwatch drinking?' Sal asked, propping his glasses up and rubbing his eyes.

'What?' Edward asked. He regarded Sal with a bemused expression, almost sympathetic. *The kid with the hair has lost the plot*, his eyes said.

Sal said, 'Were they drinking? I figured they'd be drinking.'

Luke was at the keyhole, crouched. 'Citizens,' she said quietly. 'There's someone in this room.'

'Who?' said Dalton.

She gave Dalton a blank look. 'You expect me to know these people, Your Mightiness?'

Dalton checked the corridor they'd passed along. *No sign of Streetwatch out here*. 'Edward,' he said. 'You and Scarlet go to the next entrance. Take Luke. Me and Sal will try and get past –' he placed a fingertip lightly on the door – 'whoever that is.'

Edward bit his lip. He didn't look convinced.

'We haven't much time' Dalton said. 'If we stick together and they find us – they find us all.'

Edward unfolded his arms. 'I can be round at the next door in a few minutes,' he said with a curt nod. 'If we're split up, we all rush the chamber before the twelfth bell.'

'That's the plan, fat-pockets?' Luke said, arching an eyebrow. 'We rush the chamber before the twelfth bell? And say what, exactly?' She grinned. '"Hold your horses, citizens; we've got some news"?'

Scarlet laughed. 'Anything but that,' she said.

Dalton shrugged. He'd never thought they'd get this far. And, consequently, he'd never considered what the final moments might look like. He wished he'd rehearsed some booming speech befitting a Duke, all dignified and clever.

'I'll think of something,' he said.

Scarlet raised a hand – a gesture of farewell. 'Don't get shot again, poison boy,' she said. And then she was gone, moving swiftly into the shadows with Edward and Luke.

Dalton turned to Sal. 'Ready?' he said.

Sal Sleepwell nodded.

THIRTY-EIGHT

They had no time for gentle and silent any more. A strange, fearless strength was hardening in Dalton now. Isis Holt's betrayal hadn't killed him. Pallis Tench couldn't kill him. Jessamine couldn't kill him. There was only a matter of minutes until midnight and, somewhere below them, the senators would be listening to Gabriel Applefell's opening remarks.

Dalton smashed the door open with the heel of his boot. It swung crazily on its shattered hinges. His ankle roared in pain but he could live with it. He and Sal strode in, ready to take on a baying crowd of Streetwatch guards intent on tearing two foolish p-boys limb from limb. But there was only one figure in the room.

It was a young man, curiously dressed. He turned, alarm on his face. Doone De Bello. And he was wearing the ceremonial robes of state. He was waiting, dressed in the robes of the Duke of Highlions, in a wood-panelled antechamber – waiting for his name to be announced by the senators somewhere beyond and below them in the chamber. In minutes, he would be Duke. And he looked, Dalton thought, arranging his shocked impressions, utterly ridiculous – like a child at a fancy dress party, a kid kitted out in a man's clothes. There was a long red robe, which gathered in folds on the rug beneath his boots; a staff of white wood, topped with the head of a golden kite: a hefty, fist-sized display of wealth with stones glittering in the centre of the eyes above its cruel hooked beak; and, beneath his cloak, De Bello wore a fine suit in deep blue with a ceremonial belt and decorated pistol. There was a silk sash in green; there was a ring like a flattened coin, gold bangles and a pendant.

De Bello was shocked – so pale around the temples that his veins looked like fine blue tracery. He seemed lost for something to say – clearly having expected never to see the troublesome poison boy and his misfit gang ever again. *Pallis Tench would have dealt with them, surely? The trap had been set and sprung, hadn't it?* Dalton read all of this as it raced across his features.

Dalton grinned. 'Your friend is dead,' he said flatly.

De Bello's eyes fired suddenly. He became instantly furious, swept up in a storm of rage. 'You bastard upstart!'

he shrieked, spittle exploding from his mouth, and he swung at them, arcing the heavy ceremonial staff in a great half circle.

Dalton leapt back, ducking away from it. Sal was struck across the chest, the heavy gold bird thudding into his ribs. He went down in a crumpled and groaning heap, the air knocked from him.

De Bello had changed. The calm arrogance he'd shown them when they had last met on Midwater – the causal way in which he'd smiled and muttered something about the worst mistake you'll ever make – had abandoned him utterly. He was moments from everything he had plotted for, and he wasn't about to let it go. He raised the staff like a club, ready to bring it down on Sal Sleepwell and shatter his skull.

Dalton threw himself at De Bello with all the strength he had left to muster. The two of them crashed backwards into the fireplace, the staff thudding into the ashes. De Bello's scrabbling hands found a poker and brought it down hard against Dalton's back as they wrestled. Dalton pushed De Bello's teeth away from his ear. The boy was champing wildly, thrashing in a frenzy. Dalton kicked free and retreated. De Bello was up and at him, holding the poker up like a crude sword, his clothing twisted and misshapen now.

Dalton glanced about him, hoping for some sort of weapon or shield, trying to control his breathing. A table and six polished chairs of dark wood. A decanter and a wine flicker.

Sal was moaning, pulling himself clear of the rug before the fireplace, trying to escape a pummelling. He looked as if he wouldn't be getting up any time soon. Dalton swung a chair up and held it before his body, jabbing with the legs. Doone De Bello managed an airless laugh and thrashed at it with the poker. Wood shattered against fire-tempered iron and Dalton was forced to drop its broken remains and retreat further.

Then he heard it – a sound which came like the dumb beating of a distant heart and drifted through the open windows: the church bells of Downholland and Angles, almost in unison, measuring out the first of the midnight chimes, one just behind the other.

De Bello heard them too. He grinned, wiping the sweat from his brow and smoothing his hair. 'You're flogged, poison boy,' he said. He dropped the poker. It clattered against the stone of the fireplace, leaving a dissipating cloud of wood ash to drift across the rug. 'I'm going in,' he said, gathering himself up to his full height. 'They're expecting me.'

The second chime, then the third.

De Bello straightened his ruckled robe and stooped to pick up his staff. He didn't make it that far. Dalton threw himself on to the boy's back, knocking him against the wall and tumbling with him in a thrashing heap. He got a punch in, a good connection to the other boy's face. De Bello struck him back, fierce and merciless. Somewhere in that rolling scramble, Dalton lost the advantage and De Bello was above him, dropping hard punches against his forehead and temples. Dalton raised a hand in protection. The blows kept coming.

The fifth and sixth bells were drifting over the city's roofs now.

Then, the punches stopped. Dalton opened his eyes to see De Bello pulling the gun from his belt. He was no first-timer, Dalton saw immediately. De Bello knew how to use a pistol, even a fancy silver-butt like the one he had here. And no one could miss from this range.

Seven. Eight.

For the third time that evening, Dalton thought his moment had come. There was no pack of cards to save him now. Sal was only half-conscious, balled up under the table and breathlessly spluttering. This was it.

Then, on the ninth bell – exactly on the ninth bell, as if the two actions were somehow inextricably connected – something blurringly swift struck De Bello hard on the temple. There was a sickening thud and his eyes rolled immediately backwards. He went down with a senseless crash. Above him, Dalton saw the head of the mighty golden kite of Highlions regard him coldly with those glittering eyes. He focussed, blinked.

The tenth bell tolled.

Isis Holt was holding the ceremonial staff, standing above the two boys, his muscles tight and his jaw firm and determined. De Bello was a crumpled heap, his cloak splashed about him like a great pool of blood.

Isis managed a desperate smile and held out a hand. Dalton, dizzy and disorientated, was pulled up to standing. Sal was groaning, nursing his ribs.

Eleven.

Isis let out a breath, wiped the sweat from his eyes and steadied himself. He held the staff out. 'I believe this is yours,' he said. He pointed at the doorway that led off from the room. It was decorated in stained glass: thin lead outlining owls, kites and eagles over a tangle of wax-leaved ivy. There was light from beyond so that the coloured glass glowed.

'That way,' said Holt.

Dalton took the staff, ran for the door and burst through it.

Twelve.

The great chamber dropped away below him, like a deep bowl, to a central table where a distant group of figures was sitting, their faces upturned. Across from him, Dalton was aware of a second door being thrown open and slamming backwards on its hinges. A ruck of figures bowled in and gathered themselves: Edward, Scarlet, Luke.

There was a moment's uncertain hush in which the echoes of their movement played out into nothingness, chattering across the rows of empty seats.

One of the figures down below them was at the head of the table and was standing. A second stood up, his chair clattering backwards as he did so. Dalton could make out the tall figure at the head of the table – Gabriel Applefell – stiffen and straighten himself, and the second senator whip his body round to stare at the intruders.

Applefell took a moment before speaking. He placed his hands on his hips. 'What's the meaning of this?' he said, his voice rising up to them. Dalton recognised at once the power and control invested in the man's voice. He'd heard the tone and inflection before. Applefell sounded just like his brother, the undertaker.

Around him, then, must be the senate. Dalton could see a number of figures – the second standing man who glowed with coiled hatred and anger; the man who'd arrived with the two dogs; the younger woman with the cropped hair; the old man and his papers.

Dalton wondered what to say. He felt the weight of the staff in his hand. He placed a palm over the golden head of the kite. He never dreamed he'd make it this far. If only he had something to say – something of dignity and gravity. There was such a lot to explain. He looked across to his companions. They stared back. He was vaguely aware of the fact that he was blushing furiously. Scarlet looked pleadingly at him, biting her lip. He needed to say something. Anything.

He cursed himself silently and cleared his throat. 'Hold your horses, citizens,' he said. 'We've got some news.'

THIRTY-NINE

Once the foolish echo of his voice died, Dalton began moving down towards the table at the centre of the chamber. He found, to his surprise, that, far from weakening him, the exertion of the fight with De Bello had strengthened his courage and determination. He continued downwards towards the gathered figures below, ignoring the pain and lengthening his stride, straightening his back. He balanced the weight of the staff in both his hands, kept his gaze steady.

The senate was silent: eight faces watching his progress.

Then the man facing Applefell – the furious one, standing over his tipped-up chair – bellowed. 'Where in

Kite's name are my guards?' he spat. 'Tench!' he roared, looking up and around him at the empty chamber. 'Guards!'

This was Stephen De Bello, Dalton realised, pressing a hand against the stiff-backed pew nearest to him and pausing a moment. De Bello continued to wheel about, a strong-featured man with a steel-grey beard, his thick red neck heavily veined. 'Guards!' he yelled again. 'Tench!' He looked about him, expectant and confused. No one came.

'Where are the Streetwatch?' Applefell said flatly, regarding his assembled senate. There was a strained silence. One man stared at his fingernails. The younger woman with the cropped hair raised her eyes to the roof. No one spoke.

'Tench is dead,' Dalton said by way of answer, his voice calm and firm. He continued downwards, vaguely wondering where the Streetwatch had gone. Applefell had asked a reasonable question. Only a matter of moments before, up in the corridors above them, Edward had said the place was crawling with guards.

'Dead?' De Bello said.

Dalton was close enough now to read each of their faces in turn. Those nearest to him, he noticed, were recoiling slightly, as if frightened to hold their positions at the table. One senator's chair shifted as he pushed back on his heels. They didn't want him too close. No wonder, Dalton thought. Here was a bloodied boy, blackened with chimney dust, descending towards them holding the Duke's ceremonial sceptre as if it was his.

'Your son won't be coming down,' Dalton said. He tried to hold De Bello's gaze. It took all his courage. 'We had a disagreement.'

De Bello squirmed for an instant, then exploded. 'How dare you?' he bawled. Dalton couldn't help but jump; the man's voice was a battering ram. De Bello lurched forward, reaching out a huge arm, his fallen chair spinning as he kicked it away.

'Stephen,' Applefell said with calm certainty. 'Stop this.'

The effect was immediate and remarkable. De Bello glowered and slunk back a step. Sweat beaded his forehead and he bit his lip. The other senators shifted uneasily. Dalton noticed Senator Dropmore for the first time. Icily beautiful and poised, she placed a hand on De Bello's arm to calm him. He shrugged it off with a sneer of contempt. *Right here*, Dalton thought, *amongst this group of people, fester the divisions that have torn the city apart.* It seemed nothing short of insanity that he might soon have to organise this bitter crew of hissing cats.

'Excuse me!' came a small voice from somewhere above them.

Applefell looked up, scowling. 'What is this?' he said. 'Who are you?'

Dalton looked upwards too. The silhouette of Sal, slightly hunched, came lurching through the doors above. He was nursing his battered ribs. His tangled hair over such a skinny frame made him look like a mop, Dalton thought. Preposterously, Sal seemed to be raising his hand in a polite wave.

'I'm Sal Sleepwell,' he said, his voice a painful wheeze.

Applefell examined the faces of his senators, looking for help. There were embarrassed glances, shrugs, silence. 'Am I meant to know that name, boy?' he said, directing his attention upwards again.

'I fed the guards a sleeping draught,' Sal said cheerfully.

So that's where the Streetwatch guards had gone. They were all dreaming off a potion somewhere. How was that possible? Dalton allowed himself a broad smile of admiration as he figured it. Sal's question, up in the plush palace corridors, came back to him: 'Were they drinking? I figured they'd be drinking,' he'd asked. Sleepwell had planned this all along. The room in the cellar – the serving room with the decanters and the wine. It was for the guards on duty. *Sal must have lurked there after Tench had gone. What had he used? Mandragora perhaps?*

'You did what?' De Bello said through his teeth, his face a fierce red.

Applefell crossed his arms. 'Listen,' he said. One of his senators, the hook-nosed man with the dogs, cleared his throat to speak but Applefell halted him with a glance. 'Everybody, listen,' he said. He raised his voice and pointed imperiously upwards at the group of figures above him. 'I don't know what's gone on tonight, but I want you all down here now,' he announced to the clutch of figures by the door. 'Down here,' he repeated firmly, his lips tight and thin. He indicated Dalton. 'You – don't move. Are these your friends?'

Dalton watched Scarlet, Edward and Luke descend.

Sleepwell was coming down too now, wincing. He was absurdly proud of them all. He felt a big broad smile growing. 'Yes,' he said. 'They're my friends.'

'All of them? The one there with the hair, as well?'

'Him too.'

'Right. All of you come down and stand next to the boy, here,' Applefell told them. He rolled his eyes as he spoke.

Perhaps he too recognised the utter madness of the situation, Dalton thought. Or perhaps he saw here a way out of his predicament – an escape from what had looked, only moments ago, like the inevitable accession of Doone De Bello to the position of Duke. Applefell was an impressive man, a solid and reassuring presence. He had control. The other senators, frozen in their positions around the table, respected him even if they hated him – that much was clear. Dalton looked down at his clothes, his bloodied fingernails, his scuffed and blackened boots. He swore then to be more like Applefell. These people would need him to be. These and others.

Then, as his friends came closer, a ripple of shock passed across the faces of the senate members. Senator Dropmore's face creased in confusion. She touched her neck. 'Scarlet?' she said, her voice nothing more than a tremor.

Scarlet raised a hand and tried an easy smile, but she was blushing and fearful, Dalton could tell. 'Good evening, Mother,' Scarlet said.

'Scarlet Dropmore?' Applefell was taken aback.

'Shouldn't you be with your marcher?'

He looked at his senate. Here, suddenly, was an unexpected and mystifying complication. Again the group stared back, helpless. Applefell pushed a hand through his hair, regaining his composure.

'What in Kite's name is happening here?' he said. 'Scarlet? What is this?'

Afterwards, when Dalton recalled that night – something he did many times in the days that followed – it was the next few moments that most occupied his thoughts. So much happened, and yet so little. It seemed as if so many secrets were briefly glimpsed, and yet so much remained hidden.

His memories of that evening alternately clouded and cleared, clouded and cleared, so that only passing instants of clarity remained. In one such moment, right then, standing motionless on the final few steps near the assembly and waiting for his friends to descend, the senators appeared to him with a sharpness and colour that didn't last long. In the long days that followed, his memory kept tugging him back to that tableau: De Bello, his face a red bloom of outrage; Scarlet's mother, beautiful and frightening, her skin pale and her shocked eyes wide and black; two older gentlemen with deeply wrinkled skin, one with grey, gnarled hands and heavy rings on each index finger; the man who owned the dogs, the square-jawed, hunched figure with the hooked nose and the expression of grave disbelief.

And next to him, the woman with the short hair. The one who, right then, got up and left.

Whenever Dalton recalled those swiftly passing moments, his memory kept returning him to that point, slowing to re-examine the precise moment at which the senator – he barely saw her at all, let alone knew her name – rose from her chair and moved quickly out of sight, nothing but a sweep of flapping robe and jacket. She was one of the women he had seen from his vantage point in the walled garden: a swift and purposeful figure descending from a horse-drawn carriage and helping an older senator, guiding him up the steps. Her shape and posture were the same. The one with the cropped hair, cut short and close to her neck.

Strangest of all was the response to her leaving. Senator Dropmore rose a little, as if about to speak. The look on her face – What was it? Pity? – lasted only a moment before her features were suddenly closed again, snapped shut like a locket, and she took her seat and looked at her hands. Two of the others, Dalton couldn't be sure which, closed their eyes. One placed his forehead in his hands before recovering and resuming his previous position.

Something of significance had happened – just then, in that moment. Something important recognised or learnt. Applefell raised a hand and lowered it gently, palm downwards, his meaning clear: sit still. Do nothing. Let her go.

'What?' Scarlet said. She'd noticed it too.

Applefell took a stride away from the table, approaching the lowest step, his eyes passing quickly across the faces of the intruders. 'Who's in charge here?' he said to the group.

'I am,' Dalton said. He planted his feet apart, raised himself, stood tall. 'Senator Applefell,' he continued. 'Can I say how much you sound like your brother?'

Applefell looked at him, utterly motionless. The principal senator seemed frozen in the cold silence that followed; he didn't even blink, just regarded the soot-blackened boy before him. Dalton was vaguely aware of the other assembly members behind him, still like statues. Then Applefell brought a hand up to his mouth and pressed it across his lips, biting his index finger, his eyes burning, intense.

'Who are you?' he said. Except his voice failed him and it came out as a dry whisper – the voice of a man who knew the answer to his own question. Someone behind them, a senator, drew breath sharply.

Dalton snapped the buckle box from his belt. All eyes followed the movement. Everyone saw his scabbed and soot-black hands as he raised the box and pushed open the lid with his thumb. He produced the letter – what was left of it – and held it out. Applefell took it gently from him.

'I don't know,' Dalton said as the senator unfolded the single piece of paper. 'You tell me.'

FORTY

There was a knock on his door and Dalton heard the bolts drawn back and the heavy hinges grumble. It was Ketchie, the guard who had stood, day and night, outside Dalton's room. What had begun as a relationship of complete silence had improved a little over the three days Dalton had been held. They exchanged words each morning as his breakfast was brought. Yesterday, before lights out, they'd even had a brief conversation about the progress of Senator Applefell's investigation.

'Marcher Gellis to see you, sir,' said Ketchie. Dalton couldn't help but smile when his jailer addressed him so formally. The man was hedging his bets, waiting for the outcome of the investigation. He didn't want to risk displeasing the filthy poison boy prisoner, just in case the rumours were true.

Dalton nodded his understanding and moved quickly to tidy his room. It was comfortable and clean: a bed with good sheets and blankets, a desk and chair, a high window. It had carpets and was kept warm. No fireplace, though, Dalton had noticed the moment they had marched him in. They weren't ready to risk escape.

He made his bed hurriedly, straightened his chair and scooped up the journal he'd been working on. Applefell had been insistent upon as detailed account of his life so far as he could get. It occupied most of Dalton's days, writing being a slow and painful process for one with so mean an education and such bruised and battered hands. The rest of the time he slept and took small meals and strong, foul medicines. He was feeling better than he had for a while. He'd even had the courage to unwrap the bandage and examine his ankle. The skin was black and yellow but the swelling was down. There was going to be a ragged, milky scar. Looking at it had made Dalton recall Tench's torn face, and wonder for the first time what life must have been like for the big man, recovering from such horrific injuries and living with their ugly legacy.

'Dalton.' Marcher Gellis was framed in the doorway. She seemed smaller than Dalton remembered, older, tired. He motioned for her to sit. She took the chair by the desk. 'You're still black,' she said simply. 'Have they let you wash yet?'

'A little,' Dalton smiled, looking at his hands. They were grey with chimney grit, his nails filthy crescents. He'd scrubbed at them a good deal over a brass bowl of cold water, but nothing had shifted.

Gellis straightened her jacket, preparing herself, Dalton thought, for delivery of important news. His heart tightened with anxiety. 'I wanted to tell you about your marcher,' she said. She cleared her throat, adjusted her posture. 'He would have wanted me to let you know.'

Dalton had been given a lot of thinking time since the night in the debating chamber. And he'd thought about the undertaker – about Applefell – a great deal. He'd dreamt about the moment Tench had pulled the trigger of that flintlock and Applefell had fallen to his knees, choking. That wide-eyed look of shock and regret as he crashed forward.

'Marcher Applefell was my friend,' said Marcher Gellis, her face tight. 'But he wasn't a perfect man. He was troubled by many things. Mostly, he was troubled by guilt – about you.'

Dalton swallowed hard. His throat felt dry and rough.

Gellis continued. 'When you were born,' she said slowly, weighing up each word, 'it was important that you were kept a secret. Elber chose Marcher Applefell as your guardian.' Gellis sighed. 'It was a complicated time, you see. A few weeks after your birth, your father suffered a stroke. He nearly died and the city was thrown into chaos. There were potential heirs – two high-born boys of the right age – and the senate began to make arrangements, but both of them died suddenly. It was the work of the House of De Bello – we could all see how desperate they were to remove the wrong successors and ensure they took the throne instead. It was impossible to prove, of course. All sentaways – as they came to be called – had to stay in hiding from then on. The Duke recovered, but he was only frail. If he were struck down a second time, all high-born children would again be in terrible danger. Especially you.' Dalton remembered Scarlet's account of Duke Elber's illness. She had been in hiding ever since. She had, in a way, lost her childhood just as he had. He nodded for Gellis to continue. 'Marcher Applefell – your marcher – was a man with problems. A fever-tea addict. A gambler. He'd concealed this, of course, and your . . .' She paused and licked her lips, staring at the rug under her boots. 'Your father trusted him. But your marcher was a man in a great deal of debt. And trouble. And he wasn't ready for the responsibility.' She looked at him and blinked. Dalton nodded for her to continue. 'I've told this story once already today,' she said with a mirthless laugh. The senate had summoned her, no doubt. She cleared her throat. 'Applefell sold you,' she said simply, swallowing back some great surge of emotion. 'To slave traders. He returned to the senate and he told your father . . .' There, she faltered.

I told them you were dead. Applefell's final words.

'I know,' Dalton said. 'He told me what he'd said.'

Gellis looked up. She mastered herself again. 'Years later, he recovered,' she continued, 'and he became possessed by this idea that he could find you again. That he could correct his error. He spent a long time abroad, pursuing the men he sold you to.' Gellis wiped her eyes. 'But without luck. He had no idea you had never left the city, of course. No one did. Until I saw you.' She smiled. 'Remember when we first met?'

Dalton shook his head. 'Belladonna,' he said. 'The night Jinks got ghosted, I swallowed a dose. When I came round in Scarlet's house, I couldn't remember anything. I only remember bits, even now. Mostly, Sleepwell's my memory.'

Gellis nodded her understanding. 'That makes sense. Your friend, Sal, wasn't there when we met ten days before Scarlet's party,' she explained. 'It was me, you and the boy called Jinks. I was telling you what you needed to do. You don't remember any of this?' Dalton shook his head. Gellis gave a pale smile, recalling the meeting. Her eyes filled. 'As soon as I saw you,' she said, 'I knew you were the one Applefell was looking for. There's something in your face, Dalton. Your eyes, too. And your voice. You sound like an Elber. And those fingers of yours. Card-player's fingers, like your father's.' She took a long breath.

Dalton stared at his hands, at the thin fingers he hated, and thought about the cards, punctured and blackened, cradling Tench's bullet.

'When Applefell returned, he wanted to see you straight away,' said Gellis. 'He didn't want to wait. I counselled him against it, but he . . .' She broke off, remembering. 'He was possessed,' she said with a tilt of the head. 'He had to see you. You have no idea. He went searching for you at night, wandering the streets. In the end, I arranged for him to meet up with you after the tasting but then everything . . . changed. We lost you.'

Dalton recalled those first encounters with the undertaker again. The old man had looked shocked, frightened – amazed, that was it – at seeing his boy again for the first time in fourteen years. He had recognised the baby he'd lost. Dalton stared at himself in the mirror. Did he really look so much like an Elber? Surely not. Surely there was more to this.

'Who was my mother?' Dalton asked.

Gellis' face closed up. She stared at the wood of the desk. She straightened the papers Dalton had piled up there. 'I don't know,' she said.

Dalton tried another tack. 'So, what was meant to happen?' he asked.

Gellis seemed lost in thought for a moment. 'What do you mean?'

'Where was Applefell taking me before . . .'

'I see. To his brother. Gabriel Applefell was to be your guardian. You were to be his nephew – that was the story Elber had prepared. That way, he could still have you close – still see you. There was a letter, apparently, explaining all this.'

'Yes. It was in my buckle box. Some of it, anyway. Senator Applefell has all that at the moment.'

'To check it's not faked, I suppose,' Marcher Gellis said. 'He has to be sure you are who you say you are.' She was troubled, Dalton could tell. She shifted position on her chair, wiped her hands together. 'Senator Applefell asked me to pass on some news,' Marcher Gellis said eventually. 'It concerns my charge.'

'You mean Scarlet.'

Three days had seemed an age without his friends. Dalton had spent hours wondering where they might be and what they might be doing. Sleepwell was being treated for broken ribs, Ketchie had reported. And somewhere in the Palace of Justice, doctors were attending to Doone De Bello, who was recovering from severe concussion. Scarlet was with her mother, apparently, though there had been no news other than that. Luke had vanished, the last Dalton had heard, though the Streetwatch were searching her out. Edward hadn't been mentioned. Nor had the traitor, Holt.

'Yes. I mean Scarlet.'

'Go on.' Dalton felt nervous, suddenly. This wasn't going to be good.

Gellis spoke slowly, drawing a circle on his desk with the tip of her finger. 'One of the issues Applefell needs to clear up is the fractured nature of the senate. There's a lot of bad blood between them, Dalton.'

Dalton remembered Dropmore placing a hand on De Bello, the sneer of contempt that had crossed the man's face as he shrugged her off.

'I saw,' he said. 'And Scarlet told me once.'

Gellis nodded. 'Right. The Duke of Highlions must be neutral. Not aligned with either the House of De Bello or the House of Dropmore, do you see?' There had been a question there, but Gellis continued without waiting for an answer. She wanted this over with. 'If you are to accede, Dalton, it is my duty to advise you that you will not be consorting in any way with my charge. Any further contact with her, either personally or in a professional capacity will not be acceptable to the senate. Or, indeed,' she added, her voice colder now, 'to myself.'

Dalton couldn't speak for a moment. His throat felt dry and tight again, as if the jessamine had reached its hand up and clamped his gullet shut like it had that night in the garden.

'If I'm the Duke,' he said, matching the marcher's coldness, 'can't I just do what I want?'

'It's not as simple as that,' Marcher Gellis said flatly. 'It's curious to think it, but, as a Duke, you will have less freedom than a poison boy, not more. You are bound by duty and responsibility – to the city; to your citizens.'

Your citizens. The phrase sounded laughable. Dalton swallowed back the bitterness of some sniping remark, afraid of sounding too much like Luke. He needn't argue this now. Gellis had said what she had come to say.

'Ketchie,' he said, his voice raised.

The bolts of the door snapped back and the man's face bobbed into view. 'Yes, sir?'

'Marcher Gellis will be leaving now.'

AFTERWARDS

The water was hot. Dalton slipped down under the surface and stayed for as long as his breath would allow, his shoulder blades pressed against the copper base. It was the first time he'd ever had a hot bath. It felt good. He broke the surface, lungs bursting, and he wiped his eyes. His hands were clean at last, scrubbed to a raw, pale pink. His ankle was healing. His vision had been clear for days now and his breathing was steady and strong. A parade of doctors, each bearing a chinking bag of glass bottles, had come and gone since his release. He'd dutifully swallowed a sequence of grim tinctures and treatments and thanked each of them for their help.

Ketchie, who in the last few days had somehow become his unofficial chamberlain, had arranged for the burning of his old clothes and the provision of a fine black suit and boots for Bennie Jinks' funeral. A man had come to cut his hair and another to measure him for clothes.

Ketchie had left a bottle of wine and a single flicker next to the lamp on the low table next to the bath. On a dresser nearby was the treaty, folded and still sealed, waiting for his signature. Dalton tried not to look at it, but to stare instead at the swirling patterns of the ceiling roses. The document would wait until tomorrow. Or the next day.

His thoughts returned anew to his friends. Surely he would be allowed to see them soon? He was eager to check on Sleepwell's progress, to help with the search for Luke, to see Scarlet . . . He closed his eyes. There it was again. The problem of Scarlet. If he put his name to the folded paper on the dresser, it would be official: no further contact with the foremost sentaway of the House of Dropmore. Complete neutrality to be observed and maintained at all times. The way it had been presented to him was simple: if he signed, he'd never see her again. And, if he didn't, she'd take his place, and he'd never see her again.

But then – Dalton always reached this point – did she even want to see him? Despite himself, he couldn't help thinking it through over and over, prodding and probing it, looking for a clever way through it. Elber might not have been able to unite the warring factions of the city's senate, he found himself thinking, but that didn't mean *he* couldn't. There had to be a way.

The room was colder than it had been. His water was cooling too.

One of the curtains drifted a little in the night air. Ketchie must have left the windows open. Dalton shifted in the water and wiped his eyes again. Something made him straighten a little, as if a cold finger had drawn a line down the back of his neck. He blinked, his body still and taut. There was someone in his room, he was sure of it. His skin tightened and cooled and the hairs rose on his arms. He wished he'd left his pistol nearby, but it was in the pocket of his jacket.

His heart was charging now, his pulse a drum in his ears. There was a movement near the window. *What was that? The careful placing of a foot?* Someone had climbed inside – up the ivy, perhaps.

Dalton was rigid with fear. He needed a defence. Anything. He licked his lips, trying to keep the rising panic from his voice. 'I'll shoot you, if you move,' he bluffed, hoping against hope it would work.

Silence. Then a low laugh. A laugh he knew well. There was a great fire suddenly in his chest and a surge of pins and needles along his arms. It was Scarlet. She stepped out from behind the curtain and raised a hand in greeting. She was wearing a white dress, like the night of her party, and had silver rings in her ears. Her hair was at her shoulders.

'I wondered whether you might be in trouble,' she said with a shrug.

Dalton brought his knees up, wishing he could remember where he'd dropped his robe. He was blushing with a furious heat he'd never felt before.

Somehow he managed to find enough air to suck in a breath and make words. 'Well, thanks,' he said, and his voice, he realised with relief, sounded calm and firm. 'But if there's someone in trouble here, it's probably you.'

Scarlet grinned.

The Language of Highlions

belladonna (poison)

bone (money)

chinkers (coins)

deck (kill)

dipper (pickpocket)

dreck (curse/shit)

dreckwit (idiot)

fever-tea (drug-like drink)

flicker (drinking glass)

flogged (broken/messed up)

flog things up (mess things up)

fuller (the channel running the length of a blade into which poison is put)

Gannet (Blackjack Gannet/curse)

ghosted (died)

gutted (killed)

Kite (God/curse)

lackbrain (idiot)

Marcher (the guard of a sentaway)

needled (poisoned with a blade dipped in the poison)

poison boy (a taster of food to check for poison)

scut and feathers! (curse)

sentaway (a child living away from his/her important parents, for protection)

shotpowder (gunpowder)

shutter (poisoner)

silver-butt (pistol)

stagged (caught/killed)

torn it (blown it)

wet yourself (get out of here/get stuffed etc)

ACKNOWLEDGEMENTS

Many thanks to everyone at Chicken House for their encouragement and support. And a special thanks to a trio of exceptional editors and teachers; Imogen Cooper, Christine O'Brien and Penelope Price, who patiently pointed me in the right direction over and over again.